THE
KENSINGTON
KIDNAP

KATIE GAYLE

THE
KENSINGTON
KIDNAP

bookouture

Published by Bookouture in 2020

An imprint of Storyfire Ltd.
Carmelite House
50 Victoria Embankment
London EC4Y 0DZ

www.bookouture.com

ISBN: 978-1-80019-106-8
eBook ISBN: 978-1-80019-105-1

AUTHOR'S NOTE

We have taken a few liberties with the geography of Kent, for which we apologise.

CHAPTER ONE

Pip woke to the crashing of chords and the shrieking of violins. *WTF, an orchestra?* Where on earth was she? And then she realised – *Oh God, it's Mummy.*

Her brain had woken enough to put the pieces together: crashing chords + 'Ride of the Valkyries' + Wagner = Mother. It was her mobile phone, and that was her mother's signature ringtone. Pip had chosen it as a joke a few months ago and now she couldn't remember how to change it back, so she was constantly harangued by Wagner. It had long since ceased to be funny, especially now, given the Mother Situation.

She retrieved the phone from the tangle of sheets and killed the call before dropping it back onto the bed. Where it rang again – more bloody Vikings – and again lit up with the name Mummy. She rejected the call a second time. From experience, Pip knew there would likely be a third. Mummy was not someone who readily took no (or two nos) for an answer, but Pip was not in the mood to talk. Certainly not to Mummy, or as Pip liked to call her, Ex-Chancellor of the Exchequer, since she had withdrawn her funding. She put the phone on silent and watched it light up again, which was more bearable without the Valkyries.

Pip sighed. She should really be used to Mummy's yoyo-ing funds by now. Mummy might have enough money to keep Pip in the manner to which she would like to become accustomed, but she also had strong ideas about Young Ladies Being Independent. Which meant Pip had both a chequered financial history and a chequered employment history. You never really knew which way the wind would blow with the bank of Mummy, but right now it was clearly closed, and Pip didn't know where her next latte was coming from. Or, more troublingly, the rent.

Pip lay back on the pillows and turned to face the other side of the double bed where, if her love life were in a better state right now, a gorgeous and devoted lover might be. Maybe even Tim, although she was beginning to give up hope that he would be anything more than a friendly and very decorative flatmate/landlord. Instead, on the lover's side of the bed was a large and glossy celeb magazine (Pip's shameful weakness – that and Twitter), and a three-legged tabby cat who was diligently licking his nether regions and purring.

Sighing, she picked up *Hello!* and indulged herself with an eight-page photo feature about movie stars and their kids. She knew she was a bit old-fashioned in her love of magazines, when the whole internet was bristling with up-to-the-minute gossip and pics. She followed all the celeb news subreddits and Instagram accounts, of course, but for Pip, nothing beat the smell and feel of a magazine.

The article about the celebs and their kids was very satisfying, although it certainly came down heavily on the nature side of the nature/nurture debate – every child was gorgeous, straight-toothed, silky-haired, and smiling for the camera. Even the teenagers looked remarkably pleasant. This one, for example – golden-haired, wrapped up in moss-green cashmere and posed against a forest of snow-tipped firs, spoke of his love for the clarinet and cross-country skiing, and how he wanted to make a difference in the world by teaching cross-country skiing to less privileged teenagers, and to help save the forests and trees. Pip thought about the months she'd spent skiing trails in Whistler when she worked there as a chalet girl. Mummy always said that every young lady should be able to ski. She had a moment of longing for the snow, the speed, the always-surprising cold, the smell of pines. If only Mummy weren't so unreasonable about credit cards; a trip back to the mountains would be just the thing to cheer her up.

Above the slurping and purring, Pip heard Tim going about his morning routine: his slippers padding down the passage, the kitchen tap running, the click of the kettle. Then back down the passage to the bathroom and the rush of the shower water hitting those smooth shoulders, running down his back and those firm thighs. At least this morning there was only one set of padding feet: no sleepover pal, then. Pip sighed, tossed the magazine onto the floor, pushed the cat gently out of the way, and got out of bed. Ten minutes later she was at the kitchen table, the cafetière full of coffee for her and Tim.

'Hey, Pip, you made coffee, thanks.' As he reached for the pot, she admired the way his wrists emerged from the cuffs of his work shirt, the dark swirl of the hairs and then the creamy skin of the inner forearm. She pulled herself back to reality when she realised that Tim was talking. It looked like he was talking to his coffee, because he certainly wasn't looking at her. But he seemed to be addressing her.

'Listen, Pip, I'm really going to need that rent this week. I wish I could give you more time, but it's three weeks overdue now and, you know, it's…' He tailed off, blushing with embarrassment. Pip could feel her own face burning at the shame of it.

'Absolutely, Tim, I totally understand. Thanks for the breather, I'm on it now.' She put on her confident face and improvised. 'I'm starting with some temp work today, in fact. So it's all good for the end of the week. I'll have both months' rent for you on Friday.' She felt terrible lying to Tim. She didn't like lying to anyone really, but lying to Tim was particularly bad, with those trusting puppy-dog eyes of his.

'That's great, Pip, I'm really pleased for you.' He beamed, shining his genuinely happy face towards her, those soft wide lips and his teeth so straight and white they could be American. He really was so ridiculously nice, in addition to being gorgeous. Pip felt even worse lying to him about the work lined up for today. The only thing she had lined up for today was finishing *Hello!* magazine and trawling Twitter. And perhaps a shower, if she could be bothered.

'Better go get myself ready, in fact,' she said, taking her coffee cup and heading for the door. 'Don't want to be late on my first day.'

'Yes, you'd better do something about that bed hair, even though I'm generally a fan of it,' said Tim. 'I'm off to work too. Good luck, I hope it goes really well. See you later.'

Pip considered his parting comment. Had he been flirting, or just telling her that her hair was a mess? She sighed. It was so hard to tell with men, but she was almost sure he had been telling her to tidy it up.

With Tim gone, at least she could drop the charade. There would be no dressing for work. She slouched back to the kitchen table, still in her jammies, with her coffee, her phone, a notepad and a pen. Lying to Tim had made her realise what a mess this all was. If she didn't pay the rent, even kind-hearted Tim would throw her out. And then, instead of this wonderful flat in Kennington – even if Mummy always turned up her nose and said, 'one letter and a whole world away from Kensington, darling' – she and Most would be living on the street. Or, even worse, with Mummy. Pip would brainstorm her options, make a list, prioritise, decide what to do. This irresponsible approach to life had been all very well in her twenties, but she needed to start behaving like a responsible adult.

Opening a fresh new page, she wrote at the top: *OPTIONS.*
1.
Pip wrote firmly, the biro scratching into the paper. She paused. She tipped back in her chair, staring at the ceiling for

a long moment. She could still see the mark from that time she'd made the toaster explode. No point letting it distract her now. Then she tried looking out of the window, but it was just a view of the neighbour's drainpipes. With a sigh, she tilted the chair forward until the front legs hit the floor with a smack. She looked down at the paper and wrote next to the numeral: *Loan from Mummy.*

2.

Again the biro scratched the number into the paper, again with rather more certainty than Pip felt. Next to the number 2 she wrote: *Get a job.*

3.

She pressed more lightly. *Kidney?*

Slightly more realistic than a loan from Mummy, but really a very last resort that Pip would prefer to avoid. And she wasn't sure they would accept her kidney after that bout of hepatitis when she'd been stuck in the swamps in Botswana.

4.

For option number 4, nothing. Nada. That was it. Those were her options.

She crossed out 'Loan from Mummy'. Mummy had made it clear where she stood on this.

Then she crossed out *Kidney?*

There was only one thing for it: get a job. Again. Despite her singular lack of success in gaining and keeping employment – really, just a lot of crazy misunderstandings, mistakes and disasters not of her making – she was going to have to try once again to find work. It wasn't that she didn't want a job, or to work for her crust, but the jobs never seemed to pan out. Steeling herself, she reached for her phone and began scrolling through the contacts hoping for ideas, stopping at anyone who looked like a possibility: someone who could help out, give her some work, suggest a solution.

Bill Beekeeper – not likely after that incident with the hive and the tractor which, frankly, could have happened to anyone.

Someone just called J. *Wonder who J is, or was?* Could it be worth asking J for a job? Certainly more likely than a loan from Mummy.

Neighbour Across the Road – except the road was in Madrid, from her stint there; that was no use.

Tall Alice – who was she again?

Temp Agency – Sharon.

Pip sighed. She really didn't want to phone Sharon, after the way things had ended last time, but she didn't want to phone Sharon marginally less than she didn't want to phone Mummy. Maybe Sharon had forgotten about the cat thing. Pip sighed and pushed 'call' next to Sharon's name, and was somewhat surprised when she answered. *People do start work at the most ungodly hours.*

'Sharon, hi, it's Epiphany Bloom here – Pip. How are you?' One thing about Pip: she could really perk up that voice, even if she was disheartened and sitting at her kitchen table in her PJs.

'Well, this *is* a surprise. How's the cat?'

Not forgotten then. Snippy woman.

'How kind of you to ask. Most is doing very well, thank you. He's really settled in.'

'Most?'

Pip hesitated. 'That's his name. He's most of a cat, not a full one… the missing leg… So, um…'

The cat's name was rather like Mummy's ringtone – funny at the time, but probably not as clever as it had seemed at first, in retrospect.

After a pause, Sharon sighed out a sentence: 'What is it that you want, Epiphany?'

'Well, I'm hoping it's what I can do for you! The good news is that I've just finished a great consulting contract, and I'm between jobs at the moment, so I'm available for temp work if you have anything on your books.' She didn't feel bad lying to Sharon the way she felt bad lying to Tim.

'Are you kidding me? After the last time? That disaster with the vet? They swore never to use us for temps again after, and I'm quoting here, "That crazy girl made off with the cripple cat."'

'Yes, I'd like to apologise for that, I'm really sorry that they're not using you. Honestly, I couldn't be sorrier. But, Sharon, I did explain that there were extenuating circumstances.'

It was true. The people who had run over the cat and brought him in to the vet had scarpered after they heard the surgery to save the leg was unsuccessful, the cat was now one leg short, and the bill had run to many hundreds of quid. Bastards. They didn't fetch him or pay the bill, and the vet was going to put the cat down. If those weren't extenuating circumstances, Pip didn't know what was. Pip had abandoned the front desk where she was stationed, grabbed the cat from his cage in the recovery room, tucked him under her arm, and run for the door.

'You stole a patient from the veterinarian. I'm not interested in the circumstances, Epiphany.' Sharon sounded distinctly distracted. Pip heard the tap of typing through the phone, but she continued nonetheless.

'You are quite right, no point in rehashing the whole thing. It turned out quite well in the end. I mean, Most is very happy and, you know, alive, so that's a good thing. I for one would be prepared to let bygones be bygones and re-establish our professional relationship.'

The clicking of keys filled the silence. And then Sharon sighed again and said, 'You know what? If you can start today, something's just come in and they seem rather desperate. Possibly even desperate enough to put up with you.'

CHAPTER TWO

In what might have been the fastest personal grooming turnaround in recorded history, Pip was showered, made up, hair dried to a shine, and dressed in just under nine minutes. Thank goodness she'd recently decided against pink hair and stuck with her natural colour – a dark blonde – because this didn't sound like a pink hair sort of job. Whatever, a few highlights were definitely on the list for payday.

Some might say she was overdressed, and by quite some measure, for the job of temporary filing clerk. But this was a fresh start and a good impression was imperative, so she broke out the good suit she'd had made by a tailor in Singapore when she'd thought she'd bagged that media relations job at the Singapore Stock Exchange. The job didn't come through, but the suit was magnificent.

She had tapped the link on Sharon's email (the body of the email consisted mostly of warnings and threats) and Google-mapped it. The client, Boston Investigations, was in Elephant and Castle, about a fifteen-minute walk away; a sure sign that the job was meant to be. The name of the new workplace also sounded intriguing, like an American PI firm in one of the dog-eared old paperbacks she used to pick up by the dozen at the second-hand bookshop when she was in her teens. She'd adored them – the intrigue, the smoking, the implied sex, the damaged bad guys, the plot twists that even aged fifteen she could see coming by page fifty. Seriously, she was like a clairvoyant. Even Mummy thought her ability to tell what was going to happen in TV shows and movies was uncanny. Pity she couldn't get paid to do *that*.

Sharon hadn't said what the company did, but it was probably some sort of deathly dull accounting and audit outfit, investigating expense account infringements or something. *Aha, Bill, I see you bought the two-ply lavatory paper, when company policy specifies single-ply.* It didn't matter much; filing was filing.

Anyway – *RENT MONEY, Pip. Keep your eye on the pay cheque,* she told herself as she bobbed and weaved through the pedestrians and cars, trying not to be tempted by the mouth-watering smells coming from the cafes and empanada stalls, managing to get only briefly stranded on a large roundabout. She was tall and long-limbed (gangly, Mummy called it) and a fast walker, so she was always coming up behind a slow walker and trying to scoot by. More often than not, this resulted in her walking straight into another person on the overtake. Having been raised in a mid-sized village, the sheer number of people in London still amazed her. On a country lane, if you found yourself stuck behind a slow cow, you could just give it a sharp tap on the bum and it would move out of your way. But you couldn't do that with a slow walker in London. Pip had discovered the hard way.

Boston Investigations was in a small office building, set, rather strangely, between a trendy-looking juice bar and an old-fashioned dry cleaner's just hanging on in the rapidly gentrifying neighbourhood. She'd probably walked past it a hundred times without noticing. Pip quickly sent Sharon a message that she was here, and that she hadn't let her down or run off with a cat, and then rang the bell. 'Hello, I'm here from the agency to—'

She was buzzed in before she'd even finished the sentence, and she walked up two flights of stairs to an opaque glass door with the company logo etched into it.

'They've been waiting for you,' the receptionist said, giving Pip a once over. She looked impressed. Pip was glad that she had decided on her good suit.

'Come on.' She walked round her desk and led Pip down the passage. She knocked on a door and opened it without waiting for an answer.

'She's here,' she hissed in a stage whisper to a man standing in front of a screen, looking as if he was about to present. 'From the agency.'

'Ah, come in. I'm Doug Bradford, we spoke on the phone,' the man said, gesturing Pip towards an empty chair on the far side of the conference table. A pile of three or four files was stacked neatly in front of her seat. It did not seem like a sufficiently large stack to require a temp filing clerk.

'We did? I'm—'

He talked right over her. 'You're late. Take a seat, I've just started.'

Pip sighed and sat down. *Men who don't listen. Nothing new there.* To her left was a tough-looking young man about her age, the forehead of what would have been a model's face cut diagonally with a silvery scar that was more *Texas Chainsaw Massacre* than Harry Potter. On her other side was a bespectacled older woman with a laptop open in front of her. Two more men sat across from her, closer to the presenter. They all had similar stacks of files, three or four. Even cumulatively, there didn't seem to be enough to justify a temp.

On the screen flashed a picture of the same clarinet-playing cross-country-skiing teen she'd seen in the magazine, this time in jeans and a fashionably distressed T-shirt.

'That's Matty Price!' The words popped out of her mouth. 'He's the son of Madison Price, the actress, and Ben Price, the novelist.'

Doug turned to her in surprise. 'How did you know that it's Matty Price who's missing? I didn't mention his name, or his family. No one knows but the people in this room.'

'You have a great big picture of him up on the screen,' Pip pointed out. 'And, I was reading…' She stopped, embarrassed to admit to her *Hello!* habit.

'Glad to see you've done your homework,' Doug said, ignoring both her unfinished sentence and the fact that she hadn't done any homework at all. He gave her a look of what seemed to be grudging admiration. 'That's good. As you can imagine, we are under enormous pressure on this one. Not a moment to lose. Let me fill you in on what we know so far.'

What Pip knew so far was that this was a very strange filing assignment. Doug Bradford launched into the most intriguing story. Matty Price, it seemed, had gone missing. Disappeared without a trace, apparently. The parents assumed that he'd left home in a huff, or gone off with a girl, or to some music festival or something, and would be back. But it had been a week so far and no contact. No credit card transactions. Nothing from the kid's friends. The Prices didn't want to go to the police, which is why they'd called Boston Investigations.

Pip scribbled the key points on her notepad. She wasn't sure quite why she was involved with this discussion. But she was certainly having a better time than she had expected, and she wasn't going to spoil things by asking about the filing.

'So, Ms du Bois, what are your initial thoughts? Where would you start?'

Pip turned expectantly to the bespectacled older woman – the only other female in the room – but she seemed to have nothing to say for herself.

'Ms du Bois?'

Why was Doug looking at Pip?

'Me?' she asked in surprise.

'Yes, you,' he said. 'Isn't that why you're here, to share with us your professional opinion? As an expert in adolescent psychology, with experience in runaways?'

Pip was about to clear up the confusion, but as often happened to her, she started speaking without thinking. 'Ben and Madison separated for a while last year – that must have been difficult for the boy, and could definitely lead to him acting out.' Pip remembered the confusion and bad feelings that had accompanied her own parents' break-up. She ran away from home pretty much weekly at one point – once to join an actual circus, believe it or not, but it turned out she was too tall for the trapeze. And the mix-up with the elephants could have happened to anybody.

'How much do we know about the couple's relationship now? And about the specifics of his relationship with his parents?' Pip was asking out of curiosity as much as anything else. Let's face it, this was fascinating, celebrity gossip just about first-hand! A lifetime of reading *Hello!* magazine, celebrity mags and Twitter had prepared her for this moment.

'We didn't talk about the parents' relationship in the initial interview, but that's a good point and we should have thought of that. We will have to get more info from them.' Doug Bradford glared around the room as he said this, and Pip was glad that she wasn't the one who had failed to get the information.

She reckoned it was probably time to fess up to what seemed to be a case of mistaken identity. Pity. It had been fun. She took a deep breath. This was bound to be awkward. 'The thing is—'

Doug rode right over her attempted interjection. 'There's no time to waste. The Prices are expecting a call from us to set up an interview with you. They know we've brought you on board.'

He turned to the table. 'Ms du Bois came to our assistance when we were looking for young Livi James a couple of months back. Her agency was retained by BI and she worked remotely. Ms du Bois's input was most valuable in establishing that the young woman was, happily, alive and well and living in South America.' There was a polite chuckle from the end of the table.

'I hope you'll have good news for us on this one, too,' he said, turning to Pip. 'You can deal with the family through Madison

Price's personal assistant. He's been tasked with communicating between us and them.'

He handed Pip a card. 'Here are all his details – you can make an appointment to go round to the house. There's no time to lose.'

She was going to tell him then. Really, she was. Yes, he was an irritating mansplainer who had hired an expert he didn't allow to speak, but still, he needed to know that Pip was not the expert in question.

Until he said, 'Those files there are for you. Absolutely top secret, you understand. You will know things about the Price family that nobody else in the country knows. If the press got hold of any of this, it would be a disaster. We don't want a repeat of the Princess Ann incident.' He glared at the rest of the room again. Then, turning back to Pip, he said the words that sealed the deal. 'Your payment is in there, in the envelope, in cash. The family does not want a paper trail. It's the agreed fee, plus some extra for expenses – just keep a record.'

Pip reached for the files and the envelope that might just save her bacon. Or bring home the bacon, depending on how you looked at it.

CHAPTER THREE

Was it illegal, impersonating a medical practitioner and taking the money and the files under false pretences, Pip wondered as she descended the stairs from Boston Investigations, having given them all the telephone numbers where she might possibly be found. Or where Pip du Bois might be found. She'd never actually *said* she was Ms du Bois, to be fair. Was it impersonating if you hadn't said a word? And anyway, where *was* Ms du Bois? And what was Pip going to tell Sharon? Bloody hell, this was another fine mess, as Laurel – or was it Hardy? – would say, and it wasn't even her fault. She'd turned up to do an honest day's temping and next thing she knew she'd been hired to investigate an actual disappearance, with an envelope full of cash to show for it. And really, when you thought about it, it could have happened to anyone, mistaken identity. Although probably not quite as often as it happened to her, she thought with a sigh.

She should have cleared things up right away, but she didn't and it was a bit late now. But then what to do? It was one thing winging it through a meeting, but quite another interviewing the family, investigating, or even solving the mysterious disappearance of Matty Price. And when the real Ms du Bois turned up, there'd be hell to pay. Old Sharon would probably regard this as worse than the cat. And there was no doubt that the real Ms du Bois *would* turn up. Pip sighed. She'd have to tell them the truth. Even though she had a really strong feeling that she could help. And it would be so lovely to actually do something useful and good for a change.

Exiting the heavy glass door onto the street, Pip barrelled straight into a woman standing on the pavement, surveying the names on the intercom. The incomer was small and slight and Pip was big and rangy, so Pip barely noticed her before her chest collided with the woman's head. She could see the woman's greying roots.

'I'm so sorry!' said Pip, helping the woman to her feet. 'You all right?'

'Fine. My fault. Wasn't looking,' she said, brushing herself down. 'I'm having the Most Awful Day.' You could hear the capital letters in the way she said it. 'I'm an hour late for an appointment. But here they are, Boston Investigations.' She made for the door, which was still ajar.

'I work there,' said Pip with unusual foresight, slamming the door behind her and inserting herself between the woman and the intercom. 'Who were you meant to see?'

'Doug Bradford,' said the woman. 'He's expecting me.'

'You're Ms du Bois? The psychologist?'

The woman looked at Pip, surprised. 'Yes. Are you part of the team I'm working with?'

Pip barely hesitated. 'We were waiting for you. You are too late, I'm afraid. We've got someone else. Turns out we won't be needing you after all.'

Ms du Bois went white and pressed her hands to her cheeks. Pip felt sorry for the poor woman, what with being late and having her job stolen by an imposter (although Ms du Bois didn't know that part of the Most Awful Day, of course), and then having said imposter knock her off her feet. Pip knew all about Most Awful Days. In fact, this seemed like the sort of thing that would happen to her. She almost told her everything then and there. But she didn't.

'Oh shit,' said the real Ms du Bois. 'This is a disaster. Think, Sophie, think.'

She actually looked quite shaky, like she might faint. Pip felt bad for her. She wasn't a young woman, perhaps Mummy's age. On impulse, Pip took her arm and said, 'I was going to get a smoothie at the juice place before I head home. Let me get you one too? At least your trip won't be completely wasted.'

Which is how the real Ms du Bois and the fake Ms du Bois landed up on adjacent bar stools at a wooden counter in the window of the juice bar next to Boston Investigations, watching the people spewed from the surrounding offices at lunch hour. Pip hadn't planned this part, but then again, she hadn't planned anything that had happened so far that morning. But, as Mummy would say, in for a penny, in for a pound. And since they were here, she was going to make the best of it. Maybe she'd even find a way to get out of this misunderstanding.

They surveyed the menu – really, it was extraordinary what they made milk out of these days; no longer just cows, that's for sure – and ordered their smoothies.

'Excuse me a moment,' said Ms du Bois, and she dug around in her copious bag and pulled out her mobile phone. 'I just need to check my messages.' Pip sat and observed the other woman, who seemed to be regaining her composure, sitting up straighter. The waitress brought Pip's drink – the Big Green Whiz, as it was called, rather oddly. Then suddenly, Ms du Bois turned back to her, calmer now, giving Pip her full attention.

'Tell me about you, what is it you do there at Boston Investigations?' When they'd bumped into each other in the doorway, Ms du Bois had seemed like a slightly flustered older woman. But now she seemed different. Her eyes were sharp and focused on Pip. There was something hard about them, something that made Pip feel almost nervous. If she was going to come clean, it wouldn't be to Ms du Bois.

'I help out with research when they need me,' Pip muttered into her drink, fiddling with her bamboo straw, scraping what looked like pond sludge off the side of the glass and licking it. 'I'm just finding my feet really. I'm quite new to the company and to the investigations game.' Which was true, if something of an understatement.

'And you're working on this missing teen investigation? Who's missing? What's the story there, do you think? Do they have any ideas, hmm?' Sophie leaned forward, her bright eyes fixed on Pip. 'I really was looking forward to getting my teeth into this mystery.' She added, almost as an afterthought, 'And helping that poor family be reunited, of course.' Something about the last part sounded off, but maybe Ms du Bois was one of those empath sorts who find it hard to talk about other people's suffering. Poor Ms du Bois. Having her job stolen from her, and being an empath. It really was a lot to bear. But Pip wasn't going to let her guard down and tell her everything.

'I can't say. It's an American celeb's kid, a teenager. But I don't know much. I'm the lowliest member of the team, really. I'm quite lucky to be involved in the actual investigation at all. I was hoping to make an impression, get into the investigation side of things. It seems such exciting work,' said Pip and then added, truthfully for once, 'I'm not sure if I'm cut out for it though – there's so much at stake. What if we don't find them? And I don't always have good instincts for people.'

'Don't be hard on yourself. Just take it step by step, you'll learn quickly on the job. No need to panic,' Ms du Bois said soothingly, sipping on her Berry Almond Blaze. 'And you can just keep me updated with what you're doing, hmm? I might be able to help.'

What a kind woman, willing to help even when she'd lost the job. It made Pip feel a bit better, knowing there were no hard feelings.

'So what's the deal with these teen disappearances?' Pip asked in what she hoped was a casual voice, between slurps of her apple, cucumber and spinach smoothie. 'I hear that's your beat?' She hoped she'd hit the right note of nonchalance. 'What's it usually turn out to be? Fights with parents? Or what, drugs?' Pip was fishing, but she tried to look like this was just small talk, although she wasn't really sure what an 'I am making small talk' face would actually look like.

'The former, mostly. That and romantic entanglements. But family problems – with parents, usually – that's the main one.

Often it's just the regular stuff: arguments about curfews and rules. School marks. Money. Parents fighting, or just not paying attention. Simple really. Honestly, as a psychologist, I'd say most of them need a few therapy sessions, not a private investigator. You could probably actually just leave it and he'll be back, you know. Do nothing and get all the credit, hmm?' She gave a little laugh, presumably to show that she was joking.

Now that she'd got over the shock and the Most Awful Day, Ms du Bois reminded Pip of some sort of small bird, with her bright eyes and straight back and brisk, direct manner. A sweet-looking bird, but possibly ruthless with a worm. Sophie went on to describe the common profile of a runaway: depression, doing poorly at school, messing around with drugs, no-good friends. She seemed very sure that this was just a case of a runaway. Pip thought of that picture of Matty Price in his moss-green cashmere sweater, his hopes and dreams, the clarinet, his skiing and his do-gooding. Glossy mags with their stylists and sharp photographers might not offer an entirely accurate picture of reality, but still, he didn't sound – or look – like a kid with a lot of those kinds of problems.

'What about kidnapping?' she asked.

Sophie gave a wry smile and an odd chuckle. 'With teens? Almost never. Parents tend to think of children being lured away, but mostly they walk out under their own steam. Look, you get the odd one – a girl usually – who's been taken by some awful cult or sex ring or drug dealer. And quite often there's a love interest involved – some dodgy older boyfriend. But I always work from the assumption that the problem is at school or at home, they've left of their own accord, and they'll turn up. Really, you don't need to worry about kidnapping, hmm?'

'So where do they go? How do you start looking?'

'My first call would be to a boyfriend or girlfriend, then to friends; they often turn up there. Be thorough, you know. Don't accept the first version. Keep going back. You know, he's in no trouble, so don't worry if you don't figure it out immediately. Take it slowly. Also, kids head for the bright lights. You might want to be looking at big towns. The kid is probably right here in London. Hard though, needle in a haystack. But be thorough, as I say. It's all about the motivation. Most often they're not even serious about staying away, they're just cross and want to teach the parents a lesson.'

Pip realised – admittedly rather late in the day – that she was completely unqualified to do what this smart, dedicated professional did for a living. Not only was she doing Sophie out of a job, she was jeopardising the safe return of Matty Price and extending the family's worry. Sophie, with her psychology degree and experience, might be able to track him down. Pip, with four-fifths of an English literature degree, very probably could not find a missing boy in a haystack – even given that her area of literary interest had been mid-twentieth-century detective stories. Sophie had made it sound like painstaking, patient work, and Pip knew that she wasn't painstaking. Or patient.

Pip's life was distinguished by more than the average number of very dubious decisions – Mummy would be able to enumerate them, no doubt – but this one might just be the corker. Her heart was beating fast, and her palms were sweaty. What the hell had she been thinking?

She rested her chin glumly on her hands. 'I don't know. You've got so much experience. I'm just starting out. I don't know if I'm cut out for it…'

'Look,' said Sophie. 'I know I've missed out on this job, but you just call me if you need to chat about the investigation. This business is such a boys' club – I'd be happy to help a clever young woman like you get a start. Just remember, he'll probably come back on his own, and as long as you've looked like you're busy, they'll think you did it, hmm.'

'Really? You'd help me? Wow, that's so decent of you.'

She handed Pip a business card printed with just her name and number. 'Take this. If you want to bounce anything off me, just phone. And don't be too worried – he'll probably turn up just fine.' Sophie looked at Pip expectantly, and after a pause, Pip wrote her number on a paper napkin and gave it to Sophie, hoping that was what Sophie had wanted. Sophie glanced at the number and nodded. Then she picked up her coat and briefcase and left.

Pip settled into her seat and checked her phone, which had been vibrating in her pocket.

I'm trying to phone you.

> *I am Very Busy. I have a Job. That pays Money.*
> *As you know, I need money.*

I don't like your tone, Epiphany.

> *It's a text, Mummy. It has no tone.*

No need to be snippy.

> *Must run. Been great chatting. Xxx*

Don't take that attitude with me, young lady.

Epiphany?

Dammit Epiphany, I can see the tick things.

You always were the most infuriating child, Epiphany.

Pip sighed and put her phone away, picked up the bill, and headed for home. She was going to prove herself to Mummy and do this thing. She was going to prove herself to everyone. She had work to do.

CHAPTER FOUR

Most wound himself around and between Pip's ankles. She looked down at the striped grey wedge of her cat's head and felt a surge of pity-love at the way he listed, as always, a little to the left because of the leg. She hadn't worked much since the vet incident, so he'd become quite accustomed to having her around for most of the day. He was ecstatic to see her (and to see supper, of course). It was nice to be missed. It would have been nicer to be missed by an actual human. An actual male human. An actual male human like Tim. But still, it was nice to be missed by Most. Pip spooned out Turkey Chunks in Rich Gravy. Most lunged at the food before it got to the bowl.

'Greedy boy! Wait a sec. Here you go, now you can eat it.' She stood up. 'I'm sorry I wasn't here. But a girl's got to earn a living, you know. Bring home the bacon. Or the turkey chunks. You have a working mother now.' It felt good saying it, even if it was just to the cat. She tried not to think about the part where it was all based on lies and deception.

Having seen to the cat's needs, Pip saw to her own. She poured a big glass of Chardonnay from the half-bottle in the fridge and grabbed a packet of pretzels from the cupboard. As an afterthought, she added a packet of chocolate Hobnobs. The upside of her long-limbed, gangly frame was that she never put on an ounce of weight, no matter what she ate.

She settled at the kitchen table, the wine, pretzels, biscuits and files within reach. On the way home she had decided on a course of action. She would take a look at the files, do a bit of her own stalking – sorry, online research – and then decide what to do next. Which could well involve coming clean before she was in too deep, she told herself, unconvincingly. Just because she'd run away once in her teens did *not* make her an expert. Just because she *wanted* to make things right didn't mean it was right to make things right. So to speak.

She took a deep breath. She was hyped up from the busy day and the adrenaline, and her head was buzzing with questions and ideas. She couldn't wait to get her eyes on the contents of those files, but she sipped her wine and took a moment to savour the suspense. Inside she knew she'd find money, and who knew what secrets and revelations about Matty Price and his celebrity family. If this was a movie, the buff envelope would be glowing gold with promise and there would be suspenseful dum-dum-dum-DUM music playing in the background as she reached for the envelope. Then again, if this was a movie, Pip would have had a manicure. Personal grooming had taken a bit of a dive in The Lean Years, but things were on the up and up. It would be manis and pedis all round once she'd paid her rent and taken care of her other expenses.

Pip tore the top off the envelope and upended it onto the kitchen table. A wad of fifty-pound notes hit the surface with a satisfying thud. She pushed that to one side. Half of it was going to go to Tim for rent – if she kept it, of course. There was always a chance that she was going to come clean, she told herself again, her inner voice sounding irritatingly virtuous, if somewhat unconvincing.

The files were thinner than she'd hoped, but Pip scanned the pages eagerly. In the first file, most of the pages had been printed off the internet – bits and pieces from celebrity gossip sites, pictures of Matty and of the rest of the family. There was an entertainment news snippet about Madison's new movie, the one she was going to be shooting in London, but it was nothing more than speculation; all very hush-hush. Any halfway decent celeb stalker – Pip, for instance – could have come up with this lot in about fifteen minutes. Bloody useless.

Somewhat more usefully, the second file held only one document, but it was a copy of something called the Client Contact Sheet, presumably a standard form that BI used to capture information. It was dated two days previous, and Matty had already been missing five days when it was completed. So he'd been gone a week. The client was listed as Ben Price.

Personal info was scant. Matty had turned seventeen a few months ago. He was enrolled in a local crammer-type school while they were living in London, and continuing with the American syllabus via correspondence. Hobbies, she knew about: cross-country skiing, clarinet. She hadn't known he was the youth ambassador for the Save the Forests organisation.

In the final file, there were personal documents that the Prices had presumably provided. There was a report from the school – middling marks, pleasant remarks from the staff, he was 'settling in nicely and making friends', no discipline issues. He sounded like a nice kid who wouldn't shoot the lights out. Pip knew all about that. There was a list with names, contact details, addresses of friends and family. She ran her eye down the list. Ben and Madison. This must be what Doug had meant by the files being full of confidential information.

'I have Madison Price's personal phone number,' Pip told the cat, who lifted his head momentarily from his bowl. She had a strong impulse to phone Madison, just to hear that honeyed American drawl. Then, remembering that she was not twelve years old, and that she was a professional with a job to do – though admittedly, a job premised on what might kindly be regarded as a case of mistaken identity, and less kindly as downright duplicitousness – she moved on through the list.

Three of Matty's friends (one girl, two boys), two domestic staff members and a bi-weekly gardener (how the other half live!), the principal of the school. And Fredrick Gold, the family's assistant and liaison with BI, the one she was to phone for tomorrow's meeting. Decision time. Was Pip going to go ahead and ring him up, make the appointment, continue with this investigation? Be the hero of the day, just for once? Or was she going to chuck it all in, take whatever flak came her way for it, and move on? Be the idiot loser that she always managed to be, whatever her good intentions?

The first option both frightened and excited her. She wanted to meet the Prices, that was true. Imagine, a little sit-down with the famous American TV star! But that wasn't all of it. She wanted to achieve something, to solve a problem, to make things better. Recently – well, for the last few years to be honest – she hadn't done much of that. She had generally made things worse. It felt as if Pip had lurched from one disaster to the next. Things started well, but then deteriorated. Misunderstandings. Unexpected complications. Poor decisions, she had to admit.

Pip took a sip of her wine and thought how very wonderful it would feel to be the hero of her story, for once. This could be her chance. It could be a turning point, a way to prove herself. She really did think she had potential in this field – she knew a lot about celebrities, she'd read her crime thrillers and she'd studied all the classic mystery novelists for her almost-degree, she had good instincts (apart from when she had really terrible instincts), she was a kick-ass solver of puzzles. She also had a very compelling need for the cash. A perfect combination for success. Of course, it could all go horribly wrong.

As for chucking it in, well, she could see why that might be the sensible option, on the face of it. Get out now before she was in too deep. She could give the money back. Explain the misunderstanding. They'd be cross, but perhaps not completely apoplectic. It might not go legal this time.

But the poor Prices. They *needed* her. With a bit of help from Ms du Bois, Pip could probably track him down in a day or two, and that would be that. And honestly, when would she ever get to meet Madison and Ben Price, or anyone of their ilk? *In for a penny*, thought Pip. Although, she thought, glancing at the pile of money, it was slightly more than a penny. She'd go to the meeting. See what the Prices had to say. And then decide. Time to phone Mr Gold.

Pip reached for her mobile and saw three missed calls from Mummy. She hadn't turned her phone's sound on, so Wagner had played unnoticed. Mummy always left a voice message, even though Pip's own message said, 'Please *don't* leave a message, but send me a text instead,' and even though Pip had personally asked her a thousand times to send a text instead. 'Don't be silly,' her mother had said, peeved, 'I'm already on the phone, I can just talk. Why would I ring off, find my glasses, and then type a message with my fingers, when you can just listen to the message?'

This time, there were three messages, her mother's rather reedy voice giving variants of: 'Phone me urgently, Epiphany, I have to talk to you about something.' There was virtually no chance that she was going to say the one thing Pip wanted to hear: that she was going to reinstate the allowance that she sometimes gave her.

Pip knew that Mummy's Gentleman Caller, Andrew McFee, was behind it this time. 'She'll never learn to stand on her own two feet if you keep bailing her out,' he'd told Mummy, right in front of Pip. It wasn't as if Pip really wanted to be bailed out. She would love to be able to stand on her own two feet, without Mummy's help. Anyway, this was all beside the point, because help would not be forthcoming. Mummy said she and Andrew needed the money for the two-month trip around South America – Peru and Ecuador, culminating in the Galapagos, where they were going to fulfil Andrew's lifelong dream of seeing the blue-footed boobies in the wild. Mummy could wait. Pip couldn't face another conversation about boobies.

Pip had flocks of butterflies in her stomach when she phoned Mr Gold, but it was all quite brisk and businesslike. They arranged to meet at eleven a.m. at the Price residence in Kensington. Tomorrow, she'd meet the Hollywood glamour couple in person.

CHAPTER FIVE

Madison Price was straight-up gorgeous. She had the golden glow
Pip had always assumed was due to make-up, lighting and good
photographic angles, but which, now that she was sitting in front of
her, appeared to emanate from Madison herself. It was as if actual
sunlight was coming out of her pores. Her hair was streaked with
highlights. Each individual hair seemed to have been coloured its
own unique shade of gold, and the morning light coming in from
the huge bay window glanced off each strand. She was dressed
in similar golden hues: a loose pearl-coloured cashmere top over
snug-fitting trousers a shade or two darker. The whole effect was
rich and soft and glowing. Like a crème caramel. On Pip, it would
have been covered with paw prints and chocolate smudges after
ten minutes, but Madison was pristine.

She was tiny in real life and also very slim – she'd probably
last had a carbohydrate in the early noughties. Pip knew from her
evening's googling that Madison Price was forty-five, passing as
forty-two. She looked great for forty-two, extraordinary for forty-
five. Mr Gold introduced Pip as Ms du Bois.

'Please call me Pip,' she said – no way would she be able to live
with that level of confusion.

'And this is Ms Madison Price,' said Gold in hushed and rever-
ent tones. As if Pip – or anyone conscious and in possession of a
television in the last decade – wouldn't know. Madison had played
Dr Miranda Ray in the long-running TV medical drama series

Ray's Hospital Files for, basically, ever. Five hundred and forty-three episodes, to be precise (*thank you, Google*).

Madison turned her tawny lion's eyes on Pip and said in a low voice, 'Thank you for coming. My husband will be with us in a minute.' It was really weird hearing that voice. Pip half expected her to say, 'Nurse Bloom, it's a risky operation, but I think I can save your child.'

'I hope you can help. We are crazy worried, as you can imagine.' This was said in a calm voice, with no twitch of emotion on her face. She didn't look at all worried, never mind crazy worried, about her missing son. But, to be fair, that could have been the result of the Botox. 'Would you like some tea? Coffee?' Without waiting for Pip's answer, she waved her hand in the general direction of Mr Gold. 'Just bring both. And whatever else.'

She had an oddly languid way of speaking, letting sentences trail away as her gaze and mind wandered off. Maybe it was an acting thing. Pip didn't know much about the dramatic arts. At his mistress's command, Gold left the room, just as her husband entered.

'Good morning. Ben Price,' he said, offering Pip a firm handshake and a weak smile. 'We're grateful for your help, Ms du Bois.'

'Pip,' she said quickly. 'Please call me Pip.'

'We are beside ourselves with worry, Pip. It's just unbearable, the not knowing. I haven't slept in days. Please, whatever you can suggest. We'll do anything. Just to know where he is.'

Ben put his hand on Pip's arm and his eyes welled up. Unlike Madison, Ben *did* look crazed with worry. He had bags under his eyes, and his hair didn't look like it had been brushed. *One* parent seemed genuinely distraught, at least.

'Ben,' said Madison, rather sharply. 'Let's just see what Ms… what Pip… odd name… what Pip has to say.'

'I guess we should go over the basic information on file first, just to confirm it's all correct, and to fill in the gaps. And then we can go from there,' said Pip.

Go from there to where? That was the question. No bloody idea, frankly, how she was going to get to the meat of the matter, which she thought might well be the golden couple's marital problems. She'd spent the evening and most of the night sucked into the spiralling vortex of online celebrity gossip. Four pages of her notebook were filled with snippets and questions. And frankly, this marriage seemed made in the PR department, rather than in heaven.

Ben joined his wife on the sofa, resting his feet on the table in front of them, where an orchid and a couple of big glossy coffee table books were artfully arranged – Pip noted a photographic history of the West End theatre district, a book on the history of London film-making, and a thick biography of Agatha Christie. Madison tapped Ben's feet sharply, and he removed them, after which Madison inched almost imperceptibly towards the far end, leaving a sizeable gap between them.

Pip warmed up slowly, going through the Client Contact Sheet, confirming names and numbers, asking for more details on the friends and staff, making sure she had everything straight. It all seemed to be correct. Ben answered most of the questions. Madison chipped in from time to time, but more with editorialising than with actual information. She got a friend's name wrong – 'It's Ned, not Fred,' Ben said with barely masked irritation.

Pip thought she'd lob a few low balls first to break the tension and warm everyone up. Hobbies seemed like a good start. 'Where did… does…' She struggled with her tenses – *how does one refer to the disappeared? Bet the real Ms du Bois would know.* 'Tell me about the boxing. Has he been doing that for long? Where did… does… he go to train?'

Madison answered that he had been boxing for about six months and he went to a boxing gym rather inconveniently far from home. 'I don't know how he found it originally, but he insisted that it was the only place he wanted to go. And then he went three or four times a week.'

'Did you think it was a strange hobby? I mean, the clarinet, the forests, nature… It's not a picture of a boxer.'

'Now you mention it, I suppose. But you know how teenagers can be, they experiment. Then get obsessed with things…' She trailed off, seemingly losing interest in the sentence.

'Was there a particular trainer he went to?'

'What was his name, Ben?' She turned back to Pip to explain. 'Ben often went to watch, he met the man. *I've* been busy preparing for filming.' She said this with an air of importance.

'Jimmy,' Ben muttered. He'd hardly said a word since the boxing discussion started.

'And the address?'

She took down the trainer's name and address in her notebook. Very PI-like. 'I'll go and have a look at the place, have a chat to Jimmy.'

It was time to get a bit more personal. Pip cleared her throat.

'I understand that you had some, um, family issues last year.'

'Family issues?' Ben asked, wrinkling his forehead as if trying to discern what she could mean. 'Not until this.'

'I mean between the two of you, what we might call marital differences. It was in the gossip mags. Excuse me for intruding, but I have to ask.'

'That's all water under the bridge, isn't it, darling?' Madison said brightly, turning the thousand-watt smile to her husband, and reaching her arm across the acre of sofa to rest her hand on his leg. For the first time since the interview started, Madison looked awkward, her arm stretched out, trying to look natural. Pip was 90 per cent sure there was a tiny flinch from Ben.

'There was a brief separation, not even a separation really, more like a… a hiatus,' she said, pleased with the word. 'A hiatus, yes.

You know, a little break, a few sessions of couple's therapy just to iron out the misunderstandings. And that's when I was offered the lead in this movie which is shooting here in Great Britain. We decided to come to live in London for a full year. I'm immersing myself in the country, the accent. And it's an adventure for the whole family. It's been marvellous, hasn't it?'

Ben didn't answer that question, but added: 'And just to be clear, that had absolutely nothing to do with Matty.'

Madison went on, 'He wasn't affected at all by the, the hiatus. Teenagers, you know, they're impervious. And his schedule – he was off skiing, and there was school and of course, clarinet. Hardly noticed.'

Remembering her own teenage angst, Pip thought this unlikely. More likely, the hours on the slopes were a good way to get out of the house where parents were fighting or absent.

'And he was happy to come to London?'

'Oh yes, it was good for us to get out of the States for a time.'

'And when you got here…?'

'He settled in fine, it really wasn't an issue,' Madison said.

That line of questioning was interrupted by a clattering at the door, causing them all to jump.

CHAPTER SIX

The noise at the door signalled the reappearance of Gold. Odd little man. He bore the tea tray close to shoulder height, and with his arms almost straight. Pip thought of the scene in *The Lion King* where Mufasa shows the cub Simba to his subjects. It was an unnecessarily grand entrance, and an unnecessarily elaborate arrangement – teapot, coffee press, cups and saucers, sugars white and brown, a jug of milk and a smaller one of cream, a bottle of sparkling mineral water, a glass with ice and lemon, a plate of shortbread biscuits, and another of carrots and celery cut up into perfectly even sticks – hardly a teatime staple, but Pip presumed they were for Madison.

'Thanks. Just put it here.' Madison didn't even glance at Gold, but moved the photobooks to one side to make space on the table. Gold fussed about, slowly placing the saucers out, and then the cups on top of them. Pip wondered if he was deliberately delaying – so he could listen in? Or just to impress Madison with his diligence?

Pip's mind ran back over the file's scant info on Gold: four years in the family's employ, taking care of the household and their arrangements – travel, staff, admin, online shopping. It was Gold who had come to look at schools and houses before they arrived. Gold who had set up the meeting with Boston Investigations. But Gold was not one of Matty's parents, and Pip's newly minted PI instincts told her that the parents would be the most likely to have a gut feeling as to where their son had gone.

*

Even working at a glacial pace, Gold had finally finished setting out the tea things. He poured the mineral water into a glass and handed it deferentially to Madison. 'Coffee or tea?' he asked Pip. She took tea and a shortbread and thanked him, although he seemed not to notice. He was too busy with Madison's needs.

'Not now,' said Madison, waving away the carrots.

'If I might say,' he ventured softly, 'it is so important to keep up your strength at a time like this.'

'Really, Gold, please,' she snapped. 'This is not the time for a nutrition lecture.'

Gold held the plate out to Ben, who answered in quiet anguish: 'I can't eat. How could I, when we're in this crisis?'

Pip, who was unfortunately mid-bite at this point, tried to chew her shortbread as unobtrusively as possible, leaving her jaw in place and mushing the biscuit against her palate with her tongue. The real Ms du Bois would have known better than to eat mid-interview.

'Just go, thank you,' said Madison.

'Of course,' said Gold, looking as if he might be about to cry.

Having swallowed the soggy lump of barely chewed shortbread chunks, Pip turned to Ben. 'So, what's your feeling? Where do you think he is?' Her direct question seemed to surprise him.

'Well, if I knew that, you wouldn't be here, would you?' he said, tears welling up again. 'All I know is that he was here, he seemed fine, and then he was gone. And now I don't know what to do.'

'But you waited five days to come to us?' She liked saying 'us', as if she were part of something large and official. 'You must have been fairly sure he wasn't in danger.' She felt like one of those glamorous TV lawyers, shooting insightful questions around the room. She sat up a little straighter and adopted a strict expression. These people weren't going to pull their shiny, expensive wool over her eyes.

'We didn't know what to do. I wanted to go to the police, but Madison felt—'

'That first day, you told me his social media accounts were active,' Madison interrupted Ben. 'He was posting on Instagram. Twittering. Or whatever. Tweeting.' Madison pronounced the word 'tweeting' as if it were 'cannibalism' or 'paedophilia', and added, 'Agatha would not approve of tweeting.'

'Agatha?' asked Pip, scanning her notes for the name of an aunt or perhaps a grandmother.

'Christie,' said Madison, as if that explained everything.

'Agatha Christie, the novelist? Would not approve of Twitter?'

'Yes. *I* am the young Agatha Christie.'

Pip didn't know how to react to this extraordinary statement. The file hadn't mentioned mental illness.

'In the movie,' Ben shed some light. 'Madison is playing Agatha. That's why we're in London. It's very hush-hush.'

'Ah,' said Pip, understanding. She had read the speculation about Madison's new role in a big-budget feature film, but the actual role and the name of the movie had been kept out of the press. Pip felt a frisson of excitement. She was in the inner circle now. And it was Agatha Christie! One of Pip's favourite writers and the subject of her final essay: 'The making of Miss Marple – the mistress of murder mystery' (maybe too much alliteration, looking at it now, but Pip could never resist its powerful and potent pull).

Pip gave her head a tiny shake. Things were getting off track.

'You were saying, about his social media accounts?'

Ben continued, 'I was very concerned. Madison too, of course, but she said, and I'm sure she's right, that if his social media accounts were active at first, it meant he wasn't… He wasn't in trouble or… um…'

'It meant he wasn't kidnapped,' said Madison, losing patience with Ben. 'Or in a hospital somewhere. Or dead.' Ben blanched at the word. 'Oh, come on, Ben, we agreed he needed some space.' She turned to Pip, as if confiding in a friend. 'He's holed up somewhere with some girl or other. Frankly, these English girls adore him. Just adore. The American accent is an aphrodisiac in itself for you people, and there's the celeb angle, and he is a gorgeous-looking boy. You know young people… I'm sure he's fine.'

'We don't know that, Madison,' Ben said. 'We don't know where he is. We need—'

'What we need, darling,' she said, now without a trace of the languid drawl, 'is to keep this situation out of the papers. I have told you a hundred times that I can't have this personal hiccup blown up into something it's not. My whole film could be overshadowed by a manufactured scandal about some teenage nonsense.'

'Madison,' Ben tried to interrupt. 'He could be—'

'Ben,' she said sharply. 'I know that you don't understand what it is to be an artist, but it is essential that I now inhabit the world of Agatha. The *mind* of Agatha. The *soul* of Agatha. To *immerse* myself in her books. I can't have this sort of distraction.' She flapped her hand in the direction of Pip, in a way which made her feel like the lowliest, most incompetent little beetle. 'Anyway, I wanted a chance to research which investigation agency would be the best and most discreet. Once we had that, I let you report it, didn't I?'

Pip butted in, trying to get the conversation back on an even keel. 'And what about now?' she asked Ben. 'Is he still online?'

'No,' said Ben, looking down at his hands. 'Last time was over a week ago.'

'And you've obviously tried to get in touch?'

'DMs, email, WhatsApp. Phone calls obviously, but it goes straight to voicemail.'

'The location apps?'

'Disabled.'

All of Pip's ideas seemed to have resulted in dead ends – the gym, the marital strife, the social media. She stared down at her notebook, which looked a little less than professional. She probably should get a sturdy ring-bound job, instead of this silly thing her sister, Flis, had given her for Christmas, with a picture of a kitten, and the words 'Be GRRRReat today!' on the front cover, and then in light grey type on every page. She put her hand over the GRRRReat part, but Ben had already noticed it. He looked embarrassed on her behalf, but then met her eyes with a little smile.

What would a real detective do? What would Miss Marple do? Snoop, that's what. In the movies, they were forever finding clues in medicine cupboards. Bottles of incriminating pills. Pregnancy tests. That sort of thing.

'I think I have what I need for now,' she said, in what she hoped was a decisive voice. Not the voice of a woman who had a kitten on her notebook. 'Could I please use the loo before I go?'

CHAPTER SEVEN

'Left out the door up the passage, and there's a guest bathroom on your left,' said Ben. She could tell that he already felt let down by her ineptitude. Usually, it took people a bit longer.

Pip stopped briefly at the guest loo that Ben had directed her to. Miss Marple always managed better than a guest loo, and she would too. *More than one person can channel Agatha Christie*, she thought, as she glanced around before heading upstairs.

Which room was Matty's and which bathroom would he use? She picked the first door on her left and struck lucky – it was definitely a teenager's bathroom. Hair gels and creams, all a very expensive eco-friendly range. Face wash. Spot-be-Gone – not that he seemed to have even a blackhead from what Pip had seen on the many pictures she had scrutinised for hidden clues. About four towels hung from various hooks, towel rails and over the shower door. Enough bamboo eco toothbrushes for a small orphanage. Wherever Matty had gone, it seemed he hadn't packed his toiletries. Pip wondered if this was significant, and made a note of it in the kitten notebook, before realising that a celeb like him would probably have duplicates or would just buy new stuff.

She closed the bathroom door and opened the medicine cupboard to find… nothing. A bottle of vitamins. Some aspirin. Odds and ends: nail clippers, scissors, a comb. She held a nail file up to her face and tried to channel Miss Marple. But even Miss Marple would be stumped for inspiration from this lot. All out of ideas, Pip sat down on the toilet seat, her elbows on her knees, forehead resting dejectedly on her hands. The rubbish bin next to the loo caught her eye. Inside was a small cardboard box with a courier company sticker on, a bit of paper stuffed inside it. It hardly seemed likely that this would be the kind of clue the movies served up – 'Delivery from Illegal Prescription Drugs-R-Us' stamped on the side – but in the absence of other ideas, Pip picked it up and pulled out the paper. It seemed to be a printed leaflet that had been deliberately torn up. This section had random phrases: '99.9% accuracy and a detailed report…', 'earwax, hair or nail clippings…' *That's weird – what would you need that for, witchcraft?* 'Post samples to 10 Osbor…'

Pip turned it over and hit gold: printed in small letters at the bottom of the page was a website address: www.DNAdynamix.com.

She pulled her phone from her pocket and entered the URL. It was an online paternity testing company. 'Know for sure' was the slogan. You just mailed off samples from the 'offspring' and the 'possible father' and, if identified, 'any additional possible fathers', and within days you'd receive a 'confidential report with 99.9% accuracy!'

'Ms, um, Pip?' It was Gold's voice. Right outside the door. Pip pocketed the scrap of paper, took a picture of the courier company's label and flushed the loo. Then she got up and washed her hands. She opened the door and came face to face with the odd little man.

'What are you doing up here?' he asked. His eyes were narrowed, and his nose wrinkled as if he smelled something bad.

'The usual,' said Pip. 'Would you like me to elaborate?' Their eyes met, and she held his gaze. Pip had once regaled a lesser royal with the details of her upset stomach; little Gold held no threat to her.

'You were supposed to use the guest bathroom.' He was a lot less obsequious when Madison wasn't around.

She opened her eyes wide in innocence. 'Isn't this it? Mr Price said to go up the stairs and on the left?'

'Up the *passage* and on the left.'

'Oh, silly me. It could happen to anyone, couldn't it?' She smiled at Gold. 'Anyway, done now. While we're up here, can I take a peek at Matty's room?'

He eyed her coldly. 'What for?'

'Just to get a sense of him, see what he was like. He may have left some clue as to where he was going.'

'It's not my place to give permission – you would need to ask Ms Price.'

Pip considered this. On one hand, she really *should* look at the room. On the other, she couldn't face the strange tension between the Prices again. Mummy always said that she was oversensitive to other people's problems.

'Next time,' she said in her most intimidating voice, the one she reserved for telesales people. She turned and walked down the stairs, hoping to leave Gold cringing in her wake. Instead, he followed so closely behind her that she could smell his aftershave.

Her plan to avoid another interaction with the Prices was equally unsuccessful. The couple were standing at the bottom of the stairs, as if waiting for her, but embroiled in a whispered shouty conversation, and not a harmonious one.

Pip caught Madison's throaty hiss '…because you are so jealous of my success, Ben. Maybe if you had done anything, anything AT ALL, in the last ten years other than—'

'Here we are, Ms Madison,' Gold said loudly from over Pip's left shoulder, ruining her chance of hearing anything useful. 'Ms, um, Pip was a bit lost.'

Not lost, thought Pip, *I was doing detective work.* She felt the crumpled paper in her coat pocket. A lead a last, even if she had no idea what it actually led *towards*.

'I'll be on my way then. Get to the boxing gym before it closes.' She offered a hand to Madison, who didn't seem to notice it.

'I'll show you out,' said Ben, already at Pip's elbow.

'Gold can do that,' snapped Madison, whose golden aura had frayed rather in the half-hour since Pip had first met her. 'Honestly, I don't know why I try.'

Gold obeyed with a smug smile, and in an instant inserted himself between Pip and Ben. He began shepherding her towards the front door. He walked her right to her car – did the ridiculous man think she was going to sneak back in the house and upset Madison? If she'd taken the Tube, like she'd planned to, would he have walked her all the way to the station? For once, she was pleased she loved driving so much, even in the crazy London traffic. At least she wouldn't have to walk a mile with odd little Gold at her side. Gold ran his eyes over the elderly yellow Mini, his gaze lingering on the mess on the back bumper where Pip had attempted – and failed – to remove the array of stickers festooned over the car's boxy bum by the previous owner. From the tattered remains of shiny vinyl scattered with random words and letters,

sav

he

rhino

was the only one that made any sort of sense.

Gold opened the driver's door, and then closed it firmly behind her. Pip was pretty sure that if he had his way, she would never come back.

Pip looked back towards the gracious house where the TV star, her novelist husband and, until last week, Matty Price lived. She wondered what secrets it held; the calm symmetry of its Georgian facade wasn't giving anything away.

She had so many questions. Why did Matty leave? Who had bought a paternity test and why? And how did it end up in Matty's bathroom? How did Gold fit in? And how the hell did Madison get her hair to look like that? She turned the key in the ignition and felt the little car come to life. Her eyes followed Gold back to the door. A flicker of movement in the downstairs window. It was Ben Price, his mournful eyes meeting Pip's before he turned away.

CHAPTER EIGHT

As Pip drove to the gym in Hackney, following the instructions on Google Maps as best she could, she thought about her strange discovery in the bathroom. It certainly seemed that someone in the house had used a paternity test. If it was Matty, why would he have ordered a DNA test? Was Madison right about his irresistible allure to English girls? Could he have knocked one up? That would be a disaster. Pip imagined that Agatha would approve of that marginally less than she would approve of Twitter. It might account for a young teen running away.

Or perhaps he had questions about his own father. But why would he? Granted, he and his dad didn't look especially similar. They were not one of those parent/child pairs where you immediately thought, 'Jeez, take a look at the nose on those two!' But they looked alike in the way all well-known Americans seemed to look somewhat alike: even features, straight nose, wide mouth, slim build, tallish. Ben was darker than Matty, but the boy would also have dipped into Madison's golden gene pool. He looked enough like Ben not to raise any suspicion on that score. He must have had some other reason to wonder. If that was what it was about at all.

Unless someone else had ordered the test. Ben? Madison? Even Gold, although she couldn't imagine why. She was pretty sure he wasn't in the business of fathering people; it would distract him from Madison. Unless... but she stopped that thought. Obviously Gold and Madison had not conceived a child together. She gave a little shake of disgust at the thought, almost causing the Mini to veer into oncoming traffic.

The gym, it turned out, was in a rather insalubrious part of town. Pip couldn't imagine why Matty would have wanted to train here, after the elegance of Kensington, and what his parents must have made of the place. She looked around as she drove, at the buildings in need of a paint, the dusty or closed up shops, and council blocks with hoodied figures slouching along the periphery. It was strange to think that just a few blocks further on were trendy restaurants and the sort of homes that people like her sister, Flis, had fixed up and gentrified.

Pip spotted the gym and smiled, somewhat reluctantly, at its name – The Glove Box. She drove around the block several times, looking for parking. She was just about to give up, drive further afield and risk the walk back, when a car suddenly pulled out from just in front of the gym.

'Yes!' yelled Pip, deftly manoeuvring her car into the space. Flis often commented that Pip could parallel park on a postage stamp, and Pip suspected this was true. She had no patience for people who found parking difficult, but acknowledged that some of her confidence came from the two months she'd spent driving a bin lorry. She'd loved that job and had been really sad to lose it. The accident with the piano could have happened to anyone.

Once parked, Pip shifted uncomfortably in her seat. The Mini might be a dream to park and cheap to run (aside from being the only car in Greater London she could afford) but it wasn't built for an almost six-footer to lounge about in. She was grateful to finally unfold herself and walk up to the gym. But she was disappointed. There was a note stuck to the door with a grubby piece of Sellotape. The note said, 'Back Soon'. Infuriatingly unspecific, given that there was no indication of when it was written or how long the writer considered to be 'soon'. The appearance of the note gave no clues.

Frankly, it might have been there for decades. Pip stood around for a few minutes, but the teens in hoodies on the other side of the street seemed to be getting restless, and when one shouted, 'Nice pair on you,' she decided she should rather get back into her car, cramped as it was.

Once in the car, she checked her phone. There was a message from Sophie. There was something disconcerting about having the woman you'd stolen a job from messaging you, and Pip opened it with a racing heart. 'How's it going with the investigation?' she asked. Pip took a moment. She could certainly use some advice, but she really wanted to do this alone. Show people she could. So instead of telling Sophie that she was on a stakeout, following up on her first clue – which would have sounded very impressive – she just said, 'Following your advice. Taking it slowly,' and pushed send. She felt a bit bad stealing the woman's job and now lying to her. But this was something she needed to do. Having checked that all her doors were locked, and keeping her eyes on the gym, Pip went back to pondering the paternity test. Who would be wondering, and why?

Aaaand, action. Someone was opening up the gym. Sometimes, life totally played into your preconceptions and this was one of those times. Here was a boxer straight out of Central Casting: lean and muscular, shaven-headed, light on his feet, dressed in tracksuit bottoms and trainers. Tattoos curled up from the neck of his track top and across his throat. Someone had definitely been watching too much *Fight Club*.

Pip reached across to the passenger seat for her bag, and put away her notebook and phone. Her hand was already on the door handle when she saw Ben Price walking towards the gym. Ben Bloody Price! What the hell was he doing here?

She sat rooted to the spot by indecision. Should she follow him in, or watch him and see what transpired? She reckoned Miss Marple would wait and see. But frankly, she'd had enough of sitting in this tiny car. She shoved the door open with her shoulder, grabbed her bag, and unfolded her long frame inelegantly onto the pavement. Ben was already inside. He must have dashed across town the minute Pip left. Pip hurried over to The Glove Box and stopped at the door to listen. In movies, detectives were always overhearing useful snippets of information, but in real life, all Pip could hear was indistinct mumbling. And then footsteps walking towards the door.

She backed out of the doorway, and dashed round the corner of the building. Her heart was pounding like a train. How did Miss Marple maintain her calm demeanour during investigations? Pip waited, her back pressed against the wall, long enough for her heart to ease up, trying not to think about the smell of urine, and then peeked her head round the corner. Just in time to see Ben walk into the Better Burgers Diner a few doors down. Pip processed the options, just the way a real detective would. She could either follow Ben into the diner, or go and meet the tattooed boxer. Ben would be easy enough to find if he disappeared. Jimmy – if it was Jimmy – was here now and might have some new information.

Up close, maybe-Jimmy looked even more terrifying. Muscle and sinew and ink. She would *not* like to get into a beef with him.

'Hi,' she said, in her most friendly voice. 'I'm looking for Jimmy.'

'You found him.' He slapped his open palm against his chest. Even his knuckles were inked, a letter for each finger. The right hand seemed to say 'Lily'. Maybe it was a code. Or an acronym. Or a gang sign. Were these prison tats, she wondered. Maybe he was a criminal. Did he have anything to do with Matty's disappearance? Perhaps she was in danger herself.

He interrupted her panicky thoughts by handing her a printed flier and making a polite enquiry: 'Looking to join the gym? We have an introductory special.'

'I don't think I—'

'Hey, tall girl like you? Great reach. You could be good.' As if to illustrate, he bent his knees and gave a few stabs at the air.

'Really? You think I could box?' She was flattered, in spite of herself. Imagined herself in sweats, bobbing and weaving.

'You'd have to put some work in. Get some power into those arms.' He squeezed where her bicep should be. 'Nothing much going on here. And cardio is very important too,' he said earnestly. 'What's your training programme at the moment?'

'I'm a little out of my fitness routine right now.' Yeah. Just for the last, like, five or six years. 'I've been meaning to get back into it, of course. Um.'

'No problem. When you join, I work with all the new members to put together a personalised programme of strength and fitness. Then we move on to technique.'

He was very well spoken for a hardened criminal. And speaking of hard, he really did have the most splendid arms. She wouldn't mind getting some of that shape herself. She rather liked the idea of joining the boxing gym. Better than those stupid yoga classes she'd signed up for when she was dating Wolf – or, as it turned out, Bill Smith, an Australian plumber with a guru complex. And she had been getting into karate quite seriously when that freak accident happened with the boards and the hand. Anyhow, maybe if things went well and her work was regular, she'd sign up with Jimmy. Get herself strong and fit. But right now, this conversation was getting far off topic.

'Jimmy, I like the look of this gym, and I might be keen to join. But I'm actually here to find out about one of your members. Matty Price.'

'A lot of people looking for this Matty Price today,' he responded, dropping the flier now that he realised she wasn't a potential customer. 'I'll tell you what I told the last bloke. There's no Matty Price on our client register.'

'He trained here. Several times a week. With you. You *are* Jimmy, aren't you?'

'I'm Jimmy. Don't know no Matty though. I'd know him for sure if he was a regular.'

'Did the last bloke show you a picture?'

'No. Just asked about the name.'

Amateurs! Pip opened her bag and pulled out a picture she had thought to bring along. She pushed it across the reception desk. When Jimmy took it, his other hand, she noticed, said, 'Rose'. *What sort of a gang has flower names as its tag?* It was probably ironic and meant that they were particularly violent.

'I know this kid. I've seen him around the neighbourhood. You don't get many around here who look like that. Preppy, like, I think you'd call it. Yeah. I know this kid.'

Yes!

Pip leant forward, and pumped Jimmy for details – when did he last see Matty, what was he wearing, where exactly did he hang out? To which his answers were: 'I dunno, maybe a week or two ago?' and 'Maybe jeans?' and 'Round and about.' Useless. Did the man have no medium-term memory? What was becoming apparent was that although Jimmy had seen Matty, Matty wasn't a member at the gym, let alone a regular.

'Anyway,' said Jimmy, 'why are you asking? You his mum?'

His mum? His MUM? She would have had to be, what – she gave up on the maths – she'd have to have been a teen when she had him. The man was an idiot. Probably too many blows to the head. Or drugs. Opioids. Or steroids. Did steroids shrink your brain, as well as your testicles? She couldn't remember. She explained coldly that she was a private investigator, to which he looked astonished and then impressed. 'Good on you, love,' he said. 'Just goes to show, looks can be deceiving.'

Pip decided to ignore that last remark, although she was burning to know what he meant by it.

'If you see him, or have any further information, please call me. I'll leave you my card,' she said in her most professional voice, just like they did in the cop shows, rooting in her bag. And then remembered that she didn't have a card. 'I seem to have left my cards at the office. I'll give you my number.' Her hand found her stupid notebook and pulled it out. She wrote down her number, her left hand hiding the kitty on the cover, and ripped out the page.

He looked down at it and said with his lips in a small – and to be honest not unattractive – smirk: 'GRRRReat, um, Pip. Funny name. Tell you what. I spot your guy, you come for an introductory boxing session. If you like it, you sign up. How's that sound… Pip?'

'Deal,' she said, a little flustered.

'I see him, I'll call you.' He paused, his eyes on hers – how had she not noticed until now their remarkable green? – and added, 'Might call you anyways.'

Pip headed for the bench at the bus stop at the end of the block. There were two old ladies sitting at one end, and Pip irrationally felt that they would protect her against any dangers in the neighbourhood. Anyway, she could always shout for green-eyed Jimmy. She needed to sit down and gather her thoughts before heading into the diner to see if Ben was still there. If he was, she had a few questions for him. It was exhausting, this investigating. You had to be on your toes the entire time. She would have liked to head straight for her sister's place – it was near enough, and the wine was always cold – but first, she had to deal with Ben. She took out her notebook, but before she had written her first note, she heard her name.

CHAPTER NINE

'Pip, hey!' It was Jimmy, jogging towards her from the gym, waving the humiliating GRRRReat paper in his hand. 'Just remembered something. That kid. I think I saw him with a girl who hangs around the neighbourhood.'

Praise the Lord and hallelujah, was this an actual clue? Jimmy sat down next to her, not even a tiny bit puffed from the run. 'Hippie sort of chick. Long hair, brownish. Skinny thing.'

'Jimmy, that's great! Thank you. Do you know anything else about her? A name? Where she lives? Does she work around here?'

'Sorry. That's about it.'

'Did they seem to be, you know, an item?'

'Not sure, really.'

'Come on, Jimmy, think. Anything else?'

'I've seen her in those baggy trousers from Thailand. The ones with the elephants. I noticed cos my ex had a pair almost identical.'

She filed THAT one for further contemplation.

'Great. What else?'

'She always wears the same T-shirt with something printed on.'

'A band? A slogan? A picture?'

'Words. I can't remember.'

'Anything else? Come on, Jimmy, remember, please!'

His forehead was wrinkled with the effort.

'She might be a vegan.'

'A vegan? How do you know that?'

'I dunno, she just looks like one.'

'What does a vegan look like, exactly?'

'Like a regular person, but one who needs a steak.'

Jimmy jogged back to The Glove Box, after threatening or promising – Pip wasn't quite sure – to phone her 'some time', and she walked over to the diner where she found Ben hunched over a burger like a lion over a zebra. And it was huge. Two patties. Dripping with cheese. Gherkins and tomato peeking between the layers. The sweet smell of fried onions greeted Pip before she even sat down. Her mouth watered. When had she last eaten? That shortbread at the Prices'. Coffee and an apple for breakfast.

'Fancy meeting you here,' she said to Ben.

He swallowed. 'I went to the gym.'

'As did I.'

'Jimmy hasn't seen Matty.'

'So he told me.'

Pip waited. *Another detective trick*, she thought proudly: *let them stew for a bit, see what comes up.* How would Ben explain the fact that Matty seemed never to have been at the gym at all? He didn't offer anything further, just made his way doggedly through the burger. He chewed away until she could bear it no longer.

'God, that looks good.'

'It is. Have one.'

Pip waved to a waitress who was behind the counter, determinedly examining her nails. The woman caught Pip's eye for a moment, and then pretended she hadn't. The standard of service in London's restaurant industry was appalling. Everyone was a frustrated singer-songwriter or a PhD student. Unless they were an immigrant supporting three kids.

Pip raised her voice. 'Excuse me.'

Those nails were getting a lot of attention.

Ben sighed, and called to her in his best American drawl, 'Ma'am, could we place an order here, please?'

Of course, she jumped up and came over.

'One of these for my friend, please. And same again for me.'

Pip raised her eyebrows. He certainly was trim for a guy who ate two double burgers for lunch. But then again, it seemed that Ben was not what he seemed. So to speak. He'd lied about Matty and the gym. He'd come out here without telling her. Was it possible that he was behind his son's disappearance? He was so mild – almost, well, a bit wimpy. He didn't have the demeanour of a kidnapper or a murderer. She gave a shudder at the thought. Did it have anything to do with the paternity test? Maybe it was him, not Matty, that bought the test online. Was Matty not his son after all? Her whirring thoughts were interrupted by Ben.

'Do you know, this is the first hamburger I've had in seven years. Ironic that it should be in London.'

'Seven years? Why?'

'Madison took up clean eating seven years ago. I guess I should say that *we* took up clean eating seven years ago. No burgers for me. She can smell them on me. The smell makes her nauseous, she says. Any meat does. Once a week I have an organic chicken breast. For protein. But I brush and floss afterwards.'

'Listen, Ben. Did you know Matty wasn't going to that boxing gym?'

'No.'

'But you gave me Jimmy's name. You knew him. It's not like the whole thing was made up.'

'I spoke to him on the phone about rates and things when Matty started. But I didn't meet him. I just gave Matty the money every month. Matty said the gym wanted cash.'

'But you drove Matty there lots of times.'

'Sometimes he went on the bus, sometimes I dropped him off.'

'Didn't you watch Matty box? Isn't that what Madison said?'

'That's what she said. Because that's what I told her. But no. I didn't watch Matty box.' A fat tear fell into the tomato sauce on Ben's plate. 'I wish I did. I would give anything…' Another tear, quickly absorbed into the remaining crust of the bun.

The new burgers arrived. Ben looked at his as if it were a human head on the plate, and not the direct result of him having ordered it. 'Take it away,' he said, pushing it towards the waitress. 'Please.' He was practically green.

The waitress gave a heavy sigh and took the plate, saying, 'But you still have to pay for it, you know.'

'Fine, fine, just take it away.'

'Americans,' the waitress said bitterly, 'must be nice.'

Pip waited till she was out of earshot.

'But Ben, why did you lie?'

'I just needed some time… to myself. I couldn't always be there, with Madison. For Madison. I mean. It's just… I needed to clear my head. My writing…'

'So when you were supposed to be watching Matty, you were…?' She let the question linger and bit into her burger. It was just as juicy and delicious as she had hoped. She chewed slowly and waited. And waited. Letting Ben stew. Pushing him to answer. She could swear that this is what Poirot did. Also, the burger was delicious. There was clearly something wrong with Pip's stewing technique. Her subjects literally never spat it out. She eventually swallowed her food and asked outright, 'What *were* you doing all those afternoons?'

She knew, of course. It must be a woman. Unless it was a man! But either way. No man lied to his wife and took regular two-hour-long AWOL breaks just to clear his head.

'It's a private matter. It's really none of your concern.'

Ben Price was seeing someone. More than seeing, presumably. He would drop his son at the boxing gym, and head off to meet his lover.

'Well, you see, it became my concern when you tasked me with finding your son.'

A bit rich, considering that it was in fact Ms du Bois who had actually been tasked. So strictly speaking it was her concern. But the principle remained.

'This has nothing to do with Matty. You have my word on that.'

'Look, Ben, whatever you were doing, if it has nothing to do with Matty's disappearance, it's not my business and it'll stay between us. I'm not here to judge your marriage or to make trouble.'

'My marriage?'

'I'm only interested in finding Matty. I mean, if you were visiting... let's say a friend... we can keep that between us.'

'How did you know I was visiting someone?' Ben was pale. Pip felt like a real detective.

'It's not hard to figure out that you're having an affair. Not for a person with my skills,' said Pip.

Ben looked at her as if she were speaking Urdu. 'An affair? Are you kidding? No! It's nothing like that.'

Ben looked so abject that Pip felt sorry for him. Also, she felt like a bit of a fool, but she was kind of used to that. She waited, and this time he did come out with it.

'If anything, it's worse,' said Ben. 'Completely humiliating.'

Ben muttered out the sordid details while Pip made her way through her own giant hamburger. His shameful secret? He was seeing not a lover, or a dominatrix, or a Botox practitioner, or a secret love child – but a writing coach.

'I don't understand. You're a bestselling author. *The Remains of the Night*. I once wrote an essay about it,' Pip said, lowering the remains of the burger. 'It sold a tonne. And you won that prize.'

'The Carruthers Award for Debut Literary Fiction.' Even in his dismal state he couldn't keep the pride out of his voice.

'That. I mean, you cracked it. So what do you need a coach for?'

There was a long pause. She was pretty sure he wasn't going to speak, but then Ben sighed deeply and said, '*The Remains of the Night* was a typical first novel. Bold. Overstated. Largely autobiographical. I was twenty-five, I had no expectations, no reputation. No wife.'

Pip was somewhat taken aback that the novel was autobiographical. She seemed to recall a great deal of peculiar sex and drug use. She swept her last remaining fry through the juice, gathering the crumbs and sauce, and popped it in her mouth.

'The first time it was magical,' he said mistily, as if recalling a lost love. 'I can't explain, the words just flowed out of me. I had this confidence, this ease.' Ben stared into the middle distance, as if caught in that magical time, or as if he needed to burp. One or the other.

'Five novels I've started since *The Remains of the Night*. Five!' His mistiness was gone, replaced with despair. 'Every word is an effort. It's like marching through mud. And it's pouring with rain. I can't see where I'm going. And maybe my leg is broken. It's just this difficult sodden mess with no map, no way out.'

This metaphor had done its work, Pip felt. Although she maintained a demeanour of great concentration.

Ben continued. 'I finished two. Both crap. So bad, I didn't even submit them to a publisher. It's harder when it's not your life, you know? You can't just write down the memories and polish them up a bit. But when we came to London, I felt I could do it. I had an idea. A really good idea. Now, I've submitted a proposal and synopsis to the publisher. They say they'll publish it. I've got an advance.'

He looked unusually despairing for a man with a publishing contract.

'That sounds great, Ben. So what's the problem?'

'I don't have a book. I have a concept, which is a thousand miles from being a book. And I can't write it. I just can't.'

The grumpy waitress rematerialised to remove Pip's plate.

'I'll have a beer,' said Ben. 'Pip?'

She glanced at her watch. It was four p.m. 'No thanks, driving. Carry on. It's awfully interesting.' Pip might not know much about being a detective, but she did know a thing or two about making men talk about their boring hobbies.

'Writer's block. Crisis of confidence. Imposter syndrome. Absence of Muse. I've got the lot. This is my big chance, my only chance, to claw my way back into a writing career. The trouble is, Pip, I cannot write a reasonable sentence, let alone a book.'

'A friend of mine wrote a book,' the grumpy waitress offered, along with a bottle of beer. 'Says it's dead easy once you get going. You've just got to start.'

'Thank you,' Ben said, whether for the advice or the beer it wasn't clear.

'Yeah. Bum in the chair. That's what she says. Don't be waiting for a good idea, don't be expecting that perfect word, just, y'know, get typing. Bum in the chair.'

She stood expectantly at their table. When it was clear that the discussion of writing practice wasn't going to pick up steam, she turned to leave, adding, 'Might write one myself. I've got some stories, I can tell you. Some absolute crackers.'

Ben continued, looking at Pip, 'I'm not stupid. I might have won a literary prize once, but I know half the reason they're interested now is because of Madison. The TV show, and now this movie. She is super hot right now. If I can get this book done inside of a year, it'll be the talk of the town. If not, I may as well kiss my writing career goodbye. And maybe my marriage along with it.'

'Hence the coach.'

'Hence the coach. We've plotted it out, chapter by chapter. We meet to go over everything.'

'When Matty was at boxing.'

'When Matty was at boxing.'

It was an intriguing story, but another dead end as far as Pip's search was concerned. It helped her not a jot. She knew what Ben was doing during the alleged boxing class, but she still didn't have any idea what Matty was doing in that time. And that, she felt, was the key to his disappearance. The elephant trousers girl might have something to do with it. But if he was seeing a girl, why not just be open about it? Why the whole boxing fabrication? It didn't make sense.

'You can't imagine what it's like, being the hot young talent at twenty-five and a has-been at thirty-five,' said Ben, who was now on a second beer, she noted, and still wanting to talk about himself. 'Not good. Not good at all. And Madison, well, her star is rising.' He illustrated the star, rising, by swooping his hand up towards the ceiling, following it with his eyes. Apparently clean eating excluded alcohol, because he was clearly a cheap drunk. Grumpy Waitress, who had been so desultory, was now all over them. She had returned with a cloth and was giving the table a slow wipe.

'Thirty-five's not that old, you know,' she said, her voice sounding much kinder than it had before.

'Actually, I'm forty-three,' he said. 'I've been a has-been for a few years, now.'

'Even so,' the waitress said after a somewhat awkward pause. 'You've got plenty of time. I know how you feel, though. I'll be twenty-eight next week and look at me. But I know I won't be in this dump forever. I've got me plans.' The table well wiped, she straightened up and asked, 'Anyone for ice cream?'

Ben waved her away and continued. 'You know Madison and I were at art school together?' He had that famous person thing of imagining everyone knows everything there is to know about them, although Pip actually did remember this from a mention in a feature article.

'Drama, right?'

'Yeah. I was more on the writing and directing side. Madison acting, of course.'

'College sweethearts. You must have been quite the couple.'

'We weren't a couple. Not then. Madison barely glanced at me. Man was she hot. I mean, the absolute star of the class. Prettiest, sexiest, most talented. Way out of my league. And a bit older than me, although we never mention that now. We weren't in the same circle, I don't think she ever spoke to me outside of class. Until the book. It was a few years after we graduated. I was living in New York, scraping by as a production assistant, writing on the side. Madison was living in the city too, doing improv and experimental bits and pieces in friends' lofts. I saw her on the town once or twice. Anyway, my manuscript was picked up in a crazy bidding war. Biggest advance ever paid for a debut novel. It was all over the press. It was insane! And Madison called to congratulate me, said how thrilled she was to see her old classmate do so well.'

Pip knew exactly where this was going, but she let him go ahead. He was positively forthcoming after the two beers. 'I had a dinner the next week, a book event. It was formal. On a whim, I asked her to come with me. It was great to have her there. I was a social disaster and she was much more at ease than me. Funny and charming, and she looked stunning of course. After that, she'd come along to literary things, or help me prep for TV interviews. Then there was a book tour to Europe and I asked her to join me – the publisher was paying, of course, tickets for two – and that was it. We fell in love.'

His eyes misted over at the recollection. 'Back in New York, we were living the life. The book was flying. Her career picked up.

And then she was pregnant. Completely unexpected. Best mistake ever. We both thought so. My dear boy. Matty.' With this, Ben burst into tears again.

CHAPTER TEN

It had taken another hour for Pip to extricate herself from Ben and his tales of woe. When she'd woken up this morning, if you had told her that Ben Price would be drinking beers and sobbing on her shoulder by the evening, she would have been delighted. But the reality – as was so often the case in life – was just tedious. Eventually, she had persuaded him to go home and allow her to get on with the business of finding his son. He had tearfully agreed and hugged her as if she were his last friend on earth. Which, she suspected, might not be far from the truth. She folded herself back into her Mini, and pulled into the heavy evening traffic, her mind turning over the details of the case.

Pip could see why movie detectives had those walls with photographs of victims and suspects, all connected with lines and meaningful words or phrases. There were so many facts and figures and thoughts to keep in mind, and so many different ways they might fit – or not.

The movie detectives shuffled the photographs around and connected them this way and that, until the whole cat's cradle suddenly made sense and the guilty party emerged from the chaos. As far as Pip was concerned, this whole story was still 100 per cent chaos. She couldn't see how anything fitted together. She'd only been on the case a day, but already her head was overstuffed with information and questions. It felt like a swarm of bees had taken up residence in the hive of her skull. Buzz, buzz, buzz, but no honey. Rather like her short-lived attempt at beekeeping, come to think of it. She hoped this didn't end the same way, on a drip in intensive care.

By the time she'd been in the car for ten minutes, Pip had driven precisely two blocks. The traffic was moving at a pace one click above gridlock. She looked at her watch. Six p.m. At this rate, she'd be home after eight. If she headed to her sister's house just a couple of miles from here, she could have a glass of wine – just the one – and relax for an hour with Flis, miss the traffic, and be home at around the same time. She indicated right, pushed the tiny yellow car into the right lane, and got off at the next side road.

Great, now it was drizzling. Pip put her wipers on and they scraped across the windscreen, dragging a piece of paper across her line of sight. A flier for some sort of event swooshed damply back and forth. She peered through the misted glass. 'Plastic saves trees', it seemed to say. That was a new one, Pip snorted to herself – maybe she had read it wrong. The paper turned to mush and was swept aside.

Off the main road, she made slightly better progress through the wet streets and evening traffic, and soon she was at Flis and Peter's place in the middle of a row of neat terraced houses. Flis's house was easy to spot. Amongst the traditionally popular postbox red and navy blue and British racing green doors was a greenish grey rather reminiscent of a National Health hospital in 1970. A colourologist had deemed it the most soothing hue, apparently. It didn't help; the house was invariably chaotic on the inside. Any soothing properties that the front door had were soon lost. Pip rang the bell. Harry opened the door.

'Hello, Aunty Pip,' he sprayed wetly through the gummy gap where his front teeth had been, and would hopefully be again.

'Harry!' Flis's voice came from the bowels of the house. 'I told you not to open the door. What did I *say* about strangers?'

'It'th not thrangers, it'th Aunty Pip.'

Flis arrived in the hall, wiping her hands on a dish towel that was stained bright yellow, and gave Pip a distracted cheek-to-cheek kiss while imparting Stranger Danger lessons to her son.

'You didn't *know* it was Pip.'

'But it *ith* her, thee?' he said, puzzled.

'But you didn't know that.'

'But it ith.'

'Yes, but before you opened the door.'

'It wath her.'

Pip felt like Schrödinger's cat, neither dead nor alive in the box or whatever it was. And this toing and froing was not getting her any closer to a glass of wine.

'Well, it is me, and I'm here and Harry is fine.'

'Of course, yes. Let's sit in the kitchen, I was just making soup. Pumpkin, citrus and turmeric. A new recipe I saw on TV, on *Tara's Real Vegan*. Tara has the best recipes. Does the most marvellous gluten-free blueberry muffins, too. Soup's nearly ready, you can have some too. It's very healing.'

Harry turned and thundered down the passage. In the kitchen, Flis poured them both a glass of wine, turned the soup down to a low simmer, and settled across the table from Pip. 'What have you been *doing*?' she asked. 'You've been AWOK for days.'

'AWOL.'

'Away… With… Out… L… Oh, yes. Anyway. Mummy's in a state, she says she's phoned and phoned.' She raised her voice and said, in a frankly masterful imitation of their mother's ringing, plummy tone, 'Epiphany could be dead in a ditch for all I know, Felicity. The girl hasn't had the decency to return my telephone messages.'

'I haven't had a mo. I've been working.'

'Working?'

Really, thought Pip, *there's no need to sound quite so astonished.*

'Yes. I'm working for an investigation company. I'm investigating a case. A missing person.'

It was gratifying to see Flis looking impressed. Flis was considered the more together of the two sisters – she had a whole degree, a house, a husband, two kids, and she'd just started her own green parenting lifestyle blog. None of which Pip had achieved. The sisters looked remarkably similar, with the same long bones and narrow faces, inherited from their father. Their mother's bright blue eyes and thick brown hair – both of which presented a little darker on Flis, lighter on Pip. Pip was taller, Flis heavier. Pip more impulsive, Flis more neurotic.

Pip always felt this perception of Flis as the saner, more together sister was a little unfair. By some measures, she was quite significantly nuttier. Her degree was in Tantric Studies; her house was somewhat chaotic; her husband, well, OK, Peter was actually great – somewhere between a stand-up guy and a saint – and the kids were dear. And now she had the blog, which seemed to Pip to be out on the loony edge of the parenting spectrum, but which by all accounts was gaining steam and followers at a rapid rate.

'Why was Mummy looking for me? Is something up?'

'She's been planning her South America trip and the research has given her an idea for a business. She's looking at farming lemurs.'

'Farming lemurs for what?'

'Their coats. The wool is very valuable, apparently.'

'That seems odd. I've never heard of lemur wool. Maybe lemur fur coats? You'd need hundreds of lemurs though. It would be terribly cruel and Mummy loves animals. She wouldn't be able to kill them for their fur. I don't think it would work at all.'

'No, these ones are quite big, apparently. Almost as big as, say, a small donkey. And you don't have to kill them to get it.'

'A lemur as big as a donkey? You're joking.'

'No. And they look after themselves. She would just put them in the field and let them graze.'

Pip thought for a moment, her head filled with images of donkey-sized lemurs, grazing. Then the mist cleared.

'Llamas.'

'What?'

'Llamas. You're thinking of llamas.'

'Yes, like I said. Sort of like a cross between a horse and a sheep. Their faces look like that actress. Julia Roberts.'

'That's not what you said, you said lemur. A lemur is like a small monkey.'

'Really, Pip, why would anyone farm small monkeys? Think how many you'd need to make a coat. And Mummy would hate that. You are being completely ridiculous even suggesting it. Of course I'm referring to lelamas.'

'Llamas.'

'Really? You mean it isn't pronounced lelama? It's got a double L. I've always read it as lelama. Funny, that. Although I suppose there's Lloyd and Llewelyn…'

Pip took a gulp of her wine and tried to let Flis's words wash over her. Her brain was already full. She had no space for South American animals of any kind. No llamas, lemurs, alpacas or capybaras, thank you.

'I'll call her tomorrow,' she said. 'And what's up with you? How's the blog going?'

'So well! We've got thousands of followers already. Mummies love it. And I'm on Instagram, and that's bringing in new followers every day. Oh, that reminds me!'

Flis pulled her iPhone from her pocket and went over to the steaming soup. She arranged the jar of turmeric, the ginger root and the pumpkin skins artfully on the chopping board and pushed it up against the green Le Creuset pot that was bubbling away. Then she snapped a few pictures.

'Hashtag realhealing,' she muttered to herself, tapping on the phone screen. 'Done, sorry. But I have to keep posting and publishing. It never stops, that's the only trouble with the blog, and with Insta, it's just resentful.'

'Resentful? Instagram resents you?'

'Yes. Terribly.' She took a sip of her wine, while Pip tried to digest this. 'It never lets up.'

'Relentless?'

'Exactly. People just can't get enough of it. I've got so many nice messages of support. And some very rude ones and odd requests, but I just ignore those. There's such a demand for real, reliable information that's not just lies or PR for some big pharmaceutical company.'

Pip made a non-committal hhhmmm noise. From what she'd seen, Flis's blog was a mish-mash of hearsay, scaremongering, self-help and doubtful science, interspersed with recipes, listicles, and rather mawkish poems and quotes about parenting and life. And then a very popular section where parents posed questions and problems, and others answered them. Pip did not know much about medicine or parenting, but she was fairly horrified at some of the crowd-sourced answers. Cannabis oil, coconut oil, apple cider vinegar, reiki and momma bears featured strongly. From what she'd seen, Flis always encouraged people to get regular medical advice where appropriate, but she wasn't sure that anyone listened.

'There's just so much information, and it's so hard to work out what's true and what's not. Take plastic,' said Flis, now back at the table. 'Plastic's bad, right? The plastic islands in the sea. That picture of the poor turtle and the straw. And that sea thing and the cotton bud. But when you really think about it, plastic is actually incredibly important and even good sometimes. That's what this article said. Because if we didn't have plastic, we'd use more paper, and that means more trees have to die. The rainforests, and all those poor animals, the orangutans and the monkeys. Too awful.'

How did they get back to monkeys? And plastics. Pip thought of that flier on her car. Odd, twice in the same day.

'I just shared the article, and the response has been astonishing. Look…' Flis held her phone out to Pip, who could see notifications popping and pinging continuously, too quickly for her to read. 'A hundred shares already. Very controversial, though. There is a lot of arguing going on in capital letters. But I say, how can we know what's really true? It's best to just share and let people make up their own minds. The truth will sprout.'

Flis, whose own mind really was like some sort of demented insect, returned to a comment of half an hour ago before Pip could question whether truth ever sprouted.

'What investigation?' she asked.

'A missing teenager,' said Pip, trying to sound enigmatic. 'I can't say who, client confidentiality and so on, but his parents are celebrities.'

Flis was wide-eyed. 'Missing? Oh, that's terrible.'

'Yup,' Pip answered slyly, 'he's gone AWOK.' It was wasted on Flis.

'I've been reading about the child-smuggling networks. It's terrifying. I don't let the children go anywhere without an adult, even to the loo when we're out. Oh, I do hope you find him,' she said. But then she brightened. 'Pip! You should go to Chrystalla. She's one of the mums at Camelia's school. Her name's not really Chrystalla, obviously, it's Margaret, but that's her professional name. She's a psychic. She's amazing. She finds missing things and missing people. Camelia lost a shoe once, and Chrystalla found it under the bed. It was incredible. And there was a dog, too. Someone's Jack Russell I think, or perhaps it was a sausage dog…'

The list of Chrystalla's remarkable finds was interrupted by the arrival of the children. Camelia flung herself at Pip and hugged her with arms and legs. 'Aunty Pip! Will you stay for supper? Will you play Go Fish? Will you read me a story before bed?'

'I'll have supper with you, love,' said Pip, stroking the little girl's head, 'but we might have to wait until the weekend for Go Fish.'

'I'm thtarving,' said Harry. 'Can we have thupper now?'

'It's ready,' said Flis, getting up from the table and making her way over to the cupboard. 'We won't wait for Dad.' She laid out four bowls and ladled the lurid soup into them.

'What is it?' Camelia asked warily. 'Why is it so… bright?'

'It's bright with goodness! Vitamin C from the oranges. Turmeric, which is a natural anti-inflammatory. Pumpkin, full of antioxidants.'

'I don't want ants and oxes for thupper, can't we have macaroni cheese?'

'I don't want ants either!' Camelia joined in, letting her spoon clatter to the plate. 'Yuck!'

'In some countries, they eat insects all the time. Crickets. Grasshoppers. Different sorts of worms. They are high in protein. Good for the environment, too. I should do a blog on it.'

'Grath hoppers? Are there grath hoppers in here?' Harry said, starting to cry. 'I'm not eating it.'

'I'm not eating it either. I don't want grasshoppers.'

'CHILDREN!' Flis said, arguing in capitals herself. 'There are no grasshoppers or insects of any kind in the soup. It is made of pumpkin. Pumpkin!'

The children stared her down, their spoons resting on their side plates, their soup untouched.

'We want proper supper, Mummy,' Camelia said, her eyes like pools of suffering.

Flis sighed deeply, casting her eyes to the ceiling as if for inspiration.

Pip had slurped her soup down, ignoring the cajoling, the negotiation, the bizarre detour into insectivorous culture. She was exhausted, but felt a bit stronger after the wine and the antioxidant soup. She put her hand on Flis's shoulder and said quietly, 'I'll make them a sandwich, shall I?'

While she buttered the bread, Pip thought about children. Having them. Looking after them. Loving them. Feeding them three times a day. She adored her niece and nephew and hoped, in a general way, to have her own kids someday, but gosh it was a major thing. It was remarkable that so many people did it. All that work. All that money. For twenty years. Just to pass on their DNA.

Her thoughts turned back to the paternity test. And the boxing gym. And the mystery girlfriend/friend-girl. She had work to do.

CHAPTER ELEVEN

It reminded Pip of a school project, cutting and gluing, making little labels. Except instead of The Pyramids of Giza or Australian Marsupials, Pip's project was Find Matty Price. She'd seen it done a million times in detective dramas, but Pip realised she didn't actually know what to do next. First she'd tried to find an app. There were apps for everything – surely there must be a murder board one? You know, you'd input the information and the app would tell you who had done it. But strangely, there didn't seem to be anything. Then she got briefly distracted by a thread on Twitter about whether or not Meghan Markle had been seen drinking from a plastic straw, and whether or not that was OK. People had strong opinions. Pip could have spent all day on this stuff – and often did – but she reminded herself that she had a job to do. Then she did what any sensible person would do: she googled murder boards. Top hit: 107 Best Murder Board Images on Pinterest. She scrolled through for ideas.

String was obviously essential. She didn't have any, but she did find some thin silver wrapping ribbon she'd kept from a Christmas gift. That would work. They used pins on TV and on Pinterest, but she didn't have a corkboard. Blu-Tack would have to do. And Post-it notes for names and addresses and clues. Luckily she had loads of those, left over from that time she decided to improve her Spanish by reading *Don Quixote* in the original and marking every word she didn't know. After three pages, she'd realised that maybe she didn't actually know any Spanish at all, and improving it had been somewhat overambitious.

She held Matty's picture in one hand. There he was – thanks to *Hello!* magazine – with his movie star looks in the moss-green pullover, against a forest of green. She rolled a piece of Blu-Tack between the fingers of her other hand and pressed the softened blob onto the back of the picture. She pushed the picture against the wall, where it would be the centre of her clue board, with the other clues dotted about, secured by the Blu-Tack, connected with the silver ribbon, annotated with the Post-it notes. Clarity, that was what she was looking for.

Pip looked into his eyes, almost covered by his long golden fringe. Where was he? Why did he leave? She felt sure that whatever he was doing when he was supposed to be at the gym, that would be the key to the mystery. That, and maybe the girl. Oh, and maybe the paternity test. Or maybe none of it. It was hard to tell.

She took one end of the silver ribbon and attached it, using a tiny bit of Blu-Tack, to the edge of the picture.

'Hey, hello Pip.' It was Tim. She hadn't even known he was home. The flat had been quiet when she woke up, and she assumed that he was at work. Like a normal person would be at eleven in the morning.

He pushed the door open and popped his head round the door. 'I thought I heard you come in. Good day at work yesterday?'

'Very good. Busy, busy.'

His gaze moved to the picture of the blond teenager in the centre of the wall, with the silvery ribbon hanging off it.

'Doing a bit of decorating?'

'No, it's just…' She didn't really know how to explain to Tim why her bedroom wall was now covered with bits of silver ribbon and her David Hockney poster was lying on the ground, acting as a small worktable.

Tim stepped up to the picture of Matty. 'Is that a young Justin Bieber? I wouldn't have thought he was your type.' His eyes crinkled in gentle mockery.

'No, it's not. I mean, he's not.'

'Huh?'

'It's not Bieber, and he's not my type. Definitely not.' She could feel herself blushing.

'Well,' said Tim slowly, his dark eyes holding hers. 'You don't go for the pretty golden boys. That's good to hear. I was rather worried about sharing a flat with a rabid Belieber. We all know how crazy they can get.'

He was definitely flirting.

'It's not a fan wall,' she laughed, regaining a bit of composure. 'It's something I'm working on for the new job. Just putting some thoughts together.'

'Ah. Well, I'm heading down the road to the shops and then to the pub for a ploughman's.'

She could picture him, smiling his broad smile, surrounded by nubile young office workers, sipping his drink.

Then he added, 'Hey, why don't you come? We could have a drink, hang out.'

For a moment she inserted herself into the mental picture, firmly between Tim and the nubile wenches. She was about to agree, but to her surprise, when she opened her mouth to speak, she said, 'No, thanks. I've got to get on with this. But I'd love to some other time.'

Tim didn't even blink.

'No problem,' he said. 'Next time. See you.'

Finally, he'd asked her out (sort of), and she couldn't go. And from his reaction, it would never happen again.

But funnily enough, she didn't even mind. She was so engrossed in Matty and his disappearance that she couldn't drag herself away; didn't want to, even for dishy Tim. And anyway, it did seem a bit early for a drink. She would just stay here with Most, her faithful companion and eternal admirer. She looked down at the cat, who was staring up at her with adoration. She scratched him behind the ears, sending him into a passionate frenzy of purring, and then went back to work.

What next? Ben, probably. If anything, he was the most likely to have something to do with Matty's disappearance, or at least know something about it. He'd already lied about the boxing. He could be lying about other things too. She put up an old picture of him arriving at the Daytime Television Awards. She'd cut Madison out of the picture, feeling like a jealous new lover excising her predecessor.

He was a bit of a mystery, Ben. He loved Matty, that was obvious. Unlike Madison, he seemed appropriately worried. But he had lied to his wife and to Pip about watching Matty. And then, there was the question of the paternity test. The more Pip thought about it, the more she thought he might have ordered the test. Maybe he suspected – or even knew, if the results were back – that Matty wasn't his son. But then how had the test ended up in Matty's bathroom? Unless she'd got that completely wrong and all the eco bamboo toothbrushes actually belonged to Ben? Even so, he didn't seem like a man capable of murder. She picked up her Post-its and wrote 'Paternity?' on the top one, before peeling it off and sticking it next to Ben's picture.

Pip needed more pictures. She would search for them, and then print them out later. She reached for her phone and opened Twitter. She realised she hadn't really investigated Matty's Twitter feed, just taken Ben's word for the fact that he'd been posting until last week. If he was lying about that, he would certainly be a prime suspect. But as it turned out, he'd been telling the truth. The last tweet was four days ago. She decided to go back a few months into his timeline, see if anything caught her eye. She scrolled quickly though his feed from the US, just before the Prices came to London. God, teenagers were boring. Their social lives. Their predictable opinions. Their holidays. Matty's feed from months ago was thick with skiing references.

'Hitting the slopes! #skiingislife', alongside a picture of Matty in goggles and a beanie, looking like a giant bee.

Her eye skimmed the comments.

'Yo!'

'Powdeeeerrrr'.

About twenty of those, and then:

'Mountains are not just playgrounds for rich kids. #saveour-mountains #earthforall'.

After the skiing, Pip was briefly sucked into some of the forest-related links Matty tweeted as a Save the Forests Ambassador, about the depletion of the forests, about trees and oxygen. The usual hearts and applause and occasional off-beam responses:

'If you want to save the forests, use plastic #plasticsavestrees #plasticsaveslives.'

'You're kidding, right?'

'Nope. It's the only way.'

'Everyone knows plastic is killing the earth.'

'Read this article,' with a link to an article. And another and another.

'Read the science,' said someone called @MaverickGirl. The handle rang a vague bell. Pip scrolled back through Matty's feed. Yes, @MaverickGirl was the #saveourmountains tweeter too.

'DMd you,' was her final comment on that thread. DM, direct message. So they'd taken their conversation out of the public eye.

Pip clicked on the girl's profile. @MaverickGirl's bio described her as a 'scientist and free-thinking eco-warrior'. She looked young, but older than Matty, early twenties perhaps. Pretty, in a plain sort of way. No make-up. Long straight brown hair. Bored, Pip scrolled dully through her feed, barely concentrating, as she succumbed to the ravenous Twitter Black Hole.

And then Pip saw something that made her sit up. It was a picture of @MaverickGirl. And she was wearing elephant-print trousers.

CHAPTER TWELVE

Somehow, you never think you'll spend eternity crunched up inside a yellow Mini parked outside a laundrette. But yet here she was. To be honest, it had only been fifteen minutes, but it *felt* like eternity, with her knees in her armpits and the spongy roof of the old Mini resting on the crown of her head.

Pip was on a stakeout. She was on a mission to find Elephant Trousers aka @MaverickGirl. She had finally had her first real breakthrough, identifying the girl Jimmy had told her about. Trawling through @MaverickGirl's Instagram feed, she couldn't believe her luck when she spotted a picture of her in those Thai trousers. And when she scrutinised the picture she recognised, there in the background, the dodgy diner where she'd had that burger with Ben. *Take that, Miss Marple!*

Somewhat overeagerly, Pip had leapt into her car immediately. Thank God she had a car. You couldn't do a stakeout from the Tube. Flis always laughed at Pip's insistence on driving around London – well, this would show her. She stopped by the print shop to print out a batch of photographs for her photo wall – Matty, his parents, @MaverickGirl, Gold – and now here she was, without a plan and without coffee. First stop, she'd decided, was to show Jimmy the picture and confirm that this was the girl he'd seen with Matty. But he wasn't at the gym. Some huge bloke was putting a bunch of smaller blokes through their paces – punching, squatting, lunging, jumping. It was exhausting to watch, so Pip returned to her car, having been assured by the huge bloke that Jimmy would be in soon.

The first part of the stakeout was spent reading a very long and detailed message from Doug at Boston Investigations, full of rules for how often he needed Pip to check in with him, and how often he needed written reports, and all sorts of details about fonts and single spacing that Pip found too tedious to absorb. She sent him a quick response. 'Instructions noted. On stakeout!' That done, she pondered the mystery of Elephant Trousers from the discomfort of the driver's seat. She and Matty seemed to have connected online and, if Jimmy was right, subsequently in real life. What was she, a girlfriend? A pregnant girlfriend? A friend? Someone with a shared interest in forests and environmental issues? Or was there some other connection? Ms du Bois did say that there was often a love interest in the picture. Maybe the two of them were just shacked up somewhere. Pip thought it quite likely that if she could find Elephant Trousers, she might be able to sort this thing out quickly and simply.

Thinking about Ms du Bois – Sophie – made Pip feel guilty. She'd stolen that woman's job and then promised to keep in touch, and she had barely even managed that. She scrolled through her phone until she found the message from Sophie. 'No progress. Searching that haystack, like you told me. X Pip,' she wrote. That made her feel better.

Pip was exhausted. She had ended up staying late at Flis's, and while sleeping in had helped, her murder board and the descent into the Twitter underworld had left her feeling drained. Even crammed into the tiny car, her eyes started to close.

A sharp smack to the driver's side made her start, and a big face loomed at the window, inches from her own. She slammed her head hard against the roof, and her knees hard against the steering wheel. The car door was wrenched open from the outside.

'Bloody hell, Jimmy,' she said, for the looming face was indeed his. 'I nearly had a heart attack.'

'Sorry. Didn't mean to give you a fright. What are you doing here?'

'Waiting for you. I need to show you something.'

She unfolded herself from the car seat and stepped onto the pavement. 'Hang on,' she said, reaching for her envelope of prints. She found the picture of @MaverickGirl, held it out to Jimmy and said, 'Here. Is that her? The girl in the elephant trousers? Is she Matty's friend?'

'Yup, that's her. Where did you get the photo?'

'I tracked her down,' Pip said with a deliberate casualness. 'That's what we investigators do.'

'That was quick. I'm impressed. So what's the next step? How do we find her?'

Pip rather liked the sound of 'we', even though she had no idea what use Jimmy would be to her. He wouldn't easily fit in the Mini, for a start. And why was he so eager to help find a boy he'd never met? Unless, of course, he had, and had been lying when he said Matty never came to the gym. She gave him what she hoped was a searching look, but his green eyes just seemed full of curiosity. And hope. And maybe a tiny bit of something else that sent a shiver down her spine. A good shiver, not an evil serial killer shiver. She decided to trust her instincts, and trust Jimmy.

'Look,' she showed him. 'This photograph was taken round the corner there, you can see the edge of the diner. And you've seen her around. So I'm guessing she must live or work or study around here. My plan is to hang out here, investigate the neighbourhood and see what kinds of places she might be coming to. Schools and so on.'

'Right. Well, I'm the man for the job. Know the place like the back of me hand.'

'Speaking of the back of your hands, who or what are Rose and Lily?'

'Ah,' he said with a twinkle. 'That would be telling. You're the investigator, innit? You work it out.'

'I've got my hands full already,' she punned. 'Yours'll have to wait. So how about I buy you coffee and you share your local knowledge?' Maybe it was better that she didn't know the origin of the tattoos anyway.

Five minutes later they were back in the diner, ordering coffees and toasties from yesterday's Grumpy Waitress.

'Must have enjoyed your dinner, coming back so soon,' she said. 'And with our friend Jimmy from the gym. Hello, Jimmy. Small world.' She gave Pip a look of cool appraisal, mixed with a hint of admiration.

'Isn't it just, Daisy?' said Jimmy. 'Small world indeed.'

While Daisy headed for the kitchen, Pip drew out her notebook. Jimmy began to list places where a young woman might be studying – an art school, a marketing college; or working – a language school where tutors taught English to foreign language speakers, various shops and offices. Pip made notes, a bulleted list of possibilities. He continued.

'And then there's the squats and communes. A few streets back from the main road there's some big old houses scheduled for demolition. They're rented out cheap-cheap, and filled with students and young people.'

'That sounds promising,' Pip said. 'I'll go see what I can find out about them.'

'I know those squats. What d'you want to know?' Daisy, who was surprisingly light on her feet for a big girl, appeared silently behind Pip's shoulder with her coffee.

'I'm looking for someone.' Pip hauled out the photograph of Elephant Trousers. She thought about showing the one of Matty too, but had suddenly remembered the confidential nature of his disappearance. She made a mental note to remind Jimmy not to blab.

'Seen her around. Not for a few days though, far as I can remember. But she does come in here a bit.'

'Do you know her name? Or where she works? Or where to find her?'

'I can't say I do, let's think…' Daisy frowned into the distance.

'Bloody hell,' Jimmy said, pointing to the window. 'That's her.' And sure enough there she was jogging past the window of the diner, earphones in her ears.

Pip leapt to her feet, making the coffee slosh about. 'I'm going after her. Grab my stuff,' she told Jimmy, heading for the door.

By the time she got to the street, the girl was a block ahead, moving fast, her mousy ponytail swinging rhythmically left to right. She was small and slight, and clearly fit. None of which could be said about Pip, who was also hampered by her clothing: tailored trousers and a pair of pumps with a small wedge heel. She'd dressed for work, not for running around the streets like an idiot. Two blocks in and her chest was about to burst. How did she get so unfit? OK, she'd never been what you might call an athlete. But she'd surely been fitter than this.

She dodged an old woman who was walking her Yorkie, and leapt over the leash, her size eight pumps only just missing the ball of fluff. 'Watch what you're doing, you maniac,' the woman shouted after her, shaking her fist. 'Decent people use these streets, y'know.' Pip heard a burst of laughter, which she recognised as Jimmy. She turned her head without stopping and there he was some feet behind her, with her handbag over his shoulder swaying and bumping as he ran, and her precious envelope of photographs in his hand. He didn't seem to have broken a sweat. She took a moment to admire his muscular frame, when her shoulder smacked hard into something solid. Bloody hell, it was a postbox. It was a disgrace the way they just left them standing around. She yelped and dropped to the pavement, landing painfully on her knee. She sat there, clutching her shoulder with one hand, rubbing her knee with the other.

'You all right?' asked Jimmy.

'Yes,' she muttered, even though she felt like crying from pain and humiliation. 'Go. Don't let her get away.'

'Yes, ma'am!' he said, dropping her bag and envelope on top of the inelegantly mangled heap of Pip as he carried on running.

'Less haste, more speed,' said the old woman, marching past with her head held high. Her Yorkie lifted its leg to the postbox, just inches from where Pip sat.

Pip got up to avoid the thin stream of dog wee flowing towards her and set off after Jimmy at a swift walk, each step jolting her throbbing shoulder and knee. She couldn't see the girl, but she did catch a glimpse of Jimmy way up ahead. Even in her injured state, she had to appreciate his grace and athleticism. And also, his bum. He ran like, well, like a runner. Someone built to run. She ran like someone built to smash into postboxes and get peed on by Yorkies. But she kept going, hobbling as fast as she could. She saw Jimmy waiting up ahead, leaning nonchalantly against a street light.

'She's in there,' he said, gesturing with his head. 'Look.'

And there she was, in an unexpectedly chic little restaurant called Tara's Clean Food Factory, leaning up against the counter, upon which jugs of icy cucumber water and a green glass bowl filled with lemons were tastefully arranged. @MaverickGirl was barely puffed, Pip noted bitterly, while Pip herself was still rasping like a rattlesnake. She really needed to get in shape. Maybe she'd join the boxing gym. Maybe Jimmy could take her in hand. Pip headed for the door.

'Wait,' said Jimmy. 'Just let's watch for a bit.'

'No way.'

'Trust me. Boxing wisdom. Take your time. Observe your opponent before you go barrelling in with the first move.'

Pip was about to ignore his advice and go barrelling in, but then she saw something that stopped her in her tracks. A cool blonde in a wafty white smock dress and an artfully faded cotton apron came out from the kitchen and kissed @MaverickGirl on both cheeks.

'I know that woman,' Pip exclaimed. 'She's that celebrity vegan chef from the telly. Tara somebody. My sister is a total fangirl. I wonder why she's meeting her? There's only one way to find out. I'm going in.'

But before she got to the door, Tara put her arm around their quarry, and led her back into the kitchen, out of their sight.

CHAPTER THIRTEEN

'Oh my God!' Flis was beside herself. 'I can't believe you saw Tara! Oh, she's the best. I was just this minute thinking, I should make her buckwheat granola pancakes. They're so easy. You take a cup of—'

'Flis!' Pip interrupted her sister's gushing. 'Just listen, it's important. Tell me everything you know about her.' And then amended her instruction: 'Not everything. Not the recipes. But about her business.'

Flis was tapping away at her computer and murmuring, 'Interesting… gosh, well, who'd have thought… Well, you would say that, wouldn't you… Hmm, maple syrup, that's a good idea…'

'*Not* the recipes, Flis. Focus!'

'Sorry, yes. Gimme a sec. I'm just checking out her food blog and some of the vegan newsfeeds.'

Vegan newsfeeds? Who knew? Pip could not believe she'd lost Elephant Trousers. It seemed impossible. Pip and Jimmy had gone into the restaurant to wait for her to emerge. While they sipped on their fresh vegetable juices – carrot, beetroot and ginger for him; kale, apple and celery for her – Tara appeared from the kitchen. Alone. No sign of Elephant Trousers.

She and Jimmy had the same thought. Just as it entered her head, she saw it dawn on his face.

'Shit,' he said, and was out of his chair in a second, heading for the door. Pip saw him disappear around the corner at a run. Minutes later, he reappeared slowly. 'No sign of her. I checked out the back alley and peeped into the kitchen. Not there. She must have gone out the back door. Sorry, Pip.'

It wasn't his fault, of course. It was hers. So stupid of her. Of course there was a back door. There was *always* a back door. Any halfway decent investigator would have gone there instead of sipping some vegetables through a biodegradable straw with a rather attractive boxer while her main lead – let's face it, her only lead – slipped out the back. She could kick herself.

'Well, Maverick Girl is all over Tara's Twitter feed.' Flis's excitement cut through Pip's glum reverie. 'They've got a good old love fest going, those two, lots of common ground – vegetable gardening, animal rights. It's not all about food, her social media. Lots of environmental issues. Packaging is a biggie. And plenty of links to articles about defenestration.'

'What? Who's throwing people out of windows?'

'I have no idea what you are talking about half the time. Trees, Pip. Forests being cut down.'

'Deforestation.'

'Yes. That's what I said. Defenestration. #SavetheForests.'

'Forests. Now that's interesting.' Pip paused, trying to decide, then she continued. 'Listen, Flis, I'm going to tell you something very confidential. But you need to promise me that you won't mention a word to anyone. Not even Peter. OK?'

'Ooh, secrets! Of course not. I'll be as quiet as a bat.'

'As a mou— Never mind. OK, so Maverick Girl isn't the person I'm really looking for. She's just a lead. I've been hired to find someone else. Matty Price.'

'Never heard of him.'

'You know Madison Price? The actress?'

'Dr Miranda Ray? Oh my God, you know how I love that show. I've been watching it for years. And she's in London right now, did you know that? They're shooting—' Flis seemed to be settling in for a celebrity gossip session. Usually Pip would've been happy to comply. But there was business to be done.

'Flis, please. We can't talk about that now, we need to get on with this. Matty is her son. He's the one who's missing. And the odd thing is, he's a youth ambassador for Save the Forests. So it's something they have in common.'

Flis let out a shout. 'Woo hoo! Well, what do you know!'

'What?'

Flis turned her laptop towards Pip and pointed to the comments on Tara's Twitter feed. 'Look who's here.'

It was Matty Price. He was a regular on Tara's feed, him and @MaverickGirl – Pip really wished she could find her real name; her handle and descriptors were so unwieldy. Pip scrolled and scrolled, looking for Matty's name. Tara had over 100,000 followers, which meant thousands of comments. Most of them complete drivel.

'Why don't you just do a search for him?' Flis asked. 'It'll save you a fortune of time.'

She leaned over and hit a few keys. Matty's comments popped up, a steady stream.

'You are a bloody genius, Felicity Bloom.'

Mostly they were likes or reshares, occasional messages of support: 'Preach, sister, preach!!!!' and 'You tell them, @Tara-Vegan!'

Matty's comments stopped, just like all of his social media activity, a week ago. She went back a bit, and noted that his more recent comments seemed a lot more personal.

'Wow Tara, meeting you has really opened my eyes'.

And then his last one, seven days ago. He shared Tara's open invitation to a vegan picnic potluck in the park in Hackney. 'See you there! Come on guys, join the movement! #veganeats #savetheforests #goodplasticforlife'.

Pip went back through her notebook, checked the times and dates of his social media accounts. As far as she could see, this was the last time Matty Price was seen online.

Now that she'd told Flis the basics of the investigation, Pip could bounce ideas off her. Flis was actually very clever, although she appeared deranged at times with her creative grip on English and her gnat-like concentration span. Together, they outlined what they'd learnt today. Pip made one of her lists:

1. *@MaverickGirl is Elephant Trousers.*
2. *@MaverickGirl knows Vegan Tara online and IRL.*
3. *@MaverickGirl knows Matty online and IRL.*
4. *Matty knows Tara online.*
5. *Matty probably knows Tara IRL – at least they would have met at the picnic.*
6. *All three have common interests and causes – mostly environmental.*
7. *All three have active social media profiles, and lots of followers.*

Pip drew a line in her notebook, having reached the end of their insights for the day. 'I need to find Maverick Girl,' she said. 'She's the one most likely to know where Matty is. I've messaged her, of course. Told her I was looking for Matty. No response.'

'We should try Tara,' said Flis. 'She would be easier to find. She's got a public profile. She does events and things. And the restaurant.'

'You're right. I'll message her.'

'Hey, wait a minute. I've got a better idea.'

It was a flipping genius idea. Flis – as the proprietor and writer of a rapidly growing green parenting blog – was going to ask Tara for an interview. That way, she'd get some inside intel about her work, and her causes. Pip and Flis were convinced that the shared interest in environmental issues held a clue – they just weren't sure how.

'Well, no time like the present,' said Flis. 'I'll send her a message and ask for an interview.'

As Flis went to work, Pip's phone rang. It was Ben Price. 'Pip, can we meet?' he said. 'There's something important I need to tell you.'

CHAPTER FOURTEEN

It was only yesterday that they'd met at the very same diner, but Ben Price looked significantly ropier. His face was drawn and grey, his eyes bloodshot. It was strange, but it actually made him more attractive, not less.

'Welcome back,' Grumpy Waitress said to Ben. She ignored Pip entirely, which was perhaps fair enough given she had just been there a few hours before. 'How's the writing going? Did you take my advice?'

'A bit slow, I'm afraid. I've had a lot on my mind.'

'What can I do for you today?'

'Just a mineral water for me, thanks, Daisy. No, wait. A beer.'

So much for clean eating. Pip kept her expression deliberately neutral. She ordered an orange juice.

She cut straight to it. 'So tell me. Why did you need to see me so urgently? Do you have information on Matty?'

Ben looked down at his hands. 'I've got a confession,' he said.

'I knew it,' said Pip. 'It's not a writing coach!'

Ben looked confused. 'What?'

'You're having an affair! It's not a writing coach. You can't fool a professional like me, you know.' She gave him a stern look.

'No, no, I *am* seeing a writing coach.' He sighed. 'It's about Matty.'

Pip decided it would be better not to speak this time. Speaking wasn't going that well for her so far in this conversation. But Ben hardly seemed to notice. He fiddled with the salt cellar on the table, as if maybe this – rather than Pip – could be trusted with his secrets.

'I'm sorry, Pip. I didn't tell you the whole story,' said Ben, looking up and meeting her eyes. 'With Madison, and the press, well, you know… We have to be so careful. I feel so bad about it. I hope I haven't wasted your time, jeopardised Matty's safety.'

'So…?' Pip hoped she was creating the right sort of silence, the type Poirot used to get people to speak. Not the type she seemed to specialise in, where everyone shut up and never said another word.

'There was a blow-up the day before Matty left. He and Madison had a big row. Shouting, crying, slamming doors.'

'What was it about?'

'Well, you know, they are very different people. He's very soft-hearted and she can be quite, well, I suppose you could say she's very focused. On her work, of course. And sometimes she can be, well, less than sensitive. And he's a teenager. And at the moment, with this movie in production, Madison is—'

'That's who you are!' Daisy, who had appeared behind Ben's shoulder, thumped the beer bottle on the table triumphantly. 'I knew I recognised you. You're Madison Price's husband. I've seen you in *Hello!*'

Ben went even paler.

Pip addressed Daisy coolly. 'Could we have some privacy here, do you think? We're trying to discuss a professional matter.'

'Oh, well *excuse me*. A professional matter, is it? Well then, I'll be right out of your hair. I do beg your pardon. I'll just leave the drinks here and get back to the kitchen, shall I?'

Pip watched her stomp heavily back towards the bar, shaking her head and muttering, 'A professional matter, pfff,' in a stage whisper.

She turned back to Ben and picked up where they'd left off. 'I understand. They're different people. But what set them off? What were they arguing about?'

'That's of no consequence. It's a family matter.'

Pip sighed and said sternly, 'Look, Ben. Let's not waste any more time with lies and omissions. This is no time for secrets. Spit it out. You know you need to tell me, or you wouldn't have called me in the first place.'

She could practically see his brain whizzing around, trying to find an option other than spitting it out. He gave a resigned sigh. 'Madison had an affair. It was a rough patch in our marriage. It was my fault as much as hers. I wasn't very attentive, what with my struggles with the book. And honestly, it was just a slip-up on her part, it didn't mean anything.'

He took a deep pull at the beer. 'I found out. We went for counselling. Madison insisted we go for spiritual cleansing. A bit of reiki. We decided to recommit to our marriage, to really give it a go. We had a recommitment ceremony and everything. It wasn't easy, but we wanted to make it work, for Matty's sake as much as ours. And then this London gig came up and we thought, well, fresh start, you know. We didn't tell Matty, there didn't seem any point in unsettling him. But he found out and he was furious.'

'How did he find out?'

'That I don't know. It's a complete mystery. The, uh, incident was very hush-hush, we managed to keep it out of the gossip rags. Only a handful of people knew. But apparently someone told him. I don't know who, he wouldn't say. But however it came about, he was very upset and very angry. And that's why he stormed out.'

'Not so fast. Take me through it as best you can. The whole thing from the moment he found out. Try and remember exactly what he said.'

Ben sighed. 'We were in the sitting room. Madison had just come back from a wardrobe fitting and she was telling me about the costumes, what she'd be wearing and so on. Matty came back from the boxing gym.' He paused, thoughtful. 'Well, I guess he wasn't at the gym, given what we know now. But anyway, he came home, still in his boxing gear, and stormed into where we were sitting and confronted his mother.'

'What did he say?'

'He said that people were right about her, that she couldn't be trusted.'

'What people?'

'I don't know.'

'Go on.'

'He said he'd had a hunch she'd been, um, I think he actually used the words "fucking around", which Madison did not appreciate. And now he had confirmation. He shouted at her, said that she's a liar and a cheat. That I'm weak and, um…'

He hesitated, flushed. Pip waited.

'He said that I'm weak and I'm a loser.' Ben looked like he might cry, but then seemed to rally and continued with the story.

'We tried to talk to him but he was in a total state. He was furious, said that we'd tricked him into coming to London for our selfish reasons. That he couldn't trust his own family. That he was finished with us, and was going to follow his own path, "the path of truth". Weird phrase – I remembered it, because it didn't sound like the sort of phrase he would use. You know. Sort of religious.'

Ben took another long slug of his beer and rested his head in his hands. 'We didn't even have a chance to discuss it or try to calm him down. He stormed out of the room.'

'Did you see him again, after that?'

'He turned and came back in the doorway. He looked at Madison like he hated her, and said, "I've been wondering if Dad is even my father. I guess now I know." And that was the last time we saw him.'

CHAPTER FIFTEEN

Pip pushed her thumb into Tara's glowing forehead. The Blu-Tack blob attached firmly to the wall. The photo wall was coming on nicely. Pip felt like a real detective, with her morning routine of updating the wall. OK, maybe two days wasn't a routine. But it wasn't *not* a routine.

Madison was up there on the wall. Mr Gold. @MaverickGirl. Ben. Jimmy. And now Tara, rather poorly printed on Flis's home laser printer, which was low on blue ink, giving her an unhealthy orange tinge.

'Too much beta carotene,' Pip said to herself, and barked out a laugh at her own joke.

She looked over the cast of characters. Ben Price. He loved the boy, no doubt about that. He'd fibbed a bit, but Pip was fairly sure he didn't know any more about Matty than he let on. Was it possible that he wasn't Matty's father?

And Madison. Could be that she was hiding something, but Pip suspected she was just utterly narcissistic. More concerned about her film and her reputation than her son.

Fredrick Gold. What was with him? He had a sneaky sort of demeanour, listening and lurking. He was obsessed with Madison, but was there anything more to it? Pip couldn't imagine it was mutual, that he'd been the participant in the affair, but stranger things had happened.

Jimmy. He looked like that chap from *Prison Break*, but he seemed to be just a regular decent guy with lots of tats. And his muscles. Not too much on them, just about right. Wiry, not bulky, just the way she liked them.

This, Pip told herself sternly, *is why you never get anywhere. You start off working hard at the challenge, but you end up perving over some bloke's biceps.* This is exactly how things went pear-shaped when she went into the pet-grooming business. Biceps, that was the start of the whole fiasco. She was certain Jimmy had nothing more to offer in the way of clues. That said, he was quite a handy sidekick to have around.

That left @MaverickGirl and Tara. @MaverickGirl. Elephant Trousers. What was her connection to Matty? If Pip could find @MaverickGirl, she might be able to sort this thing out quickly and simply. Which brought Pip to Tara. There was clearly also some relationship between @MaverickGirl and Tara, but what? And where did Matty fit in that?

It was Pip's hope that Tara could lead her to @MaverickGirl and @MaverickGirl could lead her to Matty. That was where Flis and her blog came in – so Pip put a Post-it between @MaverickGirl and Tara, saying 'Flis's Blog'. She felt a frisson of excitement. At least there was something on the wall that was going somewhere.

What she needed, she thought, was more Post-its with solutions. 'AFFAIR + PATERNITY + FIGHT' she wrote on a green Post-it note. At least she'd solved that one to some degree. Someone had told Matty about Madison's affair, and like a typical teenager, he'd made that all about himself. And presumed that if she was cheating now, she'd been cheating all along. Which wasn't a completely ridiculous assumption, to be fair to him. If Matty had been wondering whether Ben was his father, then that was why he'd ordered the paternity test. Not because he'd knocked up Elephant Trousers. But then the question was, who had been poisoning Matty's mind against his parents?

She took out some more Post-its and wrote down the issues. 'FORESTS'. And then 'VEGAN'. And finally 'PACKAGING' and

'PLASTIC'. She wasn't quite sure where to put them because as it turned out, they were not solutions so much as more questions, so she grouped them on the far right for later use.

The silver ribbon dangled with nowhere further to go. She couldn't decide what to connect with what. Most, who had been watching Pip work with interest, batted at the ribbon with his paw. At least the cat seemed to know what it was for. Pip sighed.

Tim poked his head around the door.

'I've figured out what you're doing,' he said. Pip froze. Had he? 'You're the Zodiac Killer. I thought there was something in your eyes.'

'It's OK, you're safe. I've got a Gemini already.'

'That's a relief. Which ones have you still got to do? Maybe I can suggest someone. There are a couple of people in my office that might be suitable. One bloke in particular. Bob. I think he's an Aries. Can I interest you in him?'

There was a bit more serial killer banter – he was so cute when he smiled; the way his dark eyes sparkled and crinkled at the edges, those gleaming teeth – and then he lingered a bit, as if he wanted to chat more. Pip felt pretty sure that he should really be at work, and that this was the second morning in a row he was inexplicably home, but she wasn't going to complain. Tim, in bantering mood, was nothing to turn your nose up at.

'What's that about packaging?' he asked, pointing at one of the Post-its.

'Something I'm working on, I'm not quite sure where it all fits in.'

'My uncle's in that business. Product packaging. They make those plastic punnets. For fruit and things. Keep them from being squashed.'

'Not a very popular business to be in these days.'

'The way my uncle tells it, they're saving the world because plastic packaging prevents a lot of food waste and damage. He says there's actually a lot of misinformation about.' Tim looked quite earnest, and Pip had to admire the clean cut of his serious jaw. She made a polite noise of mild interest to keep him talking. He really was very nice looking when he thought he was being useful.

'And some of the other so-called environmentally friendly solutions are no better than plastic.'

'Yes, I heard that,' Pip said, thinking about Flis's article.

He went on, 'They cause pollution, or use lots of water, or kill trees or bees or whatever. Something like that. He definitely said something about bees.'

Tim didn't seem to have listened very hard to his uncle.

'I'll let you get on with it then. Time I went off to work, anyway,' Tim said. 'When you've finished with your mystery serial killer project, the drink offer still stands.'

'Just a few more star signs to go, then I'm all yours,' she said. And then blushed furiously at the way it came out.

After he left, Pip resolutely did NOT let her mind wander to Tim and his drink offer and being 'all yours'. Instead she phoned Flis. Pip needed to make sure that Flis was properly briefed about what to bring up in her interview with Tara. Tara was currently the only lead that actually *linked* anything on the damn Zodiac Killer wall.

It was just as well she phoned, because Flis had worked herself into a state since the previous day.

'I mean, of course I'd love to meet her and interview her for the blog,' she said, as soon as she answered the phone, as if she and Pip had been mid-conversation. 'Tara's my she-ro.'

Pip let that one pass, limiting herself to a silent eye-roll.

'But what would I ask her? What if I make a fool of myself? What if I can't think of anything to say? What if I'm rendered moot?'

'Mute. And that's never going to happen,' answered Pip under her breath, before addressing her sister's worries. 'Flis, she's got the new book out, and the restaurant and all the other projects. Your blog's got thousands of followers. She's happy to do the interview to get the publicity and you'll have loads of questions – including the ones I need you to ask.'

Pip wished she could go with Flis to the interview. Flis could be a bit, well, erratic. Easily distracted. She was quick to panic, as this latest turn of events was clearly showing. She'd seemed so sure of herself when they came up with the plan and now she was a gibbering wreck. Pip thought she would do a better job than her sister of bringing things round to the topics they wanted to discuss – environmental causes and celebrity involvement. What she did *not* want was an aubergine lasagne recipe, and that was probably the one thing Flis would end up getting.

She tuned back in to what Flis was saying. 'It's true she was very nice when I called,' she said, apparently a bit calmer now. 'I mean, you always expect a public figurine to be, you know, a bit stand-offish, but she was very keen. We're going to do a Skype interview at eleven.'

'You see,' said Pip. 'You managed to speak to her to set this interview up, and you even managed to get it done quickly. You're a natural at this. That's why your blog is such a hit. This is going to be fine.' Pip didn't know if she was convincing herself or her sister.

Flis, on the other hand, seemed mollified. 'I'll do it. I am terribly nervous though. You know how tongue-tied I can get under pressure. You have to help me.'

Pip thought for a moment, wondering how she could possibly make sure that Flis asked all the right questions. And then it came to her. The answer was obvious.

'Just sit tight, Flis. I'm coming over – I've got an idea.'

CHAPTER SIXTEEN

No sooner had Pip put the phone down on Flis than the damn Valkyries started up again. Mummy. Pip knew she really must call her back at some point. And she would. But not now. She didn't have a moment to spare. She rejected the call, only to have it ring again immediately. No Valkyries this time, thank goodness. Her relief was short-lived.

'Bloody hell,' Pip said, showing the screen to Most, even though he was a cat and couldn't read. 'It's Sharon. Remember her? From the temp agency? The one who wanted to have you killed?'

Most seemed supremely unconcerned by his brush with death, opening a lazy yellow eye and stretching his (only) front paw to dangle off the desk where he was lying. She killed Sharon's call too, and started to gather up her notes and pens, getting ready to head off to Flis's to prepare for the interview with Tara. As she hooked her bulging bag over her shoulder, the phone rang for a third time.

'What fresh hell is this?' she asked Most, who she liked to think would appreciate an ironic Dorothy Parker reference. Most had, however, closed the lazy yellow eye and gone back to sleep. Her literary gems were wasted on him.

The fresh hell came in the form of Doug, from Boston Investigations. After a moment, she decided to decline this call too. She didn't feel quite up to donning her Ms du Bois persona, and she had a sneaking suspicion he might be phoning to take her off the case. This stream of calls was, in fact, becoming pretty hellish. While Pip was looking for Matty Price, people were looking for Pip. And she didn't have answers for them. Not for Mummy, not for Sharon, and certainly not for Doug.

Ping. Ping. Ping. Message alerts came in quick succession. She sighed. It was unavoidable. From Doug:

Checking up on your progress.

Please send an update.

> *Hi Doug. Going well. Interviewed family and others. Good leads. On the job now.*

Should be sorted by week end. Will email you report.

Good to hear. Will await email.

From Mummy:

Where are you?

> *Can't talk now. At work.*

We need to talk.

> *Can't talk now. At work.*

Did you listen to my voice message? About the llamas?

> *Can't talk now. At work.*

I know you're in there, Epiphany. Answer the phone!

Pip didn't even read Sharon's message. It couldn't be good, and she had more important things to do.

*

While she was at it, she thought she'd better send poor Sophie some news. Or was sending her updates rubbing it in? Pip was in a quandary, wanting to do the right thing by Sophie.

Eventually, she sent her a message: 'Progressing well. Met the family. Quite some drama there.'

Sophie responded instantly: 'As I said, it's usually the family! Keep your eye on that ball!'

It seemed she still didn't know that Pip had actually stolen her job, so that was one thing to be grateful for.

It was clear to Pip that this could all still devolve into another fine mess. Everyone would be furious, except for the people who would sigh resignedly, because really, what could you expect from Epiphany Bloom other than disaster? She'd have let everyone down, not least the Price family. She'd have to pay back the money, much of which of course she no longer had. She felt surprising tears prick her eyes at the thought of all the drama that was coming her way.

Unless she found Matty Price. This was her only hope, she realised. To dodge them all and keep on looking for Matty. And find him. She'd save the day, keep the money, and Matty would be safe and sound. A win-win-win situation: no one could argue with that.

Pip leaned over and stroked Most from his hard, silky head to his fluffy tail.

'In for a penny and all that, Most,' she said. 'I'm going to find Matty Price. Pronto. See you tonight.'

She tried to keep up this can-do attitude as she headed for Flis's house. Her plan was to give her sister some questions for Tara and then to sit with Flis during the interview, just in case something came up that might be useful. Pip had A4 sheets of blank paper and thick felt-tip pens so that she could write notes or instructions to hold up to Flis if necessary.

Her aim was to find out more about this little group of greeny activist types that Tara, @MaverickGirl and Matty all seemed to be part of. They seemed to have get-togethers – the vegan potluck picnic and so on – which meant they knew each other in person. She might know how to get hold of @MaverickGirl. Which might lead Pip to Matty. For a few moments, Pip held on to the happy thought that this might unfold simply – Tara to @MaverickGirl to Matty – and that Pip could find him today. Tomorrow, latest. Case closed. Money in account. A rare success story for Pip.

Flis was already set up when Pip arrived, her laptop open on her desk, a pad of paper filled with scribbles and two large glasses of iced tea next to it.

'It's ginger and mint, homemade,' she told Pip. 'It sharpens the senses, and keeps you on your toes. Also good for the digestion, and to lower high blood pressure.' Apparently Flis was back on form.

Pip felt sure her blood pressure must be elevated by the spate of harassing phone calls, the stress, and the drive across London. Not to mention the three-way interview which had to look like a two-way interview, which was due to start in five minutes. And as for digestion, well, the two cups of coffee she'd had for breakfast were churning around her stomach like socks in a washing machine. She took a sip of the ginger and mint tea. It tasted like mouthwash.

'Nice,' she said.

'Sugar-free, too. I used the xylophone.'

Pip nodded, although she had no idea what on earth Flis was on about. How would you use a xylophone to make tea? She thought for a moment, feeling like she did on the rare occasions she attempted a crossword puzzle. *Xylitol!* But she didn't have the energy to correct Flis.

The sisters settled into their chairs opposite each other, the screen between them. She smiled at Flis and Flis smiled back across the desk. It felt oddly like looking in a mirror. Pip sometimes forgot how similar looking she and Flis were.

'Don't forget to ask her about her environmental activities.'

'I won't.'

'And the youth.'

'I won't.'

'And—'

'Pip, I know you think I'm some kind of ditz, but I know what I'm doing. I've got this.'

It was as if the whole episode on the phone had never happened. Pip sometimes wondered if Flis shouldn't be on some sort of medication.

'Sorry, Flis, I'm just nervous. I don't think you're—'

'Time,' said Flis, and the distinctive dialling tone of Skype filled the room.

Flis certainly did seem to have it in hand. She started by introducing her blog, the members and page views, a whole lot of facts and figures Pip didn't really understand, but there were many thousands bandied about. She felt bad for patronising her sister. She knew how it felt to have no one believe in you.

'Those are some very impressive numbers, Felicity,' said Tara. 'And in just a year?'

'Yes, eleven months. It's been amazing and it's growing week by week. It's experiential growth, really,' Flis said, justifiably proud.

'Exponential,' said Pip under her breath, but Flis was in full flow.

'But enough about me and the blog, let's talk about you. I'm sure my readers would love to know about the real Tara.'

There was a fairly long discussion about Tara's background, and food, and restaurants, which interested Pip not a jot. Tara went off on a tangent about organic food, and how she got her ingredients straight from a farm that she could personally monitor to ensure it was all above board. Flis seemed very impressed by this and scribbled furiously, nodding so hard that Pip was worried she might injure her neck. Pip couldn't have been more bored. This was going nowhere. She scribbled a word on a piece of paper and held it up to Flis.

'ENVIRONMENT,' it said.

'As a vegan, you must have a lot of strong opinions about environmental challenges,' Flis said. 'I see from social media that you follow the issues quite closely. Tell me about some of the issues you are concerned with now.'

Tara went on at length about the forests and the trees. We must save them. The logging. The loss of habitat and so on. Pip noted to herself that this was something Tara and Matty had in common. Forests.

'YOUTH,' she waved in front of Flis, who looked baffled.

'Um, the youth, I mean the young trees, what about them?' she asked confusedly.

'People,' Pip hissed quietly, pointing to her own face for emphasis.

'People,' said Flis. 'What I meant.'

'Sorry, what was that? There was a bit of an echo,' said Tara.

'You seem to have quite a following amongst the youth. Do you see yourself as a role model?'

Tara gave a melodious laugh and said, modestly, 'I learn as much from them as they do from me. The youth of today, they are amazing. They're not won over by cheap slogans and received wisdom. They think for themselves. There's an amazing group, Green Youth For Truth. I like to think that we are in this together. But yes, I am very much involved with young people and their environmental interests and causes. And I have some wonderful young friends in the real world and the digital world, who think deeply and debate these issues.'

'MAV-GIRL,' Pip scrawled.

'People like Maverick Girl?'

'You know her?'

'Only virtually. I follow her on Twitter and Instagram. She's great online.'

'And in real life. She's very active in Green Youth For Truth. She's actually a chemist and her main interest is of course plastics.

Because as you no doubt know, it's a big topic these days, amongst the youth especially. They're opposed to littering and overuse, but they are not buying this simplistic anti-plastic stance. They know that plastic is actually a crucial element in the mix, reducing the use of trees, keeping food waste down.'

'Yes, I shared something about that just this week. It really took off.'

'It's trending right now. If you want to do an in-depth blog on it, I can put you in touch with some people.'

Pip gave Flis a thumbs up and nodded enthusiastically.

'Thank you, I'm always looking for story ideas.'

'Of course, and this is a good one. Plus, there's always more than one way of looking at these things.'

Flis was animated. 'I know! That's why my blog has grown so much so fast. You have to be broad on people's horizons.'

'Indeed,' Tara said. And added, after a pause, 'You know, Felicity, I think you and I have a lot in common. Free-thinking women, looking to make the world a better place and help others. Both influencers.'

Flis blushed with pleasure. 'That's so kind of you to say.'

'Well, it's true. And I think a person of your good sense and wide influence needs to meet some other influential people.'

'Maverick Girl?'

'Oh yes, I'd like you to meet the whole Green Youth lot, you'll love them. But beyond that, you'll find that I've got some very important and influential friends. People you will have heard of.'

'What, like celebrities?'

'You have no idea. And as luck would have it, our next meeting is this afternoon. Are you keen?'

CHAPTER SEVENTEEN

'I need to be at that meeting,' Pip said to Flis as soon as the Skype call was over. 'It's my best shot at finding Maverick Girl and then Matty.'

'But you weren't invited, I was. Tara said the meetings are private, because of all the anti-truthers and people who are trying to spread fake news and that. You can't just come along.'

'I know. But I was thinking...'

Pip paused. She had a plan, but she didn't know if Flis would buy it.

'I could go as you. As Felicity the blogger. We look alike.'

'Pip, we can't do that! Besides, we don't look alike. You're much taller. And I'm darker.'

'People used to get us confused all the time. Anyway, think about it. Tara only saw you on Skype. She doesn't know how tall you are – you were sitting down – and the quality of the video is so bad she won't have seen your face in great detail. Besides, people see what they're expecting to see.'

'I can go and ask the questions that you want me to,' said Flis, folding her arms across her chest and leaning back. 'This could be a big break for me.'

'You'll get distracted,' said Pip. 'You'll start off asking something and then someone will say something about... about, say, feeding babies almond milk, and you'll be off.'

'That would never happen,' said Flis. 'You simply can't feed babies almond milk. They'd die, Pip. I mean, I know you haven't had your own babies yet, but babies must be breastfed, Pip. It is vitally important. Anyway, think about it, Pip, how would you milk an almond? Hmm?'

'Flis—' Pip tried to interrupt.

'Plus,' said Flis, 'there was a woman in Hong Kong who fed her cats almond milk and I can't even tell you how upsetting those pictures were. It's not right, you know.'

'Felicity,' said Pip, in her most commanding voice. 'This is EXACTLY WHAT I AM TALKING ABOUT.'

'What?' said Flis. Pip watched her as she replayed the conversation in her head, and Flis realised what had happened.

'Oh,' she said, suddenly meek. 'OK. I see what you mean.'

The two sisters sat silently for a few moments – an event so rare that Pip started to feel nervous.

Eventually, Flis sighed. 'OK,' she said, sounding a bit sad. 'You go. But you'd better do me proud.'

'Of course I will.' Having got her way, Pip was magnanimous.

'And remember, I am only called Felicity in the blogging world. Don't you be using the name Flis and spoiling my street bread.'

'Your… oh, OK, got it. Felicity. Street bread will be intact.'

'Here,' said Flis, who now appeared to be totally on-side with the plan. She untied the scarf from her neck. 'Wear this. Tara said what a pretty green it is, so she'll recognise it. It'll help your disguise.'

They shared a smile at the word 'disguise'. It was pretty crazy.

'You are the best sister, Flis. Thank you. I'll make it up to you, I promise.'

Flis looked dubious. 'You probably won't. You never do. Just please don't make me look stupid.'

Tara had texted the address of the meeting, which turned out to be a unit above her restaurant. That might explain where she and @MaverickGirl had disappeared to yesterday.

Pip parked her car and followed the instructions – through the restaurant and out the back door, right into the alley and first door to the right. The door was propped open a crack. Pip stepped into a small entrance hall with a door on the left and a staircase ahead of her. She stopped for a moment, taking a deep breath. It was one thing to accidentally pass yourself off as Sophie du Bois, but quite another to deliberately set out to pretend to be another person. Her palms were quite clammy at the thought, and she hoped she wouldn't have to shake hands with anyone. 'You can do it, Pip,' she muttered to herself, and followed the stairs to a landing, where a door opened into a big room with wooden floors. The living space was occupied by ten or twelve people, some lounging on a long green sofa, the rest standing or sitting on kitchen chairs around a table set with an urn and the makings of tea. A bedsit arrangement and a small kitchenette occupied the far wall. Pip tried her best to channel Flis.

'Felicity!' Tara called from the kitchenette. 'You're here! I'm so glad you could make it.'

First Ms du Bois and now Felicity. Really, Pip hoped this would be the end of her mistaken – or stolen – identities.

Tara advanced with a welcoming smile and two platters of snacks. She air-kissed Pip on both cheeks – which had the advantage of bypassing the clammy-hand situation – and deposited the plates on the table. 'You're even more lovely in real life.' Pip decided that she wouldn't share this nugget with Flis. 'We're just getting started,' Tara continued. 'I think everyone's here.'

The people at the table dragged their chairs to the sofa, forming a rough circle. Tara grabbed two more chairs by their backs and pulled them over. 'Come and sit with me,' she said, patting the seat next to her.

Pip sat, and took a closer look at the room's inhabitants. Young-ish, mostly under thirty, some who looked no more than twenty.

Stylish in a rather ugly way, with piercings and tattoos, a couple with dreads.

A woman with a baby on her lap and hair dyed the colour of daffodils stood up and welcomed everyone in a slow drawl. 'It's so great to have everyone here, and thanks again to Tara for letting us use her space.'

'And for the snacks!' Dread-Boy shouted, to a smattering of claps.

'All vegan,' someone answered, and they laughed.

Tara smiled demurely. Daffodil Hair shifted the baby to her hip and continued. 'It's really cool to see new faces here, and welcome kindred spirits to the Green Youth For Truth group?' Pip noted she had that American habit of raising her tone at the end of a sentence, making every statement sound like a question.

A couple of latecomers drifted in guiltily and took up positions on the floor. 'Sorry,' said one in a stage whisper, raising her hands in apology. It was @MaverickGirl! Pip's pulse quickened and she had to suppress a squeal of triumph. She'd found what she'd come for. She'd actually achieved an act of detectivism! She obviously had a natural talent, and today was very likely the day she'd find Matty.

'So maybe we should, like, introduce ourselves?' Daffodil Hair suggested. 'Because of the new people? I'm Samphire?'

'Hello, Samphire,' the regulars intoned. It was like Alcoholics Anonymous. Not that Pip was an alcoholic, but she'd been once with a friend who refused to go unless Pip accompanied her. Pip had felt awful lying about being an alcoholic, and overcompensated by telling a long and entirely fictitious story about her sordid days of sleeping rough on the streets of Dublin.

'Thanks, guys. I'm the group chair this week – we have a different chair every meeting, as part of our democratic ethos. So, shall we start here and go around? And then Belinda is going to give us a short lesson on, um, social engagement techniques?'

They took turns introducing themselves and their blogs. Some were more generally concerned with environmental issues, some were specific – forests, ethical veganism. One young man with an unfortunate speech impediment was entirely obsessed with frogs. Or fwogs. 'They're weally the bawwometer of the gweater ecosystem. Wain, wivers, water quality. Any change in these and you see a wapid and wadical effect on fwog numbers…'

Tara, to his left, cut him short as soon as she reasonably could, introducing herself modestly as a vegan earth lover and a foodie.

'And a TV star,' Dread-Boy called out. Pip felt sure his school reports had made repeated reference to impulse control issues.

Tara ignored him and turned to Pip, resting a hand on her shoulder. 'And I'm very happy to be able to introduce my good friend Felicity, a truth seeker and a truth teller. Felicity, would you like to tell everyone about the incredible work you do on your blog?'

Good friend, indeed. Pip realised she should probably have made some notes about the blog numbers. She decided to go for brevity, and repeated whatever she could remember from occasionally glancing at the blog and from Flis's conversation with Tara. She must have got it sort of right, because no one flinched.

'What's it called?' a woman with what looked like a drill bit stuck through her earlobe asked sullenly.

'Oh sorry, I should have said. It's called EarthMomma.'

'Oh my God, I love that blog?' said Samphire, who now had the baby attached to her breast. 'I totally love how everyone shares their own truth? It's such a great community?'

There were murmurs of assent from others who were clearly familiar with the blog. Pip felt bad that Flis wasn't here to enjoy the accolades herself.

Tara beamed, and said, 'Wonderful work. Just wonderful.'

@MaverickGirl introduced herself next, revealing the surprisingly conventional name of Catherine Smith – no wonder she went by @MaverickGirl. She was trained as a chemist and was busy with her PhD, which surprised Pip, based entirely on the girl's Thai flea-market dress sense. She didn't have her own blog, apparently, but wrote on 'a range of interests and issues for a variety of outlets'.

Last up, probably the oldest person in the room – although she was probably not more than thirty-five – Belinda Potter introduced herself as 'a media influencer, social media expert and public relations professional, with a special interest in environmental matters'. Unlike the others, she looked like a TED Talk presenter – dark hair cut in a smooth bob, black trousers and jacket over a grey polo neck, wedge-heeled boots – and she spoke like a comms geek. Lots of stuff about 'changing the narrative' and 'speaking truth to power'.

Belinda's role, it seemed, was to outline hot topics likely to grab likes and retweets, in an effort to 'set the agenda' and 'optimise momentum'. To Pip it sounded like she was dictating what people should write about, but from the nods and note-taking, it seemed the others felt no discomfort with this. Pip nodded a few times in what she hoped was an enthusiastic enough manner.

Pip wished Belinda would wrap up smartly, give Pip a chance to corner Catherine aka @MaverickGirl, and hit the snack platters at the same time. But Belinda started to flesh out the topics in quite some detail.

'Deforestation is front of mind right now, and something that I know we're all very concerned about,' she said. 'There are new studies showing that the increased use of paper packaging is leading to more trees being lost. Of course trees reduce carbon and produce oxygen, and there's habitat loss and issues around water use, so it's really a serious problem. And then throw in what's happening to the Amazon; we just can't afford to lose more trees at this point, can we, people? I've posted some articles with the hashtags #savethetrees and #saynotopaperbags. It's important that we all use those hashtags to drive the narrative towards the optimal outcome vis-à-vis deforestation.'

Fwog Dude cleared his throat to speak and got as far as 'Um,' before Belinda barrelled over him with her second point. 'Next up, also very topical, food waste. Again, an issue close to many of us.' She nodded towards Tara. 'As you know, over a third of the food produced goes to waste. It is tragic, tragic, of course. A human tragedy. Actual deaths, you know.' Pip noted that Belinda seemed entirely unmoved by the alleged tragedy, flipping her hand dismissively as she referred to the alleged deaths, and continuing, 'If we can reduce food waste, we save food, water, fuel, greenhouse gas emissions. There's a strong argument to be made for plastic in this regard. We have to move people away from the paper narrative and towards the plastic narrative to encapsulate the zeitgeist.' Pip noticed that she always ended a point with a dump of jargon. *All the better to obscure her point?* she wondered.

However, this time a murmur ran through the crowd.

@MaverickGirl spoke up. 'As you know, I'm researching this subject for my thesis, and the science shows that it's even more complex than—'

'I know, I know,' Belinda smiled, cutting her off and holding up her hands in surrender pose. 'It's not a popular view, but as we've said before, we need to take a more nuanced approach to the issue of plastic. Plastic does an incredibly important job. The key thing is to use it wisely, reuse where you can, and recycle.' She took a deep breath, then continued.

'Lastly, for today, and related, is the need for better rubbish management. Demonising individual items like straws and plastic bags isn't helpful. We need to be promoting reuse and responsible use, and pressuring government and local authorities to enforce better separation, recycling and disposal. To this end, hashtags #ReUsePlastic and #RecyclePlastic are the driving dialogue setters.'

OK, Ms Potter, let's wrap it up, thought Pip, keeping her eye on @MaverickGirl who looked thoroughly disgruntled. Pip might have been ready to make her move, but Belinda wasn't finished.

'Remember, we need to be strategic. If we can all use our platforms to focus on these problems and their solutions, there's a multiplier effect. It means that a concerned citizen is more likely to be exposed to the message more often, and that other media will recognise these as significant issues, and social media will pick them up.'

'Excellent strategy, excellent,' said Tara. 'This is how we get to determine the agenda and spread the important messages around the *real* issues of the day.'

Fwog Dude chipped in tentatively, 'If I might just flag a concern awound the wubbish in the wivers? You see, plastic is—'

'Tea!' Tara announced loudly. 'And I brought some tasty treats from the restaurant. Everything is made with organic produce from the farm. Totally vegan. You deserve it. Activism is hungry work!'

The scraping of chair legs and a stampede to the tea table drowned out Fwog Dude's concerns. Pip went to confront @ MaverickGirl. At last.

CHAPTER EIGHTEEN

'Felicity.' Belinda ambushed Pip on her way to Catherine the Maverick, and the snack table. 'It's good to meet you. I'm familiar with your blog. I can see why it's growing in that target market – young mums – and gaining broader appeal. It's got a very unique feel, very accessible, very… refreshing.'

'Thank you,' said Pip, even though 'refreshing' sounded very much like one of those non-compliment compliments. She wondered if Belinda – like Pip herself – secretly thought the whole thing was a bit kooky.

Belinda continued, 'There's a big story to be told around plastics. I'd like to send you some literature. Ideas for blog posts. Put you in touch with interesting people to feature, experts in various fields.'

'Sounds good,' Pip said, eyeing the rapidly diminishing snack selection. These young green people were gannets.

'The packaging angle in particular will interest your readers, I think, and it's something a little edgy. It'll really bump up interest in your blog. I hope you were noting the key hashtags?'

'Mhhhm?' Pip was not interested in chatting to the PR queen; she was interested in keeping an eye on Catherine, and getting a small bite of something to put into her growling stomach, which had received nothing but liquid since breakfast.

She'd be lucky if she got her hands on a single falafel at this rate. Catherine, at least, was seated on the sofa and didn't seem to be going anywhere. Also not going anywhere, or allowing Pip to move, was Belinda. 'Very relevant to your readers, Felicity. Mothers are responsible for most of the family shopping, so they're an important target market for messaging around packaging and children.'

'Of course, yes. The children.' Pip tried to edge away. 'The recycling and everything. No straws. No packets. All that. Vital.'

'Well, you'll find, if you read the research, that it's a lot more complex than that. Plastic is in fact *good* for the environment in a number of ways. As I was saying, without plastic, food waste and spoilage would be exponentially higher. Exponentially.'

In the background, Catherine stood up, and seemed to be saying goodbye to people.

'I don't mean to be rude, but I really must go,' said Pip, trying to keep one eye on Catherine. 'Perhaps you could email me?'

Without pausing to give Belinda an email address, Pip pushed past her and looked around. Catherine was gone.

'Bloody fucking hell,' she muttered under her breath, looking round wildly.

'Everything all right?' Tara appeared at her elbow.

'Maverick Girl. Catherine. I really wanted to talk to her.'

'She's just left, but do stay and chat. You can catch up with her another time. There's so much I want to talk to you about. I feel there are so many things we can do together to make the world a kinder, better, saner place.'

Pip hurtled for the door, tossing an apology over her shoulder. No sign of Catherine. She'd been so close, and now her chance of finding Matty had sauntered off. Leaping down the stairs in twos – those long limbs did come in handy sometimes – Pip wrenched open the door and looked left and right up the alley.

'Thank you, goddess,' Pip sighed when she spotted her quarry a block away. She jogged after her, for the second time in as many days. This time without a fall, at least.

'Catherine. Wait up,' she puffed as she approached her. 'Can you stop a sec?' Pip rested her hands on her knees and drew a few breaths while her heart stopped racing. 'Thanks. Sorry.'

Catherine looked at her with interest. 'You were at the meeting,' she said.

'Yes, I wanted to talk to you but you left before I could get to you.'

'I noticed you were cornered by Belinda. Pretty forceful lady, that. What do you want?'

'I'm hoping you can help me. I'm looking for Matty Price. I'm a… a friend of the family.'

'Why are you asking me?'

'You two seem to be friends. Twitter. And, it seems from the photos, in real life too.'

Catherine looked at her, sizing her up.

'That's a bit stalkery.'

'I know it seems that way.' Pip paused and thought about how she could explain Felicity stalking Matty and @MaverickGirl on Twitter. 'But I follow you anyway, you know, shared interests. And I happened to notice you and Matty were friends. Small world, I suppose.'

'I guess. But why don't you just call him yourself then, if you're a friend?' she asked.

Pip went on: 'Well, I'm not his friend. I'm a friend of the family. The thing is, Matty hasn't been home for over a week. All I want is to be able to tell his parents that he's fine, not to worry. I'm not here to make trouble, or to force him to go home or anything like that. Promise.'

A light drizzle started up, and the two women edged towards the wall for shelter. Catherine held her steady gaze for a moment, and then seemed to come to a decision. 'It's starting to rain. I live right here, do you want to come in?' And then added, rather sternly, 'Just for a minute.'

They were mere steps from her front door, it turned out. The building was a big old house that had been rather shoddily chopped up into small flats at some point. It was in a state of neglect and disrepair: loose floorboards, chipped paint on the doors and door frames, the central ceiling light in the entrance hall hanging scarily from a wire, dust everywhere. This must be one of the squats Jimmy had told her about.

The flat Catherine led Pip up the stairs to was in a marginally better state, clean at least, although mostly furnished with what looked like dumpster finds. A pile of hardback books served as the fourth leg of the sofa. A crate covered in a bright African print cloth made a side table. Similar lengths of cloth hung from a rail over the window onto the alley. A bookcase made of three planks of wood, the shelves separated by bricks, was jammed with volumes. More tomes, a pad of paper and an old desktop computer sat on a crate turned coffee table, as if abandoned mid-assignment.

Pip tried to imagine Matty here. It was a million miles from Hollywood, and nearly as far from the Prices' posh London pad, but there was a homely kind of warmth to the place.

'Take a seat.'

Given the choices – the sofa, or the chair pulled up against the kitchen counter – Pip sat in the corner of the sofa. Catherine settled into the opposite corner.

Pip summoned up her inner detective. Well, not so much her inner detective as her inner detective-pretending-to-be-a-parenting-blogger-pretending-to-be-a-family-friend. Nobody ever said life was simple.

'So you and Matty are friends, right?'

'We're kind of friends.'

Pip got the impression there was something she wasn't saying. Or perhaps she was working her thoughts out while talking.

'Maybe not quite as good friends as I thought. He hasn't been in touch in about a week. I've texted him a couple of times, but had no answer.'

'His parents can't get hold of him either. He's not been on social media. His phone seems to be off. When did you last see him?'

'It was a week ago. There was a get-together, a picnic.'

'Ah yes, the vegan potluck picnic.'

Catherine looked surprised.

'Twitter. Stalking.' Pip shrugged and smiled and got a small smile in return.

'Anyway, most of the bloggers were there. It was a casual thing. We shared our food. Tara brought a load of stuff. Someone had a guitar and there was a bit of singing.'

Pip cringed inwardly at the thought of all that 'Kumbaya'. Catherine continued, 'I brought my frisbee. One of the guys had his dog, a cute Lab. It was a nice Saturday afternoon.'

'Did Matty seem his usual self?'

'Totally. We arrived together, actually. He came here first – he likes… liked… to chill here while I was working on my assignments.'

At least Pip now knew where Matty was when he was meant to be at boxing – at Tara's place for meetings, and at Catherine's place to hang out. She resisted the urge to do a fist pump – one mystery solved. The rest was sure to follow.

'I tease him that it's kind of funny he'd rather hang out in a squat than in his parents' fancy place, but he says he likes just being able to be himself. I think his mum's a bit of a handful.'

No kidding. 'So you went to the picnic together?'

'Yes, we walked to the park. It's not far.'

'And he was just his regular self?'

'Yes. Although now you mention it, there was a bit of a run-in towards the end, as I was leaving. He got into some kind of argument with Belinda.'

'What about?'

'I didn't hear all of it, but there was something about commitment to the cause. She can be quite bossy when she's worked up.'

'So tell me about the argument.'

'All I can tell you is that Belinda was getting het up. I heard her going on about fake news and needing people who are committed. And Matty looked really upset, even angry.'

'Is that usual for him? Getting into arguments?'

'Never. He's a really easy-going, nice guy. He's not like a spoilt celebrity brat at all. He's kind and friendly. There are other celeb kids who come to the group sometimes. This one guy, Joshua, his dad is a big football star, proper bigtime, in ads and things. He's not nearly as chilled as Matty. Thinks he's a big deal. Matty just really cares about the environment. You know he's the youth ambassador for Save the Forests, right?'

'Yes. So didn't you talk to him about the fight?'

'Actually no. I was already packed up and leaving when I saw them having their argument. I had an assignment to finish – I'm doing my doctorate in chemistry – and I told Matty I was going to leave early. I'll be honest – the politics in that group is sometimes a bit much. I didn't really want to know.'

'And did you hear from him again?'

'Yes,' said Catherine. 'He phoned me that evening. Said he was on the train to the retreat that the group sometimes go on. That he needed some time to think. And that he'd phone me in a few days.'

She sighed. 'But he didn't. I guess he's having too much fun. I guess we're not as good friends as I thought.'

CHAPTER NINETEEN

'A retreat,' said Pip, ignoring Catherine's self-pity. 'That makes sense.'

'Yeah. He had stuff going on. An issue with his parents. The day before the picnic, he came over to my place, very upset. He'd had a row with them, but didn't tell me what about. He just said that someone had told him a few truths, and now he knew where he stood.'

Pip knew of course – Madison's affair, and the question of his DNA. But who would have told him?

'So I suppose maybe it seemed like a good break, you know, get out of the house until it blows over. A few people from the group have been there. It's in the country somewhere. On a farm or something. I'm not really into these touchy-feely things, but people seem to like it.'

'But he hasn't been in touch with you or his parents? Why would that be?'

Catherine smacked her head. Pip had never actually seen anyone smack their own head in real life before. It looked rather sore.

'I'm such an idiot,' said Catherine. 'It's a screen-free zone. No phones. No internet. *That's* why he hasn't called. Not because he hates me.'

A retreat. It would explain why he had disappeared, and why his phone was off. She knew where he was. What a relief! And what a triumph! At last Pip had something to tell Doug and the Prices. This private investigator gig wasn't so tough after all. Case solved.

She reached for her own phone and typed a quick message:

Hello Doug. Sources say Matty is on a retreat.

Will check it out. But thought I'd let you know.

Great. Thanks. I'll tell Prices.

Please confirm when you have seen/spoken to Matty.

Will do.

She remembered that she owed Sophie du Bois a message too. She didn't feel like explaining all the background, so she kept it vague.

'Hi Sophie. Thanks for your advice. Seems like it was a misunderstanding and he's just taken a break. Case closed.'

Another message came through from Doug:

'Try and get him to call. Failing that, photo evidence.'

Pip sighed. This investigation business was just one challenge after the next. She knew where he was, but she still needed to see Matty.

She looked at Catherine across the expanse of the sofa. 'Catherine, I really would like to see Matty, just for a few minutes, so I can tell his parents I've seen him.'

'I don't know. If he wants to get away from everyone, we should respect that.' She looked Pip up and down. 'Your generation doesn't get that.'

Pip took a deep breath and willed herself not to react to the rather calculated insult. *Cheek!*

'I totally understand and I respect his privacy, I wouldn't bring his parents. All I want is to be able to tell them I've seen him and that he's OK.'

'What's it to you, anyway?' Catherine sounded suddenly suspicious. Frankly, Pip was surprised it had taken her so long.

Pip took another deep breath. Any more and she was going to have an asthma attack. 'Like I said, I know the family. They're beside themselves worrying.'

'I guess. Maybe. But you would have to ask Belinda. She always knows everything.'

The problem was that Pip-as-Felicity had no reason to ask Belinda about Matty. And she couldn't justifiably ask Belinda for access or directions either. Why would Felicity the blogger be interested? Pip wished she'd never started this assumed identity nonsense; it was tricky enough being one person, let alone three.

'So where is it? This retreat?' Pip asked Catherine.

'I don't know.'

'Area? County? Nearest town? Anything?'

'I just know that it's in the countryside somewhere. I'm thinking maybe Kent? I could be wrong. I remember when Mark and Livi went in the summer, he mentioned working on a farm, fishing in the river. In fact, where was Mark today? He was supposed to be at the meeting.'

'So he's one of the bloggers?'

'He's a music guy. Producer, rapper sort of person. Rather well known, if you're into that sort of thing.'

'And who's Livi?' Pip had an inkling in the back of her head, a tip-of-your-tongue feeling as if she was missing something. Catherine started to speak and it disappeared.

'Livi? Oh, Olivia James. She's really big on Insta. I haven't seen her at the meetings for ages though. In fact, I don't think I've seen her since she went on the retreat, come to think of it. Weird. She just disappeared. Maybe she got too busy with her Instagram influencer life, didn't have time for us greens. She was a sweet girl, actually. I wonder how she's doing.'

Catherine fiddled with her phone as Pip strategised out loud, 'So Livi's no help, if you're not in touch. I guess Mark is probably my best bet, if I can find him.'

'He lives upstairs,' Catherine said distractedly, eyes on her phone. She looked up at Pip. 'Now that is really weird. Livi has disappeared from Instagram. Account closed.'

CHAPTER TWENTY

The fact that Mark lived in the same building as Catherine was very convenient, and also not as much of a coincidence as Pip imagined. According to Catherine, Belinda had put both her and Mark onto the flats, as well as some others in the Green Youth For Truth network.

'Yeah, that's Belinda for you. She's quite something,' Catherine said, shaking her head. 'I don't know how she knew about the flats. Belinda always seems to have her sources. But she told us there was this big empty building and there were rooms here. It's going to be demolished sometime, but there's some hold-up. So the rent is basically nothing, compared to what you'd pay for this area.'

Handy. Pip wished she'd found such a sweet deal, although the decent and decorative Tim was a good landlord.

'So which is Mark's place?'

'Upstairs, on the right. I'll take you. I won't come in though. It's been a long day and I don't feel up to Mark.'

'Why? Don't you like him?'

'He's OK. Just a bit messianic for my tastes. I'm passionate about the environment, but I'm a scientist. Evidence-based and double-blind and peer review and all that. Some of the people who get involved in the cause are, shall we say, a little less attached to the empirical method, and more attached to broad claims and big noisy statements. Mark being one of them. Gets a bit much in large doses.'

Even in small doses, it turned out.

'Yo, Cath,' said Mark, as he opened the door. 'Is it time for the meeting?'

'Been and gone,' she answered. 'You missed it.'

'Shit, man, sorry.' He ran his hands through a mop of ragged tufts that seemed to be aiming for dreadlocks but had lost the will halfway. 'I got distracted. Twitter. Shit's going down, dude.'

Pip wondered if he was stoned, or if he was always this all over the place. Catherine cut him off.

'Listen, no problem about the meeting. This is Felicity. She's interested in the retreat. I told her you could tell her about it.'

Mark seemed surprised to see Pip on his doorstep, where she had in fact been since he opened the door. He focused his eyes on her and said, 'Oh, hi. Sure, sure. Man, it's an eye-opener. You should totally go, it's rad.'

'I'll leave you to it. Cheers, Mark. See you. And Felicity, come by my place when you're done, I'll let you out.'

Mark turned and shambled into the dimly lit room. The only light sources were from the assembled electronics – a huge computer screen, what looked like a mixing desk, other bits and pieces with levers and switches and keyboards and LED lights – and the weak evening light filtering in through the faded sheets that adorned the windows.

Pip followed, noting his dishevelled air: grubby tracksuit bottoms, huge and dirty trainers with the laces undone. Was he on something or just very distracted? Either way, he seemed almost unaware of her following him into his room.

Mark sat down at the desk with its glittering expanse of electronics, and swung on his swivel chair. Pip took a stool without waiting to be invited. She suspected it would be a long wait.

'Man, I can't believe I missed the meeting. I was working on some beats, and then I got on Twitter. Got myself into a beef there. People are so ignorant. Wow. They just believe any old thing The

Man tells them. Big Pharma bullshit. Anyway, next thing I know it's like… What's the time?'

'Four.'

'You're kidding.'

'No. So Catherine tells me you're a musician?' Pip felt a little silly using the word, seeing as there were no actual instruments around, and she felt sure there was a new and better name for whatever it was Mark did.

'Yeah.' He nodded earnestly. 'Using my words and beats to save the planet.'

'Well that's a good thing,' Pip offered gamely.

'Used to be in it for me, you know. Mainstream stuff, trying to get that break. I hit the big time, too. I was runner-up in *The Great British Sing-off*. Recording contract. But I felt the pull of the evil dollar and I knew The Man was watching me. So I chucked it in to heal the world,' he said, seemingly without any irony, humility or embarrassment.

'That's very good of you,' Pip responded, remarkably without sarcasm.

'Like, I used to sing about love and all, you know, the usual stuff. The lies that capitalism sells us. But I'm big into the environment now. That's it for me, my calling, man.'

Pip briefly considered asking him how love was a lie sold by capitalism, but gave herself a stern mental shake.

'So about the retreat?' she said.

Mark just barrelled along his own thought process as if she hadn't spoken. 'Hey, I'll play you my new one, hang on. You'll love it. The beats will groove your soul.' He turned to his decks of lights and levers, and started fiddling.

Pip surveyed the scene. If Catherine's place was homely, in a downscale studenty kind of way, Mark's was a complete tip. It was clear that whatever his winnings on *The Great British Sing-off*, he hadn't spent them on interior design. The furniture was mostly cheap skip finds – not unlike Catherine's but without her flair – though what gave the place the air of a psycho's lair was a huge pile of rubbish, mostly bottles (glass and plastic), in one corner. It looked like he'd started off putting them in a big cardboard box, but it was now buried under the bottles. Near it was a stack of newspapers and magazines.

He caught her looking at the tip. 'Recycling,' he said. 'I really need to get to that. Here, listen.'

Whereupon, for a five full minutes – or perhaps eternity, Pip wasn't sure – she was assailed by shouty industrial rap on the subject of the earth:

> *'The earth is yo momma*
> *So I'm gonna tellya*
> *Not everything you hear is good for the biosphere.*
> *There's some stuff you should know*
> *About the ice and the snow…'*

She zoned out a bit and when she next came to, she heard:

> *'We don't want them pesticides*
> *Messin' up on our insides…'*

Oh God, this was appalling.

'Mark!' she interjected loudly. 'Can we talk about the retreat?'

He muted the music. It was as if the angel of peace had descended upon her, covering her face – and most importantly, her ears – with its feathery wings. The relief.

'Yeah, that's why I was playing you that track, man. It was inspired by the retreat, the stuff I learned when I was there. Working the land, you know, being part of the great cycle of life. And what Belinda taught me, her thoughts. We talked every night, in front of the fire, just, you know, searching for, like, answers. About the world. Truth and falsity. What's, like, reality. It's cosmic, man. Belinda is tuned in to it, man. She might dress like The Man and also a bit like a man, but she's evolved, man.'

After untangling all the various men in Mark's sentence, Pip tried again.

'Where is it, the retreat?' She spoke slowly, in the hope it would focus him.

'In the country. Wow, it's so great out there. Grass and hills and this, you can't believe, this big sky. No cars. No buildings. The air, it's like totally fresh and clean. Like, you can breathe, man.'

Pip was familiar with the notion of the countryside, although it seemed to be new to Mark.

'Where exactly?'

'It feels like a different world, but it's not that far.'

Pip silently counted to three. This was like a conversation with Flis's children.

'How did you get there? Bus? Train?'

This painful game of Twenty Questions went on for quite some time, and Pip extracted the following information:

- The retreat is on a farm.
- Maybe in Kent.
- But also maybe not.
- There are vegetables, in plastic tunnels. (Apparently they are groovy.)
- There is a river and a trout dam. (With actual real-life fish, Mark was at pains to clarify.)
- There are hills and lots of grass (she sighed).
- There is definitely a sky, a big one (she sighed again).
- There are chickens, free-ranging (or, as Mark would have it, 'They were just running about the place, it was mad!').

- There are beehives with actual bees. ('Making actual, like, honey, man.')
- There is a village nearby, but he couldn't remember the name. ('Something-bury? Bury-something?')
- He and Livi had arrived there by train ('an hour or two, or maybe three') and been fetched from the station by car.

He really was the most infuriating person.

'Sorry, man, who did you say you were again?'

'Felicity. Friend of Catherine.'

'And why are you going on the retreat?'

'Speaking of friends,' Pip said quickly, 'how's Livi?'

Mark's face clouded over. 'I don't know what's up with that chick. She never comes round any more. Doesn't answer my WhatsApps. Thought we were friends.' Suddenly, he sounded really young.

'Have you seen her since the two of you came back from the retreat?'

'I got a lift back to the station with Belinda. Livi was really sick, she didn't want to travel.'

'Poor thing, what was wrong?'

'Belinda said she had a fever, maybe flu. I didn't see her. She was asleep in her room.'

'So she stayed?'

'Yeah, the people there are really cool. They said they would look after her.' Mark's brow furrowed in thought. 'You know? That's actually crazy. Now I think about it, I haven't seen her since she came back.'

'That was when?'

'A month or two, maybe? Or three? What was it, I'm thinking February, could it be February? What are we now, like, May?' he seemed genuinely perplexed by the Gregorian calendar. 'So I guess, yeah, I haven't seen Livi for like three months.'

Pip-as-Felicity felt cold. Was this another missing kid?

CHAPTER TWENTY-ONE

Tim was mumble-singing to himself at the sink. 'Oooh ooh ooh but you're ma bay-ay-beee…' Pip admired his rolled-up sleeves and damp forearms. And the way he actually did the washing up, instead of leaving it in a festering soup to 'soak', like every housemate she'd ever had, and, in fact, like Pip herself. He was a quality bloke, this Tim. The singing though… *Still, nobody's perfect.*

'Hi there,' he greeted her with his usual warmth. 'You've been busy.'

'Sooo busy,' she said, dropping into a kitchen chair. 'I'm exhausted and I still have work to do. Research.'

Most jumped up onto her lap. Poor chap, he hadn't had his stroking quota filled the last few days. He purred like a train.

'Ah, your mystery serial killer plans.' Tim smiled.

She gave a little laugh, although frankly the Zodiac Killer gag was wearing a bit thin. 'It is a mystery of sorts. I'm trying to find someone.'

'An ex? Or are you stalking someone you fancy?' He gave a mock pout and his ridiculously gorgeous eyes twinkled.

Pip thought for a moment and decided to tell half the truth, but not enough that she was breaking confidentiality about Matty.

'No, a boy who disappeared, although I think I've found him. And then a girl. Someone connected to him.'

'Also disappeared?'

'Well, she hasn't been seen around. I'm trying to find out where she is, or if maybe something's happened to her,' she said.

'Two missing people. That's strange. Cup of tea?'

'Love one, thanks.' *Proper quality bloke.* Pip sighed inwardly.

While he pottered about the kitchen counter, filling the kettle, taking mugs from the cupboard, she filled him in on the bare bones of the case. The missing boy. The green youth activist group. Livi's trip to the retreat and her subsequent silence.

'I assume you've done the usual Google search, social media and all that.'

'Yes. She's been remarkably absent on all of those. Active on Instagram and Twitter and all over until a couple of months ago, and then poof. Gone.'

'That's strange. How old?'

'Twenty-two, twenty-three, somewhere around there.'

'Yeah. It's unusual for someone to be invisible on social media for any length of time at that age. Most people pop up somewhere. Can't resist it.'

Tim gave her the tea without even asking about milk and sugar. He'd only made her tea once or twice, but he'd remembered that she liked it strong with a dash of milk and half a sugar. 'Could be some sort of digital detox, especially if she was at a retreat. Although a couple of months seems excessive for that.'

'Yes, but the odd thing is that she was part of this group, a bunch of environmental activists, that organised the retreat where she was last seen. It's quite a close-knit group and none of her friends there have heard from her. Plus, they all are very active on social media. That's their thing.'

Tim thought for a minute, and seemed to make a decision. He picked up his backpack and took out a laptop, placing it between them at the kitchen table. 'Let me poke around a bit, see what I can find.'

'I've looked, promise. As I said, all the usual searches. Really, I appreciate it but there's nothing.'

'I'm not talking about the usual searches, Pip. What's her name?'

Pip thought for a minute and answered. 'Livi. Olivia James.'

He was like a whole different Tim. Serious. Deep in concentration. Fingers flying across the keys, tapping determinedly. Quite sexy really. Muttering to himself, a stream of self-direction: 'Hhhmmm… No… Definitely not on Insta… Not since… Ah, that's interesting… Maybe… Yeah… hhhmm… What about…' He kept this up for five minutes, maybe more; anyway, it felt like half an hour. Pip sipped her tea and continued her ministrations of Most, who had drooled a large and growing wet patch on her jeans. She was about to interrupt Tim, tell him that really, she had it in hand, when he said, 'Yes!' He swung his laptop to face her.

'Missing person's report filed two months ago by a Lucinda James. Her mother, I presume. Or perhaps a sister or an aunt.'

'And you found this information where?'

'Police database.'

'You're joking.'

'No.'

'Remind me again, you're in software support?'

'Broadly speaking… Sort of… Listen, Pip, obviously you can't tell anyone about this. It's not, um, well, not strictly above board. I shouldn't really be mucking about on the police database.'

'You think?'

He gave her a devastatingly cute look, like a kid caught stealing a biscuit.

'Can you see if the case is closed?'

'No. It's not clear. She hasn't turned up in the death records, so we can rule that out.'

'God, I hadn't even considered that.'

'Let me see what I can find elsewhere. Mobile phone. Banking. Might get lucky.'

'No, Tim. That's enough. This must be totally illegal.'

'Of course it is. Hacking carries a serious sentence. Which is why you can't talk about it.'

'Hacking? You're a hacker?'

'I'm not a hacker!' Tim seemed insulted and a bit flustered. 'OK, technically that's what they call someone who bypasses security and goes into a computer system without authorisation. But I'm what they call a white hat hacker. I work for companies to try and breach their security systems, find out where their weaknesses are before the bad guys find them. But in this particular case, I like to think of myself more as a computer specialist helping a friend with an important inquiry. It's illegal, but it's a victimless crime. Unless of course you really are the Zodiac Killer and I'm an accessory after the fact. In which case I'm in big trouble.'

'That's not funny. Thanks for the information. But that's enough. I don't want you to hack into a bank. Good lord. I can't believe I just said that! I can't believe you're a hacker! I thought you were a… a… an IT nerd. Don't hack the bank.'

Pip put her head in her hands. Her heart was beating like crazy. What the hell was she doing messing around with hackers and missing people?

'OK, no hacking. But let's think this through,' Tim said. 'So, we know she was at this retreat about three months ago.'

'Yes, this guy Mark was there with her and he confirmed it. He left her there because she was sick and needed to recuperate for a day or two.'

'And her friends haven't seen or heard from her since.'

'No. And if her mother or someone in the family reported her missing to the police, that means they haven't seen her either. She is properly missing.'

Pip had a bad feeling. Where was Livi? She was last seen, very ill, at the retreat, according to Mark. And now Matty was also allegedly at the retreat. And also incommunicado. What was it with the retreat? Come to think of it, Mark was pretty barking, although he might well have been a nutter before the retreat. But they all seemed to be linked, and the retreat was at the centre of this, she was sure of it. She needed to find it. She needed to see Matty with her own eyes. And she needed to know what had happened to Livi.

Belinda and Tara were the two people most likely to know how to get to the farm where the retreat was held. She needed to worm it out of them. Use her skills. Detect things. And the place to start was at Tara's restaurant.

'Tim, I'm starving and I haven't shopped in weeks. There is literally nothing but a cheese rind in that fridge. Let's go out for a bite. My treat. I'll fill you in on some of the details, we can talk some more.'

'Now that's an offer I won't turn down.' Tim looked delighted. She hoped he wouldn't be too freaked out by her next instruction.

'There's just one thing, though. I think the restaurant is vegan.'

Tim shrugged.

'Oh, and when we're at the restaurant, you'll have to call me Felicity.'

Disappointingly, when they got to Tara's Clean Food Factory, Tara was nowhere to be seen. There was nothing for it: Pip would just have to sit back and enjoy lunch with Tim. Something had been bothering her, though.

'Tim,' she said, dropping her voice. 'You never seem to actually go to work any more. Have you lost your job?'

Tim gave a laugh, showing off his perfect teeth. 'No,' he said. 'But I guess now that I've told you most of it, you can know the rest. The work I do is… highly confidential. Sometimes I work from the office, or from the client's. But sometimes it's just safer to work from home.'

'Safer, like someone might attack you?'

Tim gave her a strange look. 'Safer like I have very high security settings on our system at the flat,' he said. He must've seen that Pip was ever so slightly disappointed. She'd rather liked the idea of Tim as a James Bond type. 'It's still very dangerous. People could sue me.'

'Ah well,' said Pip. 'That's reassuring to know. That you won't get killed and that our wifi is really safe. All good news.

'How's your food?' she asked, to change the subject, peering across the table into the dead eyes of a trout, swimming in a pond of rocket and shaved asparagus. As it turned out, thankfully the restaurant wasn't so much vegan as 'responsibly sourced'. Pip was pretty sure that Flis would have known what that meant.

'Well, Felicity, I can tell you that it's great. Thank you.' Tim had taken to her fake identity with alacrity, calling her Felicity about twenty times a sentence and acting like a person in a bad play. He'd started on the way to the restaurant, and claimed he was 'getting into character' when she objected.

He ran his knife along the side of the fish, carefully lifting the fillet from the fine bones underneath. 'I love trout, Felicity. I used to catch them. With my dad. It was our special time together – no Mum, no sisters, just him and me, fishing. We'd make a little fire and cook the trout on a stick, right over the coals. You've never eaten anything quite so delicious in your life, Felicity. Although this, I have to say, is pretty good.'

'How is everything?' asked the waiter, who sported a fine man-bun.

'Very good, as I was just telling my friend, Felicity. Reminds me of fishing in my childhood, wasn't I saying, Felicity? Caught them and cooked them.'

Pip shot him a look. His eyes were sparkling with mischief.

'They're as fresh as you'll find,' said Man-Bun. 'They came in an hour ago, they were caught this morning. Everything in this restaurant is sourced from a fifty-mile radius. Mostly from one particular farm. Local and sustainable, that's our philosophy.'

Man-Bun turned to Pip, who was inhaling a roasted pumpkin and sage lasagne. It felt like days since she'd had a proper meal. 'The vegetables too. Organically grown on the farm in Kent. They have rainwater tanks and solar power and all that. State of the art.'

Kent. Trout. Farm. Pip felt a jolt of recognition.

'My family's from Kent,' she said casually. 'Where's the farm, do you know?'

'I'm not sure exactly, I've never been myself,' he replied. 'Our owner, Tara, arranges all that, sends a van to collect them.'

'Yes, I know Tara.'

'Well, she's probably told you then. Apparently the soil is quite remarkable, and that accounts for the flavour and the high nutrient value.'

As far as Pip was concerned, there were fewer topics more dull than nutrients.

'Well, it's delicious, thanks,' she said, trying to wrap up the conversation before she heard the word 'antioxidant'.

'It sure is, Felicity,' said Tim with a smile.

'I'm sure that farm where the trout comes from is the same place where they have the retreat,' she said as they drove home, squashed into the Mini, knees touching as the car turned a corner. 'And I reckon we could find it. We've got some information, we could work it out.'

'Kent's a big place, and I suppose there are a lot of farms,' Tim said. 'But hey, I like a challenge. And a mystery. And you seem to be providing both today, Felicity.'

Pip felt herself blush. Her knee burned where it met his and a warm glow radiated up her leg to her—

'Watch out!' yelled Tim, and she swerved, saving a small oblivious mongrel from certain death.

Back at the kitchen table in their flat, Tim got his laptop up and running, while Pip took out her notebook and scribbled down the information she had gleaned from the waiter.

- The farm is within a fifty-mile radius of London.
- There is a river and dam with trout.
- Vegetable gardens or tunnels.
- Solar panels.
- Rainwater tanks.

She flipped back to the previous page and her notes from Mark's unhelpfully vague recollections.

- The vegetables are in tunnels.
- There's a village nearby, perhaps called Something-bury.
- A dam, fairly sure he said a dam. Definitely a river with trout.
- Beehives.
- Not too far from a train station.

She was more certain than ever that they were describing the same place. The retreat was on the farm where the restaurant got its trout and vegetables. Now to find the farm.

'OK, we're good to go,' said Tim from behind his laptop.

'So the waiter said everything was sourced within fifty miles, can you draw that in?'

He hit a few keys and a circle appeared, shading a big chunk of map.

'Now discount anything not in Kent.'

More keystrokes; a smaller chunk of map remained.

'Now, where to start?' He looked at her expectantly.

'Maybe with the village names. Probably Something-bury. Or Bury-something.'

He gave her a 'Really?' look.

'Hey. That's all I've got. Not my fault that my informant is a stoner rapper with poor recall. Just Google Kent towns and villages, see what we get.'

They both laughed. Pip realised she was enjoying herself. It was like one of those group projects you have to do at school, except that the topic was interesting, and for once she'd got paired with the cute, clever guy and he seemed happy to have been paired with her.

Most lay down on her paper and writhed around in cat ecstasy, obscuring all her notes. She scratched his ears.

'That's interesting. Bury is an old Anglo-Saxon word meaning a fort, or fortified place… Here we go… Villages and towns…'

She peered over his shoulder to read the list. 'Seriously, who knew there were so many villages in Kent? OK, there we go, Hawkenbury. Pembury. We should include the boroughs as well as the burys. Here's one, Woodnesborough…'

There were eight burys and eleven boroughs in all.

'Let's start with the "burys",' said Pip.

'Right,' said Tim. 'OK, so we find the villages on the map…'

More tapping, and the names appeared highlighted.

'I bet you were a total nerd at school,' said Pip. 'Games club, computer society.'

'Yes, yes and yes. Chess. Computers. *Dungeons & Dragons*. The whole lot,' he said cheerfully. 'I'm still a nerd at heart, luckily for you. So we've got the villages marked. If the fifty-mile radius is accurate, that means if we look at the "burys" we lose two of the five likely villages.'

'Great, so we're down to three. Do they all have train stations?'

Only two had stations. Tim fiddled a bit more and the aerial view of Kent came up on Tim's screen; squiggles of roads, lots of green, little blocks of roofs. 'Google Earth,' said Tim proudly, as if he'd made it himself.

'Brilliant,' said Pip, pulling her notebook from under Most's bum. 'Now we're looking for a river and vegetable tunnels; those would be the most visible I think. Maybe a dam, I'm not sure on that. A biggish house – it would have to be to accommodate the people on the retreat.'

It was painstaking work, finding the villages and checking the surrounds for likely farms. Then surveying the map, identifying possible contenders and zooming in for detail.

It was close to eleven p.m. Tim yawned and stretched. 'Hey, Pip, maybe we should go to bed, pick this up in the morning. I'm knackered.'

'Of course. You go. You've been great, really. I couldn't have got this far without you.'

'It's been fun.'

'It has. OK if I hang on to your laptop for a bit? I'll just keep at it a few more minutes, see if anything jumps out at me.'

As she continued her search, she heard him pottering in the bathroom, brushing his teeth, flushing the loo. It was oddly intimate, the sound of his night-time routine.

She went back to her task, zooming in as close as she could without losing all the detail. It was useless; it all looked the same to her. She zoomed back out and tried to stare at it as an eagle would. Take in the big picture and see what stood out. Nothing. Nothing stood out. Bloody eagles. Most took this break in concentration as an invitation to move from her lap to the much more alluring area of the keyboard. Pip knew from experience that if she let him, he would curl up and go to sleep on it, making work impossible and messing with all the settings. 'Come on, Most, play fair,' she said, reaching for him. But it was too late; his expedition across the keys had zoomed the map in again.

She was about to zoom back out and resume being an eagle, when her eye caught something unusual. Rectangles, evenly spaced. *Solar panels!*

'Tim!' she shouted. 'Tim, I think Most found the farm.'

CHAPTER TWENTY-TWO

Pip woke to the sound of the Valkyries. Mummy. Again. She hardly needed an alarm clock, with Mummy in her life. She reached for her mobile but she couldn't move her arm. Had she had a stroke? she wondered. She struggled to get up, and her legs didn't seem to want to cooperate. Was she paralysed? She'd been waiting for this since she fell off the bar and hit her head at Lacey Pointington-Simms's gender reveal party. So tacky. What could one do but drink?

No, it turned out to be another false alarm. She was just tangled in the sheets, which were anchored by Most who had snuggled right in and wedged himself next to her arm. She heaved him out of the way. He really had picked up a lot of weight since she'd got him.

The Wagner stopped and the phone rang again. No Valkyries this time though, just the usual daddle-da-da ringtone. Pip picked it up. Jimmy.

'Hello, Jimmy,' she croaked, pushing her hair out of her eyes.

'Hi, Pip. Didn't wake you, did I?'

Pip felt as if she'd just awoken from a six-month coma. 'No, of course not. Just getting my emails done before I get going.'

'Great, so listen, you said you wanted to do a trial training session, and the bloke who trains with me today has just cancelled. Turns out I've got a free morning. Well, a free day in fact, I'm not working this afternoon. Why don't you come by around ten? Sweat a bit, grab some lunch after?'

'I would love to sweat with you.' She couldn't believe she'd just said that. Her brain was still in a fog. 'Gosh, I mean, I...' He laughed.

'I mean *train*. Boxing. I'd like to train in the sport of boxing. But I've got something to do this morning. I've got to go out of town.'

'Still looking for the kid?'

'I think I've found him, but I just need to go and check in person.'

'Pity. Well, some other time.' He hesitated and then said, 'I'd really like to see you.'

Now it was Pip's turn to hesitate. She couldn't be sure, but this sounded a lot like flirting.

'Hey, Jimmy. If you've got the day free, why don't you come with me? I'm heading to Kent, it's not too far. I'll have a quick look around and we can have a late lunch somewhere in the country. My treat. What d'you think? I'll just get myself up and dressed and then—'

'I *knew* you were sleeping.' Jimmy laughed.

'Got me. I'll pick you up from the gym, OK? Give me an hour.'

Before she could begin to get out of bed, her phone rang again. Ben Price.

He started speaking as soon as she answered. 'I had a dream,' he said. 'Matty was at the bottom of a deep hole and he wasn't moving. I could see him, but I couldn't get to him. Even Madison thinks this could be a premonition. I don't know what to do, I can't breathe,' he said, gasping for air.

'Ben, I'm almost one hundred per cent sure that I know where Matty is,' interrupted Pip.

'Not in a hole? Not dead?'

'No,' she said firmly. 'Alive and at a retreat. I'm going to find him. OK?'

'Oh,' said Ben. 'Alive, you say? My darling boy! Just at a retreat.' He paused. 'Maybe I could go too. You know I've—' Pip interrupted again. At this rate, she'd never make it out of here.

'Ben, I must go,' she said, and hung up. Hung up the phone on Ben Price. Who would have thought?

An hour later, and perhaps a bit more dishevelled than she might have hoped, Pip was again in the car with her knee pressed against that of an attractive man. It was starting to become something of a habit. Jimmy was a little smaller than Tim – an inch or so shorter than Pip, in fact – but wiry, muscled, and with a kind of pent-up bouncy energy that she liked.

'So where's the kid? Where are we going?' he asked.

'He's at a retreat on a farm, somewhere near Huddersbury I think.'

'You think?'

Pip explained about the trout. The solar panels. Google Maps. Being a detective. She didn't mention Tim, which she felt oddly guilty about.

He whistled in admiration.

'That's some high-level detective work.'

'Thank you.' She smiled. 'Let's just hope I'm right. You happy to navigate?' She handed him the overhead image from Google Earth that she'd printed out, with her intended destination circled in red. He took the paper and waved his iPhone at her, grinning. 'GPS. It's the new thing, you know. You detectives should get in on it.'

That reminded her. Detectives. Doug and his need for updates and written reports. She quickly sent him a message. 'Investigating retreat situation. Will report in full.' She knew she probably wouldn't, and no doubt the message was in the wrong font, but Doug didn't respond, so that had to be good.

It was fun to be heading out of town, going off on a mission, especially with Jimmy for company. Gradually, they left the slow-moving morning traffic and grumpy drivers behind them. The car felt tiny on the open road, lorry tyres at Pip's eye level, but when they turned off the motorway they soon found themselves in the countryside, the little car buzzing along, the fields and hedgerows swishing by. She needed to get out into the country more, Pip thought. Maybe once the job was over...

She'd been avoiding that thought – the job coming to an end. It was exhausting and stressful, but she felt more alive and stimulated than she had in years. Not since she was on the ranch in Idaho, helping with the foals. She'd loved that. She'd still be there if it wasn't for that ill-advised entanglement with the head honcho. And who could have known he had a fiancé? Or that he'd react like that to avocado? But really, attempted manslaughter was a stretch.

'What I don't understand,' said Jimmy, 'is why this retreat is such a big secret. I mean, why can't you just ask someone for the address, and then pop over and check up on the kid?'

'It is weird. People are very cagey about it. And to be honest, I made things a bit tricky because I got into a bit of a muddle with them.'

'How's that?'

'They think I'm my sister.'

'Why would they think that?'

'Well, I told them I was her.'

He was looking at her with an amused smile. 'Because?'

She explained, 'She has this blog, and I went as her to interview someone so I could ask questions to get information about Matty. Maybe not the best idea, as things turned out. Because once I was her, I couldn't really start asking questions as me, and she – by which I mean me as her – had no real reason to ask, so it all got rather complicated.'

'As I see.' Jimmy was chuckling under his breath in a very annoying manner. Imagine if he knew that Pip was juggling not just two, but three personas.

'Anyway, that's beside the point, seeing as I've found it myself. Through high-level detective work.'

They drove on in a companionable silence, each thinking their own thoughts, mulling over the matter of the retreat. Pip let her eyes rest on the road ahead, and relaxed her shoulders.

'It's still odd though, don't you think?' Jimmy asked after several fields and cows had passed. 'The secrecy? Like, how do they get new customers if it is such a big secret?'

Pip thought for a moment. 'I don't think they're really looking for customers. It's kind of by invitation. A lot of the people who go there, the people in this Green Youth group, seem to be kids of celebs, or somehow well known in their own right. Music world, social media influencers, that sort of thing. So maybe that's why.'

'Privacy and safety. Makes sense.' Jimmy nodded to himself as he said this, like a man well acquainted with the pitfalls of celebrity life.

Pip had an idea. 'Do you think there might be something else going on? Like maybe it's a rehab facility or something, and they don't want that to get out.'

'Drugs?' suggested Jimmy. He probably had drugs on the mind from his gang days.

'That's what I was wondering, although I've no reason to think Matty was into drugs. Mark definitely looks like he could be into something. If it is rehab, it didn't work in his case.'

Jimmy nodded. 'Or,' he said, 'it could be some sort of cultish brainwashing thing.'

Pip laughed. 'You've been watching way too much Netflix,' she said. 'These are environmental activists, not Moonies. And trust me, I know about the Moonies. No – they care about trees. Nature. Saving the planet.'

'Well, influence is power these days. There's a lot at stake. Different interest groups wanting to get their message across. It's like being in the ring. The person who can see the whole picture, who has the information, that's the guy who's going to have the advantage, right? If I was a cult leader in this day and age, I would use social media big time. Hey, this is the crossroads. Left here.'

Pip turned into a narrower road that wound up and over a small hill. Whatever farm buildings there might be were obscured by the hill, not visible from the main road.

'Looks like about a mile from here,' Jimmy said. 'So what's our plan?'

'I think we play it straight. Just drive up to the main house, go to the door, ring the bell, ask to visit Matty Price. I only need to see him and make sure he's OK. If I could get a picture that would be great. But as long as I know he's safe and well, we can turn right around and leave. We can go back to Huddersbury and I'll buy you lunch at the pub we passed. The Duck and Hog. Or was it the Chicken and Pig? Whatever. We'll eat at a pub named after fowl and swine. Definitely.'

'Sounds easy enough. And yes, I accept your kind invitation to the Goose and Boar.'

'Oh.'

They passed a few smallholdings with modest cottages. Jimmy had Pip's Google Earth printout in hand and was trying to match up the houses with the aerial view. He muttered to himself, 'OK, so that's… yeah, OK… So two more on the right… Looks like it's just round this corner.' He looked up at the property in front of them and said, 'You might need to revise that plan of yours.'

A tall reinforced wire mesh fence stretched across the perimeter, as far as the eye could see, punctuated by a big pair of electric gates which were closed. Pip slowed.

'Look at those massive gates.'

Jimmy peered past. 'There's a guard. A uniformed guard. With a dog. Why would they have that?'

'This can't be it,' she said, continuing past the gate and pulling over into a lay-by a few yards down the road. 'I'm looking for an organic farm slash retreat. This looks like a military thing. Let me see the aerial view.'

'That's it, I'm positive – look.' Jimmy traced the printout, pointing to the road, the smallholdings, and then the bigger farm with the vegetable tunnels and the river and the Lego blocks of the outbuildings scattered about. Looking carefully, they could see the gate posts and what they now realised was a guard hut.

They needed to get into the farm. Pip hadn't come all the way out here just to turn around at the first sign of a problem. Besides, she had a plan. Jimmy shrugged, and they headed back up the road.

'Good morning,' she said cheerily to the guard, extracting herself from the Mini and stretching her legs. 'How are you today?'

'Can I help you, ma'am?'

'Yes. A friend told me about this farm and the organic vegetables, and I wondered if I could speak to someone about supply. For my restaurant. I have a restaurant. Organic.'

'Entry is by appointment only, ma'am. You'll have to phone or email.'

'That's such a pity. I'm only in the area for the day, I don't know when I'll be able to come back.'

A stony silence greeted her.

'Could you make an exception? Could I pop in, perhaps, have a quick look at the lie of the land? I promise not to pick the peas,' she said, with what she thought of as her alluring smile. It had worked that time on the Iraq border.

'No exceptions,' he said, quite firmly this time. Apparently he wasn't attracted to her. Weirdo.

'Oh, and another thing,' she said. 'My friend mentioned that there's some sort of retreat here. Is there someone I could talk to about that?'

The guard looked at her with real interest this time. 'You're in the wrong place, lady.'

'Am I? Maybe I'm mistaken. So there's no retreat, nothing like that?'

'Could I have your name, please?'

'Jenny.' Jimmy's voice came from behind her, where he'd stood silent during her conversation with the guard.

But who was Jenny? She looked around, confused.

'Your name please, ma'am?'

'Jenny,' he said again, more loudly this time, and putting his hand on her arm. 'We're going to be late for our lunch date. Just leave it. We'll phone about the vegetables and come again another time. Obviously this isn't the place. Darling.'

'And your surname, please?' asked the guard.

'Thanks for your help,' Jimmy said breezily, turning back to the car, steering Pip gently with him.

'Jenny? What was all that about?' she asked, irritated. 'This is my job, you know, Jimmy. I don't need you to chivvy me away from my work.'

'I didn't want him to know your name. And I wanted to get out of there. Pip, that guard? He was carrying.'

'Carrying what?'

'A gun. Shoulder holster. I could see the bulge under his jacket. I know enough from my time doing club security to know what to look for.'

'That's crazy. Why would you need an armed guard at an organic vegetable farm? Or a retreat? Who is he meant to be keeping out?' Pip felt a chill as she offered an answer to her own question. 'Unless he's not there to keep anyone out. Unless he's there to keep people in.'

CHAPTER TWENTY-THREE

'So you were a bouncer,' Pip said, cutting her Scotch egg into quarters, revealing rubbery white and a bright yellow centre.

'Club security, it's called. Yeah, I did that for a while. Not for me though.'

'Scary?'

'Boring. The odd moment of conflict – mostly just your usual drunks and idiots causing trouble – and a whole lot of nothing in between.'

Pip reached over for a chip from Jimmy's meal – the Pheasant and Swine's recommended lunch for the day, a venison pie.

'And the hours, of course. Not very family friendly.'

'You have a family?' Her heart gave a little lurch. She'd got the distinct impression that he was a free agent. She wasn't sure why she felt so disappointed.

Jimmy hesitated. 'Two daughters. Lily and Rose. Lily is seven, Rose is nine.'

'Your hands!'

'That's them.' He opened his hands, palms down, stretched out his fingers and looked down at the tattoos, the girls' names etched across his knuckles. 'Bit of a silly idea, really, but I had the tats done when they left.' He stopped talking and looked away.

Pip waited and poked at her egg with a fork. An old Kylie Minogue song piped from a nearby speaker filled the silence.

'New Zealand. Their mum remarried – a Kiwi. Took the kids.'

'Couldn't you stop them?'

'I tried. But honestly? I was a bouncer working stupid hours in a dodgy business.'

'I'm sorry, Jimmy.'

'Yeah,' he said. 'Me too.'

They turned their attention to their food, not quite knowing where to take this oddly personal moment of connection.

'Not bad, eh, the Hen and Bacon?' he said. 'Pie's good.'

'As pubs go, the Egg and Porker does do a reasonable lunch,' she agreed.

The mood somewhat lightened, they went back to their own thoughts. Pip replayed the visit. After hours of searching and researching, not to mention driving, now she was at a dead end. She had started the day so hopeful, but she'd learnt nothing. No sign of Matty. No proof. What was she going to tell Boston Investigations? And the Prices?

'It wasn't a total waste of time, this trip.' Jimmy seemed to have read her mind. 'The one thing we can say for sure is that there's something not right about that farm.'

'I guess. And the way he reacted when I asked about the retreat. Wanting my name, all of a sudden. That was odd. Something not right about that, too. If only we could see inside. Do you think we could get over the fence?'

'Pip, seriously, that is not a good idea. You don't know what's on the other side. And these might be dangerous people.'

'They're tree-hugging greenies! How dangerous could they be?'

'The big fence. The guard. The dog. The gun. They are hiding something. Or someone.'

'Maybe there's something valuable there. Something they want to protect. Like, I don't know. Heirloom tomato seeds for fruit the size of your head,' she joked, but only sort of.

'More like cash or guns or drugs,' said Jimmy, flexing his hands.

Pip's phone vibrated on the table, the screen lighting up with a text message. It was Catherine, who would be forever @Maverick-Girl to Pip – who would presumably always be Felicity to Catherine.

Hey. Something strange w Livi.

Can you talk?

> *Driving back to town now. I can come to you. 4ish?*

4 is good.

Pip called for the waitress, a smiley blonde with chubby red cheeks. Rural Kent was mercifully free of waiters with man-buns and grumpy waitresses with literary advice.

It was closer to five by the time she had crawled through the afternoon traffic and dropped Jimmy back at the gym. She settled into Catherine's sofa with a sigh, sinking a bit deeper into it than she had expected. The sofa had seen better days. Catherine handed her a mug of tea.

'Thanks. I need that,' said Pip. 'Busy day. And you?'

'Busy month. My PhD. The experimental phase is finished and I'm analysing the results. It's all-consuming. Fascinating, but so much to get through. It takes forever.'

'What's it on, exactly?' Pip said, hoping she wouldn't get an overload of chemistry jargon in her weakened state.

'Plastic. Degradation rates of specific types of plastic, and individual items – shopping bags, bottle tops, that sort of thing. The really exciting part is that I developed a new testing method – or a better way of measuring, I guess I could say – and the results are more accurate than previously.'

'Wow.'

'It's a bit of a big deal, actually. In chemistry circles, of course,' she said, with a smile. 'Although not good news from an environmental point of view. Plastic is even worse than we thought, takes even longer to break down. My new research shows that the old studies underestimate the lifespan of plastic items by a considerable margin. I mean, like twenty per cent. More in some cases.'

'So that means?'

Catherine explained that a plastic bottle, say, was thought to take four hundred and fifty years to break down, but her new research reckoned it was closer to seven hundred years.

'In fact,' she said, 'it doesn't ever really go away. As I explained to Belinda, it just breaks down into ever-smaller pieces. It's a real breakthrough. That's why I'm so exhausted – it's so exciting, I can't drag myself away. Not even for a retreat. Belinda actually phoned this morning and invited me.'

'Really?'

'Yes. She was quite insistent that I go. Said I should take a break. But I can't, of course. Deadlines, you know! She doesn't seem to understand about that. Although she's taken a real interest in my research. Keeps asking about it. In fact, that's kind of what I wanted to talk to you about. We got into a bit of a… not really an argument, but a bit of a spat, you could say. About the research. Just before she invited me to the retreat.'

'What about the research?'

'She disagreed with my results. She's surprisingly interested and informed about the science, for a layperson. I guess because of her environmental work. But she's been working with the old stats and studies and I know that they're wrong. Anyway, she disagrees. She claimed my numbers must be wrong, and then she changed tack and said that this sort of controversy would be really bad for the environmentalists and the clean earth activists because it just causes confusion, makes it look like our facts are not to be trusted.'

Pip thought about this for a moment. 'That's strange, isn't it? I mean, we all know that plastic is bad. And now it turns out it's even worse. But the basic message is still the same. The communications work she does for environmental groups doesn't change.'

'In some ways, this new information is better for them. It's going to be big news, not just for chemists, but for environmental academics and activists too. She kept on saying that plastic had its place. I got a bit annoyed!'

'You know, I've been hearing that a lot recently. At the meeting. And there was a spat about it on my sister's... on my blog. Someone wrote a piece about how plastic saves trees, and of course people went nuts, and the thing degenerated into a brawl.'

'Yeah, that's the argument. It's true, to a very limited extent. It has a place. We need plastic, at least until we develop new technologies. Anyway, then she went back to trying to convince me to go on the retreat and clear my head before I write up the research. But here's the thing. She said something really strange.'

'What?'

'She said, "You are so stubborn, you young women. You think you know everything," and then something about how Livi was another one who just couldn't see sense. And then she was suddenly all sunny and said, "Oh well, it's really not important." And I thought of you, and your questions about Livi. Something's off.'

Pip sipped her tea and tried to look calm as her heart raced and her brain whirred, trying to decide what to do next. Should she tell Catherine about her concerns for Matty and Livi? About the missing person's report? She was a smart woman, and Pip felt she could trust her.

She took a deep breath.

'Livi is officially missing,' she said. 'Somebody, her mother I assume, filed a missing person's report two months ago.'

'How do you know?'

Pip fudged that one a bit – *internet research, a helpful friend* – and admitted, too, that she didn't know if the case was still open.

'But why were you even looking into Livi?'

Again, Pip hesitated. 'As you know, I'm a friend of Matty's family, so I'm asking around, trying to help them track him down.'

Catherine studied Pip over her teacup. 'Why did they ask a blogger to go track him down? Instead of the police? Or an investigator?'

'Um. I'm also an investigator, in a sense. Side gig, you know. Or maybe the blog is the side gig. It's complicated. They wanted to keep things quiet, because of Madison Price's new movie, see if we could find him without going through the official channels. Anyway, that's not important. The thing is that Livi's name came up, and no one seemed to know what had happened to her.'

'Two missing people? Both with links to Green Youth? That seems too much of a coincidence.' She was smart, Catherine. Quick on the uptake. That science-y brain.

'Exactly. That, and they were both at the retreat around the time they dropped off the map…'

She wanted to tell Catherine the whole story, but could she trust her? Pip took a deep breath. 'I went to the retreat. Well, I found the farm. They wouldn't let me in. It was very strange, very high security. High fence. An armed guard.'

'Armed? Are you sure?' Catherine said.

Pip's own unease seemed all the more justified in the face of Catherine's concern. But what to do next?

'There *could* be a perfectly reasonable explanation for this,' she said. 'It could be that she went off for a digital detox or on a trip, or with a boyfriend or whatever. She might be sitting in her mum's house drinking tea right this minute. We need to get hold of Livi's parents, that's the thing to do.' Pip tried to look both decisive and reassuring. 'There's no need to panic just yet.'

'And the armed guard at the farm?'

'Oh, that could just be for the heirloom tomatoes,' said Pip. Catherine looked a bit taken aback, but nodded.

'Well, tell me as soon as you hear anything,' she said. 'Matty's my friend. I'll do whatever I can to help you find him.'

CHAPTER TWENTY-FOUR

The next day, after Pip had sent a detailed report of her findings so far to BI, and reassured Ben, in another rambling conversation, that she had just hit a small obstacle but she was quite sure that Matty was at a retreat, Tim came up with the goods again. Pip had to do a wee bit of grovelling first.

'I thought you didn't want anything to do with my nefarious ways?' he teased.

'I didn't want you to hack into a bank. Which I think is a perfectly reasonable position. But I do want you to get me a phone number.'

'An unlisted phone number.'

'Well, yes, but there's a very good reason.'

'That's what they all say. Slippery slope.'

'Seriously, there's a missing kid. Maybe two, in fact.'

'I'll get on to it. I'm walking into my office right now. I'll get back to you in five.'

Pip used the time to play with Most, who was in the throes of a complete passion attack, rubbing himself against her legs. He jumped up onto the table, butting his hard little head against her chin and then hurling himself onto her laptop and writhing around like a porn star on a water bed. She rubbed his round furry tummy. It really was getting rather portly. She suspected Tim was giving him snacks,

While she waited, she opened her notebook and went through the list of people who had been at the Green Youth For Truth meeting, and the others like Mark and Livi and Matty. To start, she googled their names. She began with Fwog Dude, whose real name was – no kidding – Hamilton Cunningham-Smythe and who, it turned out, was a superstar zoologist. Turns out Cunningham's Cunning Critters, which he launched as a 'fun thing' for fellow Life Sciences students to share pictures and videos of amazing animals, had many hundreds of thousands of followers on Facebook, Twitter and Instagram. Good lord, it just went to show that looks could be deceiving. His following was bigger than Matty's or Flis's, nearly the size of Mark's. Between them, they were in the millions. That was a sizeable market for influencers. Pip had an idea. She picked up her phone and called Catherine.

'Quick question,' she asked, without so much as a hello. 'How did you get involved in Green Youth, and Belinda and Tara? How did you find them?'

'They found me. Twitter. I was tweeting about my research and plastics and so on, and I was getting quite a bit of traction on it. Belinda started following me. Showed interest. We had a few exchanges. There's a lot we don't agree on. I Twitter-met some of the others in the group. And at some point someone invited me to one of their get-togethers. I was interested, to a degree. Belinda had some savvy in the social media world; I thought I could learn something from her, like how to promote my ideas better. I liked Matty, in particular – we hung out, even though he's a kid.'

Pip put down the phone and mulled over the rather uncanny coincidences and commonalities of the people involved in Green Youth For Truth. They were young and they were influential. Everyone she'd met or looked into had an online following. A proper following, not just a few family members and friends.

Her phone rang and vibrated, sending Most off her lap in a seething huff. It was a message from Tim – as he promised, within five minutes – with Livi's mum's mobile number.

*

Livi's mum was not at all forthcoming. Pip had started by asking for Livi's contact number, trying to sound casual and upbeat, while giving the vague impression that she was a long-lost friend without telling an outright lie.

'Who are you again?' Mrs James asked.

'I'm Epiphany Bloom,' said Pip, who'd had enough of her multiple identities and had decided to play it straight, at least with her name. It wasn't as if Mrs James would connect her to BI and Doug.

'I've never heard that name and I certainly would have remembered it. And how do you know Livi?'

Pip sighed. That was indeed the problem with her name.

'I don't know her personally, but I am trying to find a boy who seems to be, um, missing. Livi's name came up.'

'Are you something to do with that Green Youth lot?'

'No, but the boy—'

'Because I don't want anything to do with those people.'

'I'm not part of them, I promise. The boy I'm looking for is involved with them though, and I know Livi was too. Mrs James, please, I need your help. I need to speak to Livi. I know that you filed a missing person's report two months ago.'

'How do you know about that?' she cut in suspiciously.

'Public record,' Pip said in a decisive voice, and asked quickly, 'so she turned up? Is the case closed? Mrs James, where is your daughter?'

There was a pause before she answered.

'I think we had better meet.'

A grey Mercedes swung into the garage just as Pip drew the yellow peril up to the kerb. The James residence was in one of the smart new developments near London Bridge. Pip would have loved to live so near the water, with a view of the Thames, except for the swans. Since she'd learnt for herself that the thing they say about a swan being able to break a person's arm was actually true, she'd steered well clear of them. A woman emerged from the subterranean garage, carrying a briefcase and a large bunch of keys. She beeped her remote to lock the car, and the lights flashed on and off.

'Epiphany?' she asked. Pip nodded, struggling with the car key that needed just the right little jiggle before it would come out of the door lock. No central locking for her.

'Lucinda James. Come in.'

She took Pip through a shiny reception area, giving the barest hint of a nod at the doormen, and up in the lift to the tenth floor. As they stepped out of the lift, the sheer glass walls gave exactly the view of the river Pip had imagined, and she was sure she could make out some small swan shapes in the distance. How high could they fly? she wondered. Mrs James opened the door to her duplex, revealing a spotless open-plan sitting room and in the background, a kitchen in fifty shades of white.

Mrs James was younger than Pip had expected, probably in her early fifties. Her neatly tailored blazer and trousers hung a little loosely on her frame, as if she might have lost weight since she bought the outfit, and her eyes looked bruised and tired. She dumped her briefcase on a glass table, indicating that Pip should follow suit, and headed to the kitchen, straight for the kettle.

'Long day,' she said. 'I need tea.' She took out two cups and a teapot and said, without looking up from her task, 'Before I tell you anything else, I want to know exactly who you are and what you know.'

There was something no-nonsense about this woman. Pip was going to tell her the truth – or as much of the truth as she could, without revealing the inescapable fact that she was only doing this job because she'd stolen it.

She explained that she was a private investigator, working for Matty Price's parents, and that her investigations had brought her into contact with Green Youth For Truth. 'So I'm looking for Matty Price,' she concluded. 'He is missing too. It seems he might be at a retreat on a farm, and I think Livi was there. It might just be a coincidence but—'

'In Kent? The farm in Kent?' The woman went as white as the rest of her house.

'Yes.'

'That's where Livi was before she...'

Pip waited.

'Before she went away.'

'Mrs James,' Pip asked gently. 'Where is Livi now?'

Mrs James poured the boiling water into the pot and brought the tray to the table.

'Livi is travelling,' she said. 'I believe she's in Bolivia now, but it's hard to keep track. She...' Mrs James paused, and Pip could see her visibly pulling herself together. 'She doesn't contact us very much, I'm afraid.'

'Bolivia? In South America?' Pip's geography was a little sketchy, although she had spent those months as a ski assistant in Chile. That hadn't ended well. But avalanches do happen, and it was only a small one. It was ridiculous that they had blamed her.

'Indeed. South America. Bolivia. Or maybe Peru.'

'What is she doing there?'

'I don't know.' Mrs James's voice wavered.

'When did you last speak to her?'

'We had postcards...' Her voice trailed off.

'Mrs James, I'm sorry to upset you. I'm only trying to help. But can you tell me what happened before you lost contact? Where was she? Can you explain it from the last time you saw her?'

Mrs James sat down at the table, poured tea into the two cups, and gestured to Pip to help herself to milk and sugar.

'The last time I spoke to Livi, she was on the road to that farm. Very excited, she was. She said she'd been invited to this special week away. Like a retreat, but for people involved in this environmental movement she was so passionate about. The Green Youth For Truth network. It was an honour, she said. Livi has all these hundreds of thousands of Instagram followers, you know, very big on the Gram,' she said with a tiny roll of her eyes. 'It had been mostly teenage stuff in the beginning – fashion and so on. But over the last year or so, she'd been doing more and more environmental messaging. And being asked to be part of this retreat meant she'd been recognised by the leaders – a woman, I think her name was Brenda – as someone with potential, someone doing important work.'

'Belinda?'

'Yes. That was it. And a man. John, I think.'

This was news to Pip. She hadn't heard any reference to a John so far.

'So Livi and another boy had been invited. They would be gone for a week and back the following Sunday. I was worried about her studies – she was meant to be working on her thesis for Digital Media Studies, but she spent most of her time on her Instagram career. If you could call it that.'

Her eyes welled a bit. 'We had a fight actually. I said she was already spending too much time on these green issues and with those people. Since she'd got involved with them a few months earlier, I could see her focus on her studies had slipped. So I spoke my mind, and it wasn't well received. I can see now that it might have sounded like I didn't support her life choices, which is what she yelled at me before she walked out. It's hard, getting it right as a mum. Anyway, she left and I sent her a message saying I was sorry about the fight, and I hoped she had a wonderful time. She sent one back saying she loved me and not to worry because there would be no mobile phone communication for the week, but she'd ring me when she left the farm on Sunday. She never did.'

'That was the last phone call you had?'

'Yes. Sunday came and went. Monday. Tuesday. No sign of her.'

Mrs James told Pip that she kept on calling, with no answer. She and her husband didn't know what to do. They tried her friends. Her academic supervisor. No one had heard from her. They filed a missing person's report. The police asked around. They made some calls, mostly to the same people the parents had contacted. Nothing. They hired a private investigator.

'But just three days after we reported her missing, we got a postcard from Venezuela, and then a few weeks later from Bolivia. And the private investigator we hired confirmed it. So we went back to the police and said, well, sorry for all the trouble, but it turns out she's in South America. They were very understanding about it. The policeman said, you know how it is with these young people. But they didn't know Livi. It was so unlike her. She would never worry us so. And as for abandoning her thesis, her Instagram business… I thought she must have had some sort of breakdown. Anyway, we waited, thinking she'd make contact soon, or just walk in the door. There was one more postcard, a couple of weeks later, saying she was going travelling. And in the last month, nothing. Not even on my birthday. Livi is very good about birthdays. I just think maybe she didn't really forgive me for that fight. I know that I'm a pushy mother, and I think I just pushed her too far. All the way to South America. Her father always warned me that one day I'd push her away.'

'What about the green people, and the retreat? Did you speak to them?'

'We managed to track them down but they didn't know anything. That woman Belinda came round, very concerned, she'd heard Livi was out of communication. Livi had had a bit of flu, apparently, so she stayed another day, but they'd looked after her and then driven her back to the village – Hudbury? Huddlestone? I forget – to catch the train. She was so sorry, said what a lovely girl Livi is, please let us know that she's all right, all that. I did send her a message when I got the postcard.'

Pip asked to see the postcards, which Mrs James handed over with some reluctance. The one from Venezuela had a waterfall. One had a picture of Lake Titicaca. The other of the Andes. All had short scrawled messages and both were rather smudged and blotchy, as if they had been rained on: 'I'm in South America! Amazing here. I just need some space. Love you.'; 'Miss you!' and 'Wow, so beautiful! I am going travelling – next stop Peru.'

'Her handwriting?'

'Well, yes. Why do you ask? You don't think…'

'No, not at all. Just a thought.'

'A girl phoned, from the green lot, I didn't get her name. She sounded quite young. Said that Livi had mentioned South America when she was at the farm. She said she wanted to see the rainforests, and the Andes, although she'd never mentioned that to us. It all seemed to hang together, but I just don't know why she wouldn't tell us she was going. It makes no sense. I keep turning it over in my head. Wondering if there's something I'm missing, something that would explain it. Maybe there was some man. Or even – I know it sounds crazy – a cult of some sort. Brainwashing. Kidnapping. Or worse, I can't even bear to think about that. And she doesn't have any money with her and isn't using her bank cards. Sam and I are thinking of hiring a private investigator in Bolivia.'

Pip was 99.9 per cent certain that the Bolivian PI was going to come up empty-handed. There was going to be no record of Livi travelling to South America. Pip might be new to this investigation business, but she didn't buy the story. She felt sure there was more to it than a girl who'd been suddenly bitten by the travel bug.

Whatever the answer to the mysterious disappearance of Livi James, the answer lay here in England. The retreat was at the centre of the mystery, Pip was sure of it. If she could crack the mystery of the retreat, she'd find out what had happened to Livi and she'd find Matty.

Pip knew what she needed to do. She had to get back to that farm.

CHAPTER TWENTY-FIVE

'Hello, Aunty Pip. Did you know that the smallest dinosaur was no bigger than Hammy?' With which Camelia produced a hamster from her pocket and waved it in front of Pip's face. 'Say hello to Pip, Hammy. Rooooaaaarrrr. I'm a dinosaur!'

The little ball of golden fluff wiggled its tiny legs and looked bemused.

'He certainly is scary,' Pip laughed.

'Mummy's in the kitchen, doing her blog things,' she said, gesturing inside the house. 'I'm going to put Hammy back in his cage. See you.'

As promised, Flis was at her kitchen table, laptop open, her phone on the desk next to it, both glowing and pinging and vibrating like some demonic disco.

'Pip!' she said, looking up from her screen but not getting up. 'Thanks for coming. I'm so happy to see you. I've been stuck behind my computer for days. As you can see, things are crazy with the blog. But in for a penny, in for a hound, as they say.'

Pip was pretty sure that Flis was the only person in the history of time who had ever used that particular bon mot, but she didn't have the energy to correct her.

'What's going on?' she asked instead, peering over her sister's shoulder at the screen with its pop-ups and messages and pings and tings. Pip herself had been ignoring a call from an unknown number all morning, but that had only caused a few pings.

'It's been mad. I've had a blog post that has gone viral, and the numbers are just climbing experimentally.'

'Exponen—'

'Literally millions of new followers every day.'

'Millions? Really? Wow,' Pip said, astonished.

'Well, not literally, obviously,' Flis said, as if Pip were the one being silly. Pip ignored the tone.

'What was the article about?'

'Surviving your narcissist mother.'

'Really?'

'Oh, yes. Narcissism is really big, it's like the hottest trend right now. Literally everyone thinks their mother's a narcissist. Ours *is*, of course. But lots of people just *think* theirs are. Anyway, it was a really helpful piece about the importance of self-care and healing. Mindfulness and mediation.'

'For you or the mother?'

'You, of course. Nothing you can do about the mother. Narcissism is virtually untreatable, apparently. But crystals can be enormously helpful in rebalancing your energy.'

Much as she could use some energy rebalancing now – specifically, balancing the scales towards more energy – 'crystal' was a word that made Pip's jaw clench. She did manage to push out the words, 'Well, that's great about the numbers, well done.' She really was happy for Flis that her weird set of interests had somehow coagulated into an actual business. 'So are you starting to make money out of all this?'

'A bit. I mean, that's not why I got into it. I wanted to spread the message about health and happiness and to help other people, especially mums. Not the narcissistic ones. The others. But if you get enough followers and you have a high profile, you're an influencer. And some companies will pay you to use their product or tweet about it or go to their events or what have you. Mostly they just send you a lot of free stuff.'

She waved her arm behind her, where a pile of bags and boxes was stacked.

'Everyone I've come across at Green Youth For Truth is on Insta or blogging or vlogging or whatever. I couldn't believe the numbers of followers. Hundreds of thousands,' said Pip. And then she added, archly, 'Literally.'

'Well, that's how marketers or even, like, lobby groups or political parties or whoever get their message out. People don't believe ads and corporations any more. They believe people like themselves, and the people they follow on social media.'

Something worked away in a corner of Pip's brain. It felt as if she was missing something, something about these influencers and the greens.

'Oh, and something arrived for you.' Whatever had been working its way into Pip's exhausted consciousness slipped away when her sister spoke. 'Well, for me. But for you. Because of, you know, the interview and Tara, and you being me and me being—'

'Yes, yes. What is it?'

'An email,' Flis said, scrolling through what looked like pages of incoming mails. 'This is it, um, yes, from Belinda Potter. Let's see now, where are my glasses? Ah, let me finish this quick text first. You know me, I'm not one for multi-asking.'

'Tasking.'

'Hey… Joe…' Flis proceeded to read slowly out loud as she typed on her iPhone – one of her annoying habits. 'I am…' She backspaced. 'I was…'

'Just forward me the mail, I'll read it on my phone.'

'Gosh, you're a bit edgy today, aren't you?'

'Sorry, yes, long day.'

It was true, Pip was on edge. She'd been running around like a madwoman, hardly slept in days, driven up and down to Kent, and still she hadn't found Matty. In addition, she had another missing youth to worry about. At least it kept her mind off her man issues, if you could call them that. Tim and Jimmy. Her thoughts were interrupted by the ping of Belinda's mail coming through, via Flis. Pip opened it and read it out loud to Flis.

Subject: Great source for your article on plastic

Hi Felicity

So great to meet you at the Green Youth For Truth meeting the other day. You mentioned you are working on a big story about plastic for your blog (love the blog btw!). I've been working with top people in that field and there's new research out that you should see. I can introduce you to the expert – John's great, really knows his stuff, and can talk you through it in a way that your readers will relate to. Seriously, this could be a big scoop for you. I tried to call you a couple of times but no luck. Don't write this piece without speaking to me!

Best
Bel Potter.

Well, that explained all the mysterious missed calls this morning. And there was the name John again.

'So what's that all about?' demanded Flis. 'Why did you tell her you were writing a plastics piece for the blog? I hadn't planned on anything like that.'

'I was improvising. I was a bit on the spot and I had to say something. And for some reason it just seemed to send her into a tizz.'

Flis looked irritated, which was unusual for her.

'Sorry, Flis, I didn't mean to drag you and your blog into something you don't want to do. I'll sort it out with her. I do need to see her though, I think she's got information that can help me find my missing kid. I'm thinking if I can just meet her, and talk about it…'

'It's OK. I mean, maybe we could write the piece, if it's a big scoop. There has been a lot of buzz around plastics recently. That Twitter spat between the Ban All Plastic lot and the Save the Forests people. My followers would probably like a story on that, now I think about it.' She was sunny and enthusiastic again. She was a good-natured soul and didn't really have enough of a concentration span to hold a grudge. 'In fact, let's! I've just signed up with this big aggregator site and I'm getting lots of new visitors to the blog. That plastics story might be the kind of thing that keeps them coming back.'

'OK, cool. I'll speak to her sometime, although I can't imagine what she means about the so-called scoop. I mean, the impact of plastic is so well documented. We've all seen the turtle with the straw. But I'll get what I can from her, and we can work on it together just as soon as I've found the missing kid. Kids.'

'Those poor parents… How's the investigation going?'

Pip updated Flis on the developments, and her current dead end. 'I'm sure the retreat holds some of the answers to Livi's disappearance. And I'm sure Matty is there. I'm going to go back, I just need to find a way.'

Her phone rang. The same mystery number, which she now realised must be Belinda. She answered.

'Hello, Felicity, at last!'

'I was just reading your mail, thanks for that. Sure, I'd like to talk to your guy. I'm speaking to a lot of people – I want this piece to be very in-depth and to bring in all the angles. Catherine's been telling me about her research; it seems like she's on to some interesting results.'

'Catherine is doing some interesting work, yes,' said Belinda. There was a pause before she added, 'Felicity, to be honest with you, I fear there are serious flaws in her methodology. In fact, I'm going to speak to her about it tomorrow. I wouldn't want you to publish anything before you have the facts, it could reflect badly on your blog's credibility.'

Pip doubted it was any less credible than that ridiculous thing on turmeric she'd seen on her sister's blog the previous week. Still, why was Belinda being so forceful on this? There was something going on, something around this plastics issue. She said with studied detachment: 'Look, Belinda, I've got a lot going on at the moment, so I'd like to hear what you and your source have to say, but it might have to wait.'

'It can't wait! It's very topical right now. I need your word that you won't publish without speaking to me.'

This woman was a real piece of work. *I need your word? Cheek!* Not that Pip had anything to publish, but who was Belinda to come making demands?

'I need to speak to you urgently,' Belinda continued dogmatically. 'It is very important. I'm out of town today, and I've got a meeting here tomorrow. With my plastics expert, in fact. The source I was telling you about. Catherine is coming too.'

'I'm happy to talk about it, but it's going to have to wait. Maybe next week…'

'Next week is too late!' Belinda's voice was just one click below shouting. 'How about tomorrow night, I could come back from Kent in the afternoon?'

'Kent? You're at the farm? The place where you have the retreat?'

After a pause Belinda said, 'Yes.'

Pip felt a jolt of possibility. Could this be her ticket to the retreat? She knew she had to play it right. She took a moment to think and then said, 'OK, Belinda. Here's an idea. How about I come down to you?'

'I'm not sure that's the right thing. Maybe… actually, no. That won't work.'

'It's a great idea! I can meet your source. Well, I'm really keen to run this exposé. The blog has had a huge leap in readership since a post went viral this week, and I've signed up with this aggregator. I'm looking for something big and controversial to keep up the momentum. That plastics story could be just the thing. If I can get the right sources, of course. But I guess if I can't come to the retreat, we'll have to wait till I have a gap again. Maybe next month. No, wait. I can probably fit you in in September.'

There was the sound of Belinda taking a long slow breath to calm herself.

'Fine. Come to Kent. Tomorrow. You and Catherine can travel together. I'll text you the details.'

CHAPTER TWENTY-SIX

Pip felt warmly towards Catherine, seeing her leaning against the wall by the station entrance, her bulging backpack at her feet. With her rumpled Thai elephant trousers and her unbrushed hair, she looked like she'd got straight out of bed. Or perhaps never gone to bed at all. She was smart and solid, though, and Pip felt she could trust her. It was good to have a companion and an ally on this trip. Pip didn't like to admit it, but Belinda made her uncomfortable. She was so forceful and always seemed on edge, except when she was being *too* nice. It was a combination that made Pip nervous. The whole trip was a bit nerve-racking. Pip still didn't know how she was going to tackle the question of the missing kids.

After some wrangling with the inscrutable interface of the ticket machine – would a human being be too much to ask for? – Pip managed to buy two returns for the 8.55 to Huddersbury, which was already pulling into the station when they arrived on the platform. Pip had wanted to drive, but she was scared the guards would recognise her car and have her thrown out as a person of suspicious provenance. So she decided to stick with the train, which was what Belinda seemed to expect, anyway.

'So why are you going to the farm to see Belinda?' she asked Catherine, once they'd settled into their seats. 'I thought you were up to your neck in your research.'

'I am. It's crazy. I'm working on the thesis and then also this article for an international journal. Even though the thesis research isn't finished, there are some aspects of the findings on the half-life of plastics that are important to share asap with other researchers in the field. Belinda's been badgering me to come and talk about my research with this expert she seems to be working with. John. A client, I think. I told her I'd come in a few weeks, once I'd got this journal article off to the editor, but when she heard about the article she was even more insistent.'

'She is very – how would you put it? Forceful?'

'She most certainly is. And, to be honest, she did mention that this mysterious expert she's always referring to might be able to help source funding.'

'Well, that would be worth going to Kent for,' said Pip.

'You're not wrong. If I could get money for the project I would broaden the scope, get a lab assistant to speed things along; it would make a huge difference. And what about you? Why are you here?'

'Similar. This big piece we're doing on the blog. She was very insistent, wanted me to speak to her expert.' Pip's explanation tailed off. She thought for a moment and made a decision. 'And I saw it as an opportunity to go to the retreat and have a look around. There's something not right about that place. I want to check it out, see Matty with my own eyes, just to be sure. And even ask around about Livi. Maybe you can help me.'

Catherine raised an eyebrow, just a millimetre, and said, 'Sure. Why not?' She reached into her backpack and pulled out a sheaf of papers; numbers and tables scrawled with notes and markings. 'May as well get some work done.'

Pip watched the fields slide by, cows zooming in and out of view as they ignored the train speeding past them, and watched Catherine chewing her pencil and stabbing it occasionally at the papers.

Then she remembered what the little niggle in the back of her brain had been telling her. Sophie du Bois had worked on Livi's case! Doug had mentioned her and Livi at that first meeting. How could she have forgotten?

Pip sent a message to Sophie: 'Quick Q. I know you were involved in the Livi James case. Did you find her?'

Sophie replied within minutes: 'I did. Safe and sound and in love, travelling in South America with a guy she met. Case closed.'

Was it possible that Pip had been making a mystery where there wasn't one? Was Livi safe and sound with a hot Colombian, or had Sophie perhaps made a mistake? Maybe she'd been misled by someone, but who? And that still left the question of Matty Price. Today, thought Pip, was the day she found him.

Which reminded her. 'Hoping to have seen Matty by close of play today,' she quickly messaged Doug. She was rather proud of the phrase 'close of play'. Had a ring of professionalism about it. Ben was about due for a call, so she messaged him too. 'Think I will see him today. Will let you/Boston Investigations know.'

'Thank God,' Ben messaged back. 'Madison has suddenly taken it all on board and is beside herself.'

It was hard to imagine, really, Madison being beside herself. Or even slightly rumpled.

Well, Pip should be able to put everyone's mind at rest by the end of the day.

CHAPTER TWENTY-SEVEN

'Welcome, welcome!' Belinda bore down on them, reaching for Pip's little wheelie bag. 'I'm so pleased you are both here. So much to talk about. So much. Here's the car.' She swung the case into the boot, tossed Catherine's backpack in after it, and slammed the door. 'In you get. It's not far. Lovely road, too, as you'll see. Ah, the countryside. The hedgerows. Crows.'

Pip wondered if it was nerves or just the country air, but Belinda was like some manic hostess. She was still jabbering on when they turned into the huge gates Pip had seen when she'd come with Jimmy – no guard this time, she noted. 'There's lunch arranged for one. Organic farm fare, of course, Tara's recipes.' She chuckled. 'I've arranged a deep relaxation treatment for Catherine. Felicity, maybe we can fit one in for you tomorrow. We'll see.'

Belinda walked quickly through the entrance of the house – a vast wood-panelled hall filled with plinths and tables displaying expensive-looking vases and imposing busts – and up the staircase. The staircase was one of those which split in the middle, so you had to choose whether to go left or right. Pip knew from experience that this was a muddle waiting to happen, and tried very hard to remember that they turned to the left.

It was a relief to be shown to her room, which was unexpectedly calm and bright after the wood-panelled gloom of the rest of the house. It featured a four-poster bed so high off the ground that it required a small step to get into it. Pip glanced under the bed, and was relieved to see no sign of a chamber pot. That would have been a step too far. The room was furnished in white linen, and overlooked the garden and the fields beyond. And it did not have Belinda in it. She had let Catherine drop her backpack in the room next door to Pip's, and then she'd taken her away for her relaxation session. 'I won't be long. You freshen up,' Belinda said to Pip, who actually considered herself quite fresh enough, 'and let's meet downstairs in the library in fifteen minutes. It's just to the left of the front door where we came in. Help yourself to a herbal tea and we can have a good chat. John is eager to meet you.' The calm was to be short-lived, but Pip decided to savour it for a moment. Instead of unpacking her few things, she lay back on the bed and let her mind play with the facts of the case. Who was this John, anyway? Some mysterious client, who allegedly had all this important information about plastics and forests and so on. So a scientist, then?

Pip felt herself in danger of drifting off, like Goldilocks in the bear's bed. She was exhausted after her busy days and late nights working through her notes, searching the internet, tossing and turning while her brain stewed. Better get up and not be caught napping. She would head to the library. Maybe one of the herbal teas would have traces of caffeine. One could only hope.

If only she could find the library. She couldn't even find the staircase! It felt as if every passage wound up in a dead end or a tapestry, and Pip was almost sure she would have remembered if they'd walked *through* a tapestry. Really, she should concentrate. Was it left or right? She headed right, fully aware that this meant it would turn out to be left. But if she headed left, the opposite would turn out to be true. Pip dithered and then decided to go with her first instinct – right it was.

She didn't recognise the oil paintings of old men in velvet coats hanging along the passage to the right. But she didn't not recognise them either. And doubtless all the corridors had similar gold-framed elders from centuries gone by. Goodness, some of these old fellows should have got the medieval equivalent of the soft filter. What was it someone had said about someone? A face like a wedding cake left in the rain.

If this is what the paid portraitist came up with, goodness knows what they looked like after a long day hunting at hounds, or playing whist while sloshing back the port, or whatever it was rich people did hundreds of years ago.

Music was coming from somewhere. Maybe the TV was on in the library. If they had a TV, which they probably didn't, seeing as it was a no-tech retreat, apparently. She seemed to be getting closer to the source of the music, a gentle tune with a mellow and woody sound. Pip wondered what it could be. And could it be coming out of the panelled walls? No, that was ridiculous. It must be coming from a room. She followed the sound further down the passage. A recorder or a flute or something. Or an oboe. Some sort of wind instrument, at any rate.

Pip froze where she was, a realisation dawning. It was a clarinet! As in, the instrument that Matty Price played. Could it be? Could she have just followed the music straight to her prize? Her body got actual chills at the thought. Now she was following the sound, down the wide passage, past the rogues' gallery to a small flight of three stairs, past the sign that read, 'Private – No Entry'. She came to a wooden door, from which the sound emanated.

Feeling a bit like the Prince in *Sleeping Beauty*, Pip knocked and shouted hello.

'Hello, is someone in there?'

'Who's that? I said not to bother me when I'm practising.' The voice was definitely that of a young man. Deep, but still with the cadence of childhood. It had to be Matty! Pip decided to take that chance.

'Matty, you don't know me, I'm a friend of Catherine. Maverick Girl. Green Youth For Truth?'

The sound of footsteps crossing the wooden floor, and the door opened. There he was, the boy from the pages of *Hello!*. The boy from the missing person's file. The golden hair, rather dirtier than in the photos; the green eyes. It was him.

Pip almost did an air-punch, but managed to rein herself in. She'd solved the case! She was an actual detective!

'Can I come in? I need to talk to you,' she said, hoping she sounded calm. And sane.

He hesitated, then stepped back. 'I am practising, and my music can't be neglected. But is Catherine all right?'

'Yes. She's here. Listen, Matty. I don't have long and I need to tell you a few things. Your parents sent me to look for you. They were worried when they didn't hear from you.'

Matty's pretty forehead wrinkled.

'But didn't Belinda tell them? That I was here?'

He explained that he'd only come for a night or two, after the row with his parents. 'I didn't mean to stay away so long,' he said. 'But they wanted me to stay for the full programme. There was so much I needed to know and do.'

'Like what?'

'Working the land. Understanding science. How to use social media effectively. So many things. I just stayed. Belinda said she'd tell my parents. I'd handed over my phone already, so she sent them a message. Maybe she forgot. Oh man, Dad must be crazy worried.'

'It seems the message didn't get to them, and yes, he's worried. They both are.'

'Sorry, just tell me again. You are?'

'I'm Pip. Investigator. No, wait. I'm Flis. Blogger. Either way. Listen. I'm going to text your parents, tell them you're safe. Let me take a pic of you.'

She snapped a photo. He was frowning in confusion, his mouth half open – not one for Instagram or *Hello!*, but enough for proof of life. She messaged it to BI, together with a location pin drop and a brief message to say she'd located him and he was fine. And then for good measure she forwarded it to Ben and to Jimmy, Jimmy's with the message, 'I got in and look who I found!' That would show him what she could do.

'Gotta go. I'll find you later. Belinda is waiting. Don't tell her about the PI thing. In fact, don't tell her anything about me, OK? I need to figure out what to do.'

'Listen, Flip…'

She turned back from the door, her hand on the handle.

'Belinda. I think she's… strange. I mean, not in a good way. I don't trust her, really. Or John. Or his mom.'

'His mum?'

But before Matty could answer, Pip's phone pinged.

Belinda Potter: 'Where are you? I'm waiting in the library.'

'Matty, I've got to go. I'll see you later.'

CHAPTER TWENTY-EIGHT

Belinda was on her feet, pacing the library. The look on her face, Pip had to concede, *was* rather grim. No wonder Matty felt a bit wary of her. A man sat in a wingback chair, only his long crossed legs and loafers showing beneath a newspaper.

'Sorry I'm late, I got a little mixed up in the passages. And none of the old guys in the portraits were able to help.'

Belinda gave a tinkly little laugh that sounded about as genuine as a cat barking.

'Not to worry. It can be a bit confusing, the two wings look so alike. But you're here now! That's all that matters. Felicity, this is John Wade from BITE. Bio Innovations and Technology Enterprises.'

The mystery man lowered his newspaper, as if he had been waiting for his cue, and smiled.

'John is the one I wanted you to meet for input on your article. He is an expert on the issues you're writing about. An expert.' The way Belinda said this, and the way she looked at him, John might as well be God.

He stood up, extended his hand and spoke in a calm, deep voice, right over Belinda's nervous blathering. 'Very pleased to meet you. Belinda speaks highly of you and your blog, which I hear has a lot of momentum and influence in a certain sector. And it's gathering steam.'

He really was dishy, it had to be said. Like George Clooney in the Nespresso ads. Only with herbal tea, instead of coffee. And

younger, of course. And the way he said 'steam', it was sort of…
steamy. And he had that way of looking at you as if you were the
only person on earth. His eyes sort of bored into you, and not in
an unpleasant way. A girl's mind couldn't help wandering.

The sound of a thousand shrieking Valkyries broke the spell. It
was emanating from Pip's handbag. *Nice timing, Mummy.*

'I'm so sorry,' she said, flustered, digging in her bag, stirring
and scattering tissues and pens and assorted detritus. She hit the
Silent button.

'A phone?' John looked at Belinda, his dreamy eyes cold.

'Gosh, well of course. As you know, Felicity, I did mention this
is a retreat, a haven of peace, and there are privacy issues for some
of our guests, so no phones. Please hand it over.'

'You should have sorted this out on arrival, Belinda,' said John,
over the shrieking Valkyries.

'I… we… there was the other girl… sorry.' Pip was quite shocked
at how contrite and, well, small Belinda suddenly seemed.

Pip stabbed at the phone, trying to kill the call. Belinda reached
for it. Pip held on. 'I need it,' she said. 'For my work. The blog.
You have to engage.'

'It's the rules,' snapped Belinda, and snatched it from Pip's hand
with quite a surprising amount of force. 'Do continue, John. My
apologies.'

John's eyes were on Pip. The cold had been replaced by a deep
warmth and utter absorption. 'I'm so looking forward to our chat.
I'm sure we will have much common ground, you and I. Many
touchpoints.' On the word 'touch', his eyes seemed to become
more intense.

Pip blushed, feeling like a right twit. She couldn't help it. He
was cheesy but also very charming.

He continued in his low, sexy voice, 'I don't know how much
Belinda has told you about my work? I am first and foremost a

scientist, a devotee of the search for truth.' He etched a shape with his hands. The truth, Pip assumed. 'I have many areas of interest, mostly around the environment. Reducing emissions. Protecting resources. Reducing pollution. My great interest though, I could say my… passion…' His voice paused on the word 'passion', as he looked deeply into Pip's eyes. Then he continued. 'My passion is for the earth's forests – our lungs, nay, the heart and soul of our planet, and our greatest weapon against global warming.'

'That's very admirable,' said Pip, tongue-tied as a schoolgirl at her first mixed party. 'Very, um, important work.'

'As a scientist and a businessman and a citizen of this beautiful earth, I consider it my duty to reach out to important stakeholders outside our scientific community, to make sure that they understand and disseminate the facts. The real facts. I recognise the importance of an influencer like yourself in this. Belinda assists me very ably in this regard.'

Belinda beamed quietly, as if receiving the headmaster's award.

'Well, she did insist that we meet. She might have mentioned that I'm working on a big article – in fact a series – on plastics. Very big issue in our market. Parents. Mothers. Of course they are concerned with what sort of world we are leaving for our children. Their children, I mean. All children.'

John nodded in assent and made agreeable hhhm, hhhmm noises while Pip channelled Flis.

'The straws… The sea… Will there even *be* turtles when this new generation grows up? That's what they want to know. And we want to help them understand what we can do, each individual, each family, to make sure—'

'Exactly!' said John, clapping his hand on her shoulder. 'That's what we all want. All of us. Turtles. We are on the same page here, Felicity. On the same page.' His eyes did that thing again. The boring into the brain. Pip cleared her throat and swallowed. She found herself wanting to impress John, against her better judgement. Which was a waste of time. What she really needed to do was get out of this stupid room, get back to Matty, and get away from this retreat.

'Are you a scientist, Felicity?'

'I'm not.'

'Any background at all in chemistry? Marine biology perhaps? Even, say, geology?'

'Um, no.'

'Hhhmm.' He looked somewhat disappointed. 'I see the problem you are up against. This is a very complex field.' He paused and continued brightly, 'But I don't want you to worry your head about this. We can sort it out. That's why Belinda brought you here. That's where I come in. Interpreting the data, getting to the crux of the matter for you, with you. Helping you separate the chatter from the real facts.'

Pip had always been under the impression that the definition of fact precluded unreal facts, but if John-with-the-eyes thought so, she wasn't going to point it out. Also, she couldn't help but think of the warning – if you could call it that – that Matty had given her. Not to mess with these people.

'That would be so helpful,' she said. 'And of course Catherine is an expert; she can help me too.'

'No,' he said sharply. 'Catherine is, well, let's just say she's gone a little off track in her research. I'm sure she'll get back on track, once she's thought it through, but I wouldn't want you to get mixed up in anything that isn't completely solid. Peer reviewed and all that. I think leave Catherine out of it for now.'

'Oh, all right then. I suppose you know best. And you're right, I wouldn't want to publish anything dodgy. So thank you for that.' That was interesting, thought Pip. What was it that made them so jumpy about Catherine and her research? Shouldn't they be pleased to have such credible data on plastics, overseen by a university?

Belinda beamed. 'Oh, Felicity, this is excellent. Excellent. I'm going to leave the two of you to get acquainted, while I go and check on Catherine and see how lunch is getting on.'

John turned to Pip. 'You might be surprised to know,' he said in a throaty, conspiratorial tone, 'that plastic is very beneficial to the environment in many ways. Let's start there, shall we? Reducing fossil fuel usage is number one, isn't it, Felicity? How do you think we can make cars lighter and reduce fuel consumption right at the petrol pump?'

'I'm going to go with plastic,' said Pip, when it appeared that John actually expected an answer. At the back of her mind, she was chewing over what Belinda has just said. 'Check on Catherine' were her words. Why on earth would Catherine need to be checked on?

John was still talking. 'Exactly, Felicity. Plastic components of cars. You're a very smart girl. Very smart girl indeed.'

'Er, thanks.'

John leaned in, so close she could smell his shampoo – a fresh-yet-manly herbal fragrance. 'Tomorrow morning, you and I are going to sit down and have a proper talk. Come back here at ten and bring that little notebook of yours.' He nodded towards her silly glittery book. She blushed. He patted her knee. 'Just you and me. A good long talk. It's going to be GRRRReat!'

CHAPTER TWENTY-NINE

'Catherine! Wait up.' Pip sped up to catch her, her feet crunching on the gravel path. 'Hang on a minute. Wait, it's me, Pip.'

Catherine turned to look. 'What?'

'It's me. Felicity.'

'Oh, sorry, I thought you said something else.'

'Doesn't matter,' said Pip quickly, walking alongside her and taking her arm. 'I need to talk to you.'

Pip had spotted Catherine walking in the garden, from one of the endless windows in the endless passages. She'd only taken two wrong turns in her rush to get out and catch her. Luckily, for once, Catherine wasn't running. Pip glanced up to the library, and saw John looking down at them. She waved cheerfully and then stepped behind the hedge that lined the path, pulling the surprised Catherine with her. She hoped it looked natural, two women taking a quiet walk.

'In private,' Pip hissed, and sat down on a wooden bench conveniently placed in the hedged garden, beneath a rose-covered bower. Catherine joined her and waited while Pip caught her breath.

Catherine was fit, as Pip remembered from when she had chased her through London, and she wasn't the least bit puffed by a stroll in the garden. She waited, with a wry smile on her face. 'When you're ready.'

Pip allowed herself a moment of dramatic pause before delivering her big news. 'I found Matty.'

'That's brilliant! Where is he? Let's go say hi.' Catherine made to get up, but Pip put her hand on her shoulder.

'Wait a minute, it's not so easy. He's upstairs in a private wing.
He seemed nervous. Almost…' Pip hesitated. 'Almost scared. Scared
of Belinda and John. And then I had to go to meet Belinda, so I
couldn't chat.'

'She's strange all right. This whole place is strange. The whole
situation. Not to mention the so-called relaxation session. That
was truly weird.'

'How so?'

'It started off like any sort of spa. You know. The smelly candle,
the robe, the shoooey whoooey music. Whales and chimes and
whatnot. They offer you herbal tea. Foul, by the way. I poured
it into the pot plant when the therapist wasn't looking. Anyway,
there's a bed in the middle of the room, and I had to lie on my
back with a mask over my eyes while the therapist person massaged
my head and shoulders.'

'That sounds quite nice,' said Pip, rolling her tight shoulders
and stretching her neck left and right. She could use a massage.
Maybe when this was done. Maybe Jimmy, he had strong hands.
Or Tim, he'd be more gentle.

'It was OK. I almost dropped off, except the therapist was
working pressure points in odd places on my head and skull which
was a bit sore, and the music got very peculiar. No more whales.
More like chanting. Hypnotic droning. And she was speaking over
the chanting. Whispering. It was bizarre.'

'What was she saying?'

'I could hardly hear, it was very soft, but it was all about nature.
Trees and forests. "Love the trees." She said that a few times. And
once, I thought I heard her say "plastic".'

'Are you sure? About the plastic?'

'Not completely sure. No.'

'Maybe she said relax. Or practise. Or drastic.'

'Drastic? Why would she say that? It doesn't make any more
sense than plastic. Anyway, I asked her, while I was lying there. I

said, "What's that you said?" and she jumped about a foot out of the chair and said, "You're awake? Did you have your tea?"'

'What did you say?'

'For some reason, I said yes, I'd had the tea. Even though I hadn't. But doesn't the whole thing sound very strange?'

Pip agreed that it was. Very. But also, somehow not strange. Familiar. It came to her, all of a sudden.

She grabbed Catherine's sleeve. 'They were trying to brainwash you!'

'What?' Catherine laughed, but without much conviction. 'Oh, come on.'

'Seriously, I know this. Once I got lost going to a new hairdresser, and I ended up at this strange religious cult meeting—'

'You what?'

'Got lost. Turned out it was Road, not Lane, or maybe it was Avenue. Anyway, I couldn't find the place, and I asked this guy and he invited me into a… Never mind, long story. We don't have time for the details. It could have happened to anyone. Except I ended up at this cult meeting. The Moonies, we think. Never got my hair done. My point is, the brainwashing. That's how they did it. Drugs. And relaxation. The chanting. The repetition. I think these people were trying to brainwash you, to make you more susceptible to their messages.'

'Oh my God, Felicity. Do you really think so? Thank God I didn't drink that tea.'

'I know,' said Pip. 'We mustn't drink anything they offer us.'

'But then we'll die of thirst.'

Pip thought about it. 'OK, we'll only drink if everyone is drinking the same thing. Otherwise we'll drink water.'

'Great.' But with the question of what to drink out of the way, they had to face the bigger problem.

'Do you really think we're in danger, Felicity?'

'No, no,' said Pip. 'I'm sure we're fine. Fine.'

They looked at each other, and Catherine smiled weakly. 'Fine,' she echoed.

Catherine glanced down at her watch.

'Dammit, I don't want to be late for Belinda. She's going to take me to this mysterious John character who's allegedly such a big expert on the subject I'm actually doing my PhD in.' She sounded somewhat bitter. 'We're having supper in the library. Supper in the library with a mansplainer. Sounds like a blast. Maybe they'll try to brainwash me again. Or poison me. Wish me luck.'

An hour later, and Pip was *wishing* for supper in the library with a mansplainer. It would be a lark compared to her supper which was – believe it or not – held in silence. Silence! As in, you were not allowed to speak. Apparently, that was the way they did it every Thursday. Had she known, Pip would have come on a Friday. Or any other day of the week. Or brought a sandwich and eaten it in her room. But no, here she was trying to get butter for her bread using the international sign – a broad spreading back and forth movement of the right hand over the flat palm of the left.

She and Flis had been the ace team at Charades when they were young. It was as if they could read each other's minds. Flis would hold up two hands and start to unfurl fingers and Pip would yell, '*Seven Brides for Seven Brothers.*' Or Pip would puff out her cheeks and Flis would shout, '*Gone with the Wind.*' It drove everyone crazy. No one would play with them unless they were split up. They were that good.

Not so Matty Price, who was sitting at the far end of the long table they were eating at. The dining room was like something out of Hogwarts, creepy atmosphere included. A headless ghost would have come as no surprise. Pip managed to catch Matty's attention and enacted a series of jerky head movements and eye rolls intended to indicate that she wanted to talk to him outside, but he hunched his shoulders quizzically and looked to his dining companion for help. Pip thought she recognised the other boy, who was a bit older than Matty and extremely good looking. Where had she seen him before? Television maybe? Was he an actor perhaps, or a musician? Whatever, he would not be her first pick for Charades either. He shrugged helplessly at Matty. She gave up. She turned her attention to looking for people who might be Livi James, but although there were a few young women, none of them matched Livi's description. She didn't think Livi was here. Another dead end.

She focused on her food, trying hard not to think about drugged tea and Moonies. Belinda came in at eight p.m. on the dot and put a stop to the ridiculousness, announcing the end of the silence and that everyone was allowed to leave. Pip hadn't realised they hadn't been allowed to leave until Belinda said this. She quickly stood up and scooted down to the end of the table where Matty sat, but Belinda intercepted her.

She beamed at Pip. 'John is expecting you first thing in the morning, Felicity. Come to the library at ten a.m., you can do the interview there.'

'Sure, I'll be there,' said Pip, and then turned to Matty and his friend. 'Hello, I'm not sure we've met, I'm—'

'Sorry, Felicity,' interrupted Belinda, 'no time for chats. I must take these young men away. Matty, Jay Jay, let's get going, we've lots to do.'

The boys ignored Pip completely, their eyes on Belinda. The mystery boy asked, 'Can we have our phones now? You said we could have our phones back when we've finished the whole course.'

'Yes, yes, of course,' said Belinda with a brittle smile. 'Let's go and find them, shall we?' She ushered them out of the room as if there were a fire behind them. Her smooth bob swung in time to the clip, clip, clip of her boots. Matty glanced back at Pip as they left. She couldn't be sure, but she thought he gave a small shake of his head. But what did that mean? That he didn't want to speak to her? That he did want to speak to her? That he didn't think he'd get his phone back? That her outfit didn't work? Who could tell?

Pip stopped by Catherine's room on her way to her own, hoping to get the lowdown on her meeting with John, but there was no sign of her. Pip supposed that dinner with a mansplainer might take more time than a silent dinner at Hogwarts, but she felt a stir of unease. It was almost like they were trying to keep her and Catherine apart. But why would that be the case? They were both here, supposedly, for the same reason – to meet the famous John. Why would they need to do everything separately? Pip felt a chill, but that might have been the vast draughty passages.

Nothing for it but an early night. There was so much craziness going on that she'd hardly had a moment to reflect on the fact that she'd succeeded in her mission. She, Epiphany Bloom, had investigated a worrying disappearance and solved a mystery. She'd located a missing kid and brought relief to his family. For once, she could say in all honesty that she'd done a good job. But given all this, why did she feel a deep unease, as if nothing was solved at all? And why were her dreams filled with nightmares involving running away from George Clooney, who was waving a plastic straw in one hand and a turtle in the other?

CHAPTER THIRTY

Having supped at six and gone to bed at eight thirty, like a retiree in some Cornish seaside town, Pip was up and about at six a.m. She luxuriated in the cotton sheets, enjoying the calm, the wakening birds twittering and chirping, the gradual lightening through the window. In the warm morning light, her worries of the day before seemed stupid. An overreaction. She'd found Matty! She allowed herself to bask in the glow of a job well done, but her mind soon turned to her future. What next? What would she do, now that the job was over and she was pretty much back where she started – no job, money tight, and a cat to feed.

She really liked this investigating business. She could see herself doing it as a job. Could she fess up to BI? Maybe they would give her a real job, now that she'd proved herself on the Matty Price case. Or would they be furious with her for pulling the wool over their eyes and impersonating Ms du Bois? She tried not to think about poor Ms du Bois. Pip hoped she hadn't got her into trouble.

But the fact was, Pip had done a great job. What she needed to do now was to make sure she built on her success. No more bad decisions. No more unintended disasters. No more faking it. She'd been given this opportunity to clear her debts, gain some skills, and possibly find her true calling. She was going to grasp it! She was going to make her life better!

Starting with a jog, Pip thought, throwing back the bedcovers and swinging her feet to the floor. She needed to be fit if she was going to be running around the country finding missing persons (why were they 'persons', not 'people', once they were missing, she wondered). She pulled on yesterday's jeans and trainers, regretting that she hadn't brought any running gear. Except that she didn't own any exercise gear, unless you counted her ski stuff. Well, she'd have to remedy that. You can't run in snow boots. She opened the door and set off down the hall, stepping lightly so as not to wake the loser slug-a-beds who were not up at six to go jogging.

As she tiptoed past Catherine's room, she had an idea. Maybe Catherine was up early – there being zero nightlife, no Netflix, not even *Candy Crush* in this joint. You didn't even have a phone to follow some celebrity down a Twitter hole. Maybe Catherine would like to come with her. She certainly seemed to like running. Creeping up to the door, Pip opened it quietly and peeked in. The bed was empty and had even been made. That sense of unease returned, but then she remembered that she had just been thinking about how Catherine liked running. Maybe she'd had the same idea and already gone for a run. There was absolutely no way she hadn't slept in her bed, no matter how untouched the room looked. No way.

Good lord, running was hard. A few yards in and Pip's heart was already racing, pounding against her chest. She rested her hands on her knees and remembered, rather sadly, the last time she'd been properly fit. Come to think of it, she had started the Camino just about as unfit as she was now, intending to plod along for a day or two to take her mind off a horrible break-up (what was she *thinking* with that awful arms trader?). But somehow, she hadn't stopped. She'd fallen in with a group or another single traveller or trudged alone. Weeks went by, a month, two. When she finally reached the sea, she was as fit as a fiddle and happy. She could get there again. Happy and fit. It just took a bit of time and consistency. But maybe not right now.

After a rather brief jog and a shower, Pip still had some time before her meeting with John. Her jog – if you could call what she had done a jog – hadn't relaxed her so much as made her worry again, and she decided to see if she could track down Matty or Catherine before she met John. First, she knocked on Catherine's door again. There was no answer, and she tried the handle. Locked. Catherine must have been back and locked the door at some point of the morning. Pip wanted to find this reassuring, but she didn't. She set off down the passage, trying to remember which way she had gone when she found Matty. But the corridors seemed to have changed – the glowering portraits glowered in the wrong places, and around one corner, she hit a dead end in the form of a moth-eaten tapestry of a unicorn where she was sure there should have been more passage. It was all horribly frustrating, and without the sound of a clarinet to guide her, she couldn't make head or tail of it.

Glancing at her watch, she saw that it was almost ten, and she headed back down the hallways until she found the top of the large staircase, at which point she knew the way to the library to meet John. She really just wanted to go home, now that she had found Matty. Get a start on her new improved life. Buy the running gear. She told herself she was staying because it would be hard to back out of the whole blog cover story at this point, but if she was honest, it was more. That anxious look Matty had thrown her as he left the dining room. The question of what had happened to Livi. The worrying absence of Catherine since last night. Her failure to navigate the passages. She needed to put all these worries to bed before she'd be ready to move on, and become a super fit detective person.

John languished in the wingback again, his coffee cup perched on his knee and a sheaf of papers on the table next to him. While yesterday she'd been quite taken with his sexy George Clooney vibe, it seemed a bit contrived this morning. She actually suspected that the position he was in was an exact copy from one of the ads, and the room smelt of coffee – rather odd given the retreat claimed only to serve tea. 'Smoke and mirrors' was the phrase that popped into her head. Only it was more steam and one rather warped mirror over the mantel, in this case.

'Ah, Felicity. Sleep well?' he asked, boring into her with those soulful eyes. 'I do hope you were comfortable?'

'Very. Slept like a log and started the day with a run. Got the blood flowing, the endorphins going, and I'm ready to face the day. Just add coffee…' she said with a high giggle that she recognised as her flirtatious laugh, and resolved not to use ever again. Just because she'd seen through the whole look didn't mean it wasn't still sexy.

John gestured to the sideboard, where murky herbal tea and cups stood alongside a plate of sliced fruit and a basket of fresh bran muffins. No sign of the coffee she was sure John was drinking. Pip loaded up, more modestly than she'd like, and sat on the second wing chair angled towards John, her breakfast on the table next to her. She hauled out her notebook, trying to hide the cover, even though he'd already seen it. Maybe as she asked bloggy-type questions, she could think of a way to find Matty, Livi and Catherine, and put this whole retreat behind her.

John looked at her expectantly. She should have thought of some questions. She realised that now. Pip racked her brains for some suitable plastics questions. She went back to the meeting, and to the tweets and articles she'd scanned in her search for Matty. It all seemed rather mushy and indistinct, unfortunately.

'Before we get into my questions,' she said, looking down at the notebook as if there was a list of insightful questions there waiting, 'perhaps you could give me some background in your specific area of interest and expertise.'

John launched in. Unsurprising, really. Who doesn't love to talk about himself? Although the substance was quite unusual. He was descended from a chemist who'd jumped on the plastics bandwagon early in the twentieth century.

'We are plastic, through and through. My bones are plastic,' he said proudly, if somewhat confusingly. 'Plastic born and bred. We've been at the forefront of the plastics revolution since day one. All of this' – he swept his arm to indicate the breakfast, the room, the farm, and perhaps all of Kent – 'built on plastics.'

'Oh, the farm is yours?' That was odd. She'd been under the distinct impression that he was a client of Belinda's, and nothing to do with the retreat.

'Of course. It's been in the family for decades. Anyway, so plastics is my family business, and it's also my area of expertise. I studied chemistry, chemical engineering, all that. As I said, I'm a scientist. There are few people who know the industry or the science like I do. Which is why all the disinformation is so distressing.'

He took a break and looked into her eyes. 'It's why I need the likes of you, Felicity. Journalists who are committed to the truth.'

'Well, "journalist" would be stretching it, I'm more of—'

'A truth-seeker, I know. But that's what we're talking about here, isn't it? The truth.'

'Yes. So tell me, John. Why don't you tell me the truth as you see it?'

'Not as I see it, Felicity. As it is. As. It. Is.' His eyes bored into her, aiming, no doubt, for her soul.

'As it is then. Go on.'

Which he certainly did. At quite some length. As he'd told her the previous day, plastic was the new messiah. It reduced food waste. It kept food clean and free of pathogens. Heart stents featured. A confusing tangent about plastic tennis racquets. Something about the vegetable tunnel being made out of plastic.

'Plastic saves lives, Felicity. *Human lives!* Some research indicates hundreds of thousands of them a year. *Hundreds of thousands!*

'Hhhmm, hhmmm…' Pip murmured agreeably, frantically making notes. Journalism was hard. She hadn't had a hand cramp like this since her final university exams, that essay on Miss Marple. He waited a moment for her to catch up.

'I can email you the research, there's more where that comes from.'

She broke in while there was a pause. 'All very interesting, John. Very interesting. But surely, I mean, on the environmental side there's an issue to be faced.' Gosh, that sounded professional!

'Indeed, indeed, I'm not denying that we have work to do on that score. But let's look at the facts, shall we. The real facts. Plastic is actually *good* for the environment in many ways. Did you know that plastic insulation is the smartest, cheapest way to keep our homes warm? Saves on fuel and carbon emissions. And so much of it can be reused and recycled. What are we going to use instead, wood? More indigenous forests cut down?'

Was he going to list every use of plastic in the world? She cut in.

'Very interesting. Thank you. Really, I've learned so much. I think from my, um, readers' point of view, maybe plastic bags and single-use packaging are something they'd be worried about.'

John's face darkened. He suddenly didn't look like George Clooney at all. 'Bags, bags, bags. People are obsessed with plastic bags. Can I just say, for the record, that the plastic bag is greener than the cotton tote. Tote! Whoever introduced that horrible American word to the world should be shot!' He was spitting a bit by now, rather alarmingly. 'Recycling is the point, Felicity.'

'Well, isn't that sort of the problem, though,' Pip managed to get in. 'That a lot of plastic can't be recycled?'

'If people were a little less lazy and stupid, more of it could be. Good God, how hard is it to separate your rubbish? As I tried to explain to Catherine last night. Plastic is not the enemy here. But we've been demonised.'

He stopped for a moment and took a sip of his drink. 'I'm sorry, Felicity, I get a little carried away.' He smiled at her, a crinkly sexy smile, filled with rueful boyish charm. He patted her knee and leaned in towards her, still breathing a little heavily from his tirade. 'I guess I'm a very passionate man.'

Was he going to try and kiss her? Pip panicked. The man was rather sexy, although clearly a bit touched, at least when it came to plastics. She knew her weakness for the slightly crazy. The arms trader being a case in point. They all knew how that had turned out. Nonetheless, she felt herself drawn, as if by some magnetic force. The magnetic force of crazy, perhaps.

The moment was interrupted when the door was flung open and a woman stepped in. Pip couldn't believe her eyes when she saw who it was. *Oh dear.* This was going to take some explaining.

CHAPTER THIRTY-ONE

There, framed by the door, stood Sophie du Bois. The real missing child expert, the psychologist, whose job Pip had stolen. She must have realised, and tracked Pip down, using her superior investigating skills, and now she was going to confront her.

'I wasn't expecting you quite so early,' said John, whipping his hand off Pip's knee at warp speed and leaping to his feet. Gone was the lazy charm.

'As I see,' said Ms du Bois, looking at Pip, bright eyes burning into her.

Pip's brain was still trying to work its way around why John seemed to know the *real* investigator when she noticed a dazed-looking Catherine behind her, with a man holding her arm. She knew his face, too. But at least that solved one of the outstanding issues – Catherine was here. One down, Matty and Livi to go.

'This is Felicity,' John said, speaking quickly and gesturing to Pip. 'She is here to interview me. She's a well-known blogger and we're—'

'*That's* not a blogger.' Ms du Bois sneered as she said this, looking at Pip as though she were something terrible she'd found on her shoe.

This was not good. Not good at all.

'Yes, it *is*. I mean, she is. Felicity is a top blogger. EarthMomma has excellent reach and coverage in the parenting sector. This will do us great good.'

Ms du Bois sneered again. She really was rather good at it. 'Please. She's not Felicity and she's not a blogger. Her name is Epiphany Bloom and she's a lackey in a private investigations firm.'

Pip knew she should be worrying about this sudden revelation, but she'd suddenly realised who the man next to Catherine was. It was the guard from the gate, the one Jimmy insisted was 'carrying'. What was the guard doing in the house, with Catherine?

John was not similarly distracted. He was still focused on Pip's identity.

'First of all, Epiphany isn't even a name. And besides that, Mother, I assure you—'

Wait, what? Mother? Ms du Bois was John's mother? Pip's brain was scrabbling for meaning at this point.

'John,' Ms du Bois sighed. 'She's a private detective. She's looking for Matty Price.'

John looked at Pip in shock and betrayal – and then anger. Pip felt a prickle of fear. It really was the arms trader all over again.

'Good God, do I have to spell it out to you?' said Ms du Bois, who was not nearly as nice a person as she had seemed back when Pip was stealing her identity and they were sipping healthy smoothies. 'This woman is a shameless imposter. She lied her way onto the case and took the money to look for the boy.'

'Really, Mother? I don't think that can possibly be true. We've checked her blog and her background and everything. I've told you before, Bel and I have this side of things under control.'

Pip decided to come clean. All this lying was exhausting. She wanted to go home.

'It is actually true. I'm not Felicity and I do work for Boston Investigations, but then Sophie, who are you? Other than John's mother? Because I thought you were the investigator who was supposed to be hired to find Matty. But clearly, that's not true. So who on earth are you? What are you doing here?'

'I'm…' Sophie stopped. She seemed to make a decision, and pulled herself to her full height. 'I am the head of this once-proud plastics family. I am the keeper of our legacy.'

'So you were also an imposter when it came to Boston Investigations. Why did they think I was you?' None of it made sense to Pip.

'The mystery to me is how anyone in their right mind mistook *you* for *me*,' said Sophie with a sneer. 'But I was on my way to Boston Investigations to pretend to help with the investigation – keep them off our backs, really, as I did with that girl Livi, but I was late, as you know, due to unforeseen circumstances.'

'So you let me continue, and update you like a fool. But why?'

'We were nearly done with Matty, and besides, I thought you were much too stupid to do any damage. Your pathetic updates certainly didn't seem to add up to much. But it turns out that my son here and his good friend Belinda are even stupider than you. As incredible as that is.'

Speak of the devil and she shall appear. Right in the doorway. Belinda took in the room.

'Oh, you're here again, Sophie,' Belinda said coldly. She didn't seem delighted to see her.

Before Sophie could react, there was a groan from Catherine. 'Oh dear, I think I might be sick.'

'Not on the carpet!' said John.

'It's a very ugly carpet,' Catherine slurred.

'What have you given her?' asked Belinda, looking from Catherine to Sophie.

'Don't you worry about that, Belinda. You and John can just go about your little chats with your influencers and your press releases, and let me handle the grown-up business.'

'Buuuurn,' said Catherine, who seemed to be feeling a bit better, and gave a snorty laugh. She flapped her hand like someone putting out a match. Then her eyes fell on Pip. 'Oh hey, Felicity. Weird scenes, hey. Weird scenes.' She looked around to make sure no one was listening, but seemed not to notice that she was surrounded by people, listening. 'I don't think I like that Sophie woman,' she said in a loud stage whisper. 'Seems like a right cow. Gave me the bad tea. Verrrrrrry bad.'

The guard looked uncomfortable at the turn things were taking, and tightened his grip on Catherine's arm.

'I knew it,' said Belinda. 'You've drugged Catherine. You are at it again.'

Sophie rolled her eyes and imitated Belinda. 'You're at it again,' she said, in a little-girl whine. 'Listen, I gave the two of you a chance to handle it, but you didn't. And now look at this mess. We've got that Price boy here, when we should have finished the programme with him days ago. Jay Jay, another one – Belinda, you were supposed to be on top of the celeb kids' angle. And as for Catherine – John, you've failed there too. She's as stubborn as that other one. Didn't buy you for a minute. And then there's this ridiculous pseudo PI who managed to fool you two idiots into thinking she's some kind of journalist. I don't know when I've seen two more incompetent people than you, John, and your girlfriend. And then you want to criticise *me*.'

'Ooh, you two are getting TOLD!' Catherine yelled in the direction of John and Belinda, before dissolving in a fit of the giggles and burying her face in the guard's shoulder.

No two ways about it, it hurt that Sophie had called her ridiculous. And it was a bit of a shocker to discover that John and Belinda had a thing going. But even more worrying to Pip was Catherine's state. Belinda was right, she had been drugged. It was looking like she'd been right about the brainwashing. Matty too?

'What did you give her?' Belinda asked again.

'Oh, calm down. She's fine. Just a little tranq to make her more pliable while I decide what to do about your mess-up.'

Belinda turned on Sophie. There was a moment when the two women stared at each other, as if they could destroy each other simply with the power of their minds.

Pip was still putting together all the references that Sophie had made to Livi, and it didn't sound like Livi was in South America cavorting with a Colombian. It sounded like she'd been drugged too; like this whole so-called retreat was some sort of brainwashing operation. Pip needed to get herself, Catherine and Matty out of there, and then tell the police what she knew. They could get to the bottom of things, and find Livi.

If there was one thing she'd learnt from the Moonies, it was that if you stopped drinking the tea and walked out the front door, no one would actually stop you. The trick was confidence.

'Well, I can see you all have lots to chat about,' said Pip, in her most sparkly, cocktail party voice. Her Finishing School for Young Ladies would have been proud of her, for once. 'So I'm just going to take Catherine and go. No hard feelings. Right, then.'

She walked over to Catherine and took her arm. 'I've got her now, thanks ever so much for your help,' she said to the guard, who seemed unable to think of a reason not to let Catherine go. 'Come on then,' she said to Catherine, who slumped against her, but at least seemed to be able to walk.

They stepped out of the door, Pip trying hard not to run. Slow and steady and big smiles had got her across the Iraqi border, and would get her out of this place too. She glanced up the stairs as they stepped out, and saw Matty standing at the top, looking over the balustrade. 'Matty,' she said, in what she hoped was a calm and reassuring voice, despite having to shout so he would hear her. 'Catherine and I were just leaving. Why don't you come with us?'

At that moment, Sophie's voice came from the door: 'Do you call yourself a security guard, you useless piece of dog entrails? You just literally let the prisoner go without a whimper because a mildly attractive woman told you to!'

Prisoner? Mildly attractive? Cheek!

Pip gripped Catherine's arm, and walked faster. Confidence; that was the ticket. 'Come on, Matty,' she yelled.

She heard the sharp click of Sophie's heels on the floor behind her. 'You're not going anywhere, Epiphany,' she said in a calm voice.

Pip stopped and turned around. 'Listen, Sophie, we've obviously got tangled up in some private family stuff here. So we'll just leave, and you can sort it all out, right? Put it behind us.' She turned and started walking again. The front door was two metres away, and maybe someone would be out on the road and they could flag them down. She glanced to the side. Matty seemed frozen on the stairs, his mouth slightly open, like a goldfish. Then he let out a gasp.

'Look out!' he shouted, just as Sophie launched herself at Pip, wielding a possibly priceless vase that she had grabbed from a table.

'Mum, not the Ming!' was the last thing Pip heard, before the vase made contact with her head, and everything went dark.

CHAPTER THIRTY-TWO

When Pip came around, she was lying on a couch with an aching head that was not at all helped by Belinda and Sophie having a shouting match. She kept her eyes closed and listened.

'You could have killed her, you bloody lunatic,' Belinda was yelling. Pip wondered who they were talking about, and then remembered the flying Ming. It was her that Sophie could have killed, and the thought sent a chill down her spine.

'Well, I didn't. Unfortunately. Head like a brick… the lower classes are always like that,' said Sophie. For a moment Pip wished Mummy were here; she'd never stand for anyone calling Pip the lower classes.

There was a moment of silence.

Belinda spoke first. 'You know what? That's it. That's enough. You are not actually sane. I'm done with you and your drugs and your craziness,' she said. 'I'm out.'

'Bel, darling,' John said. 'Please, Mother is just trying—'

Pip would have liked to hear how this finished. *Mother is just trying to kill someone with the Ming?*

But Belinda snapped at him before he could finish. 'And as for you, John. Yes, you're charming and powerful and good looking. But you are not smart. I'm ten times smarter. And I'm tired of the way you flirt with these girls in the name of our work. I'm just another tool to you. I should never have thought I was special. I was a fool. But that's over. I'm done here.'

'Now, that's not fair,' said John. Pip risked opening her eyes a slit and saw his red face. They seemed to have forgotten about Pip on the couch in all the drama.

'It is,' said Catherine helpfully, from her position on the floor where she'd now slid down against the door frame, her head leaning on the guard's leg, her arms wrapped around it.

'I didn't sign up for this,' said Belinda. 'I signed up for PR and working with influencers. But this…' Belinda swept her hand over the whole sorry scene. 'This is unacceptable.'

'Oh, I'm sorry, it's unacceptable to you?' Sophie looked scornful. 'Well, look at Little Miss Ethics. You were happy to take our money, weren't you? And you knew what you were getting it for.'

'That's not true,' said Belinda. 'I knew that your message was somewhat dubious, and yes, maybe I went with that. But that's just *words*. I was just using *words*.'

'You certainly were. Rather brilliant words actually. You invented those hashtags, remember.'

'OK, I probably went a bit far. But all's fair in love and war and on Twitter. No harm done. But I didn't know we were going to be endangering young people. I certainly didn't know about the drugs, except for the natural herbs for the massages. Or the hitting people over the head with household objects. I should've stepped away earlier, but I thought John cared. I thought we had something. But I was wrong about that too, I guess.'

The others were so engrossed in their argument that Pip decided to take a chance. She edged along the seat, in the direction of Catherine and the door. If she made it there, maybe she could make a run for it again, only alone this time. Get out of this crazy zoo. Call for help for the others.

'*You* brought us those people,' said Sophie, glaring at Belinda. '*You* found those influencers. It was *your* idea to host the retreats so we could isolate them and brainwash them and win them over. How did you think we were going to brainwash them without drugs, you fool?' What made Sophie particularly scary was how she never raised her voice. She even had a slight smile as she eviscerated her opponents.

Belinda bristled. 'This is just bullshit. I'm leaving.'

'You are, are you?' said Sophie. 'Because let me tell you, you are in this thing up to your armpits. You targeted these people. You brought them here. You were here when Livi—'

'We went too far with Livi,' said John, interrupting his mother's flow in a decisive tone. 'I told you that at the time, Mother, when we moved the body. You agreed. We all agreed it wouldn't happen again.'

'Shut up!' said Sophie and Belinda at once.

Catherine had stirred to life and all attention was on her. 'That sweet girl Livi is dead?' she said, struggling to her feet in agitation. 'That can't be true. That's not right.' She turned to look at the guard, who she seemed to regard as her personal friend. 'That's not true, is it?' she asked him.

Pip went cold. Livi? A body? She was dead. She thought of the girl's poor mother, waiting for a postcard from Peru. It wasn't exactly a surprise, she found. It had always been clear that something terrible had happened to Livi. And they had tried to murder Pip, with the vase. For once in her life, Pip needed to think clearly. These people weren't just a brainwashing plastics cult, they were murderers. And if Pip didn't make a plan, there would be more dead.

'It was an accident. A terrible accident,' Sophie said in a strange monotone, as if she were reading from a script. 'She went swimming in the river at night, it's very deep. She'd just had supper. It was cold. Accidents happen.'

'Wait. No,' Pip said. 'If it was an accident, like you say, why didn't you tell the police?'

Sophie turned and looked at Pip as if she'd forgotten she was there at all.

'It was all a bit tricky. We're not registered, the retreat. There would have been questions about the accident. Problems with tax and insurance… indemnity… investigations.' Sophie waved her hand vaguely. 'It was easier to cover it up. No need for a fuss.'

The woman was ruthless, Pip realised. And possibly entirely insane.

'But they hired investigators?' Pip remembered Livi's mother saying so. 'Only you somehow pretended to be an expert, didn't you? You infiltrated the investigation. You told them all that Livi was fine, in South America. They knew it didn't sound right, her parents, but because the investigators had said so, they accepted it at first.'

'You said Livi was an accident,' said Belinda. 'You never said anything about lying to investigators.'

'It wasn't an accident,' said Pip. 'Sophie tried her brainwashing trick and Livi wasn't cooperating, was she?'

Belinda said, 'Well, she was very passionate about sea creatures. She insisted on tweeting and blogging about whales full of plastic. Nothing we said would make her see sense...' Belinda stopped speaking and went pale. 'She's right, isn't she? It wasn't an accident, was it?' She glanced from Sophie to John, neither of whom would make eye contact with her.

'Oh my God. You killed Livi,' Belinda said, backing away from Sophie. 'You killed her and you feel nothing.'

'It must have been the drugs,' said Pip, who had been trying to piece it all together. 'Livi wasn't buying the lies about plastic, was she? Some of them – like that Mark – are easy. Others are a bit harder to convince – you made Matty question his paternity and his family and leave home so you could lure him here and brainwash him. But not Livi. She wasn't going to be won over; in fact, my guess is she was planning to spill the beans about the whole operation, so Sophie deliberately overdosed her, threw her in the river, and then told everyone it was an accident.'

'Is that what happened?' asked Belinda, looking at Sophie in horror.

'It was an accident. I have explained this to you several times.' But Sophie stared down at her hands, fiddling with her rings.

John looked back and forth between Sophie and Belinda a few times, as if there were an invisible tennis match going on. Was John in on the murder, or had he also believed it was an accident? Pip wasn't sure. He certainly had something ruthless about him. Sophie would have needed someone strong to move the body. Was that someone John? Or the security guard, who was currently being patted by Catherine as if he were a dog.

'I don't believe you,' John said to Sophie. 'I'm with Belinda. I think you murdered that girl and lied to Belinda and me about it.'

'Well, what about you two? You helped cover the whole thing up. Moved the body downstream and weighed it down with rocks. It's a crime, you idiots. Accessory after the fact. You think you won't go down for this?'

'I could always tell the police. Tell them how you tricked us into covering it up.' He reached for his phone.

'Oh, my sweet stupid son,' said Sophie, taking his phone from his hand. 'We've gone way too far for that. Way too far. For a start, we have to deal with these two.'

And she pointed to Pip, who had finally managed to make her way over to Catherine.

'Bob, we're going to need your cable ties.'

CHAPTER THIRTY-THREE

Bob the guard let go of Catherine rather tenderly, making sure she didn't hit her head as she crumpled and then leaned against the door frame. Then he made his way towards Pip.

This, presumably, was the sort of situation you learned about in Private Investigator School, but Pip hadn't gone to Private Investigator School, and they certainly hadn't covered it at her upmarket Finishing School for Young Ladies – at least not in the time before she got expelled – so she stood there like an idiot for a moment, rigid with shock. Then she did the only thing she could think of.

'HEEEELLLLLPPP!' she shouted at the top of her lungs. 'HEEEEELLLLLP!' Bob seemed momentarily stunned by this, and she took advantage of his confusion to make a break for the door.

He grabbed for her, his arms coming at her like octopus tentacles. She darted behind the sofa. He reached for her. She lunged to the left. He followed. She lunged to the right. He followed. She felt like she was in some silly farce. One with potentially deadly consequences. Right, left. Bob too. The back of the sofa between them.

'Oh, for goodness' sake,' said Sophie, who had been watching the action impassively. 'Stop messing about. Just grab her and let's get this done.' Bob hurled himself across the back of the sofa and flung his arms around Pip's waist in a sort of rugby tackle. Pip squirmed and wriggled, while Bob lay stranded inelegantly across the sofa.

It was Belinda who put a stop to the idiocy by stepping in and holding on to Pip's arm firmly, but gently. She muttered into Pip's ear, 'Just relax, we'll get out of this. Play along.' Pip wasn't at all sure she trusted her, but she didn't see that she had much choice. She relaxed her body.

'It's OK, I've got her,' Belinda said loudly. 'You're right, Sophie. We're implicated in this. We need to stop this woman from speaking.'

Sophie gave her a long hard look, and Pip's heart almost froze in her chest. Sophie wasn't the sort of woman you could easily lie to. But Belinda was a powerful force of her own, and eventually Sophie nodded.

Bob stopped and leaned on the sofa, puffed from the exertion. His left hand rummaged in his back pocket, presumably for the cable ties. Pip noted the bulge of his gun on the right. 'Very sorry, ma'am, but I don't seem to have cable ties,' he said, patting his pocket and looking at Sophie. 'That's funny… Must have dropped them when I went out for a smoke.'

'What is the point of you?' Sophie asked viciously. 'If you can't do the simplest thing? Bring the most basic hardware?'

Belinda tried to inject some calm into the situation. 'We don't need cable ties. Let's just calm down, Sophie. I'm sure we can persuade this woman to be quiet. Everyone has a price, as you always tell me. Perhaps she'll regard it as worth her while to keep shtum.'

'Absolutely right,' said Pip. 'I've done my job. I've seen Matty is fine, and I'm happy to leave it at that and be on my way. I don't need to get involved in your business. Which seems to be a very nice family business. Just let me go and take Matty with me, and that's the last you'll hear from us. I swear, I won't talk.'

'I'm sure she won't,' said John. He beamed at Pip as if she were a star pupil. 'You see, Mother. Belinda and I have this under control.'

'No!' For the first time, Sophie's voice rose. 'You are an absolute fool. She'll have the police on us in two ticks. You wouldn't survive jail, John. Your good looks wouldn't help you there. No. We are doing this my way. Give me your belt.'

'What, Mother? My belt? Have you gone mad?'

'We need to tie these two up while I make arrangements. Give me your goddamn belt.' There was something spine-chilling about the way she said 'arrangements'.

John unbuckled his belt, pulled it from the trouser loops and dangled it uncertainly at his side. Just half an hour before, Pip would have predicted that she wouldn't have minded John taking off his kit, but suddenly it didn't seem like such a good idea.

Belinda tightened her hold on Pip. 'You're right, Sophie, as always.'

Belinda took the belt and put an arm around Pip, using the opportunity to whisper in her ear, 'Take it easy. Trust me.' Then, more loudly: 'I'll tie her hands behind her back.'

Pip passed her hands behind her and felt the belt slip over her wrists and tighten. For a moment she panicked. But although Belinda pulled the belt snug, it didn't dig into her wrists. Belinda was leaving her some wiggle room.

'Let me check that,' said Bob, moving towards them. 'You need a professional to properly secure a suspect.'

Pip's palms started to sweat. If Bob checked, the game would be up.

'A professional wouldn't have lost his cable ties,' snapped Belinda. She drew herself up, suddenly looking in charge again. 'I know how to tie a person up.' She said this as if really, this was a basic skill any half-decent person knew. Bob paused and stepped back. Pip felt herself relax slightly.

But not for long. 'Check her,' hissed Sophie at Bob. 'You incompetent idiot. Obviously you need to check her. Jesus, do I have to tell you everything?'

Bob glanced from Sophie to Belinda and made his choice. He stepped towards Pip, reaching for her. Pip looked at Belinda, their eyes met, and there was a moment of recognition – there was only one way out of this. They would have to fight. Pip hoped that she remembered her karate moves. It was so long since those idyllic three months she'd spent with Riku while he trained her in his arts. And, as she had realised in the last week, she certainly wasn't as fit as she'd been back then. All she could do was try.

Pip shifted her body slightly to the side, and summoning all the muscle memory she could, she gave Bob a strong kick to the belly. She heard something tear; could've been a muscle, but she suspected it might be her trousers. Either way, Bob dropped, surprised and winded, landing face down on the floor. Belinda pulled the belt off Pip's wrists and the two women fell on Bob. Pip sat on his back and pulled his arms behind him, while Belinda sat on his knees. Pip grabbed the belt from Belinda and fastened it around Bob's wrists before he could resist. She tightened it as much as she could before she reached around him for the bulge in his pocket. She really hoped it was a gun, she thought, and not just his natural appendages. That would be rather awkward, but she knew she needed to disarm him.

Bob was slowly trying to get up, trussed hands and all, lifting the two women who were still sitting on him. Belinda fell to the side, leaving only Pip sitting astride the groaning bull of a man.

'Some help here, John,' Belinda shouted from the floor, but John seemed to be frozen. Or, thought Pip, he didn't actually want to help. Maybe he was as bad as his mother, after all.

Catherine's voice came from across the room. 'I'm coming, don't worry, I'm just trying to…'

From the corner of her eye, Pip saw Catherine struggle to her feet and Sophie knock her back down with one shove. A semi-tranquillised environmental scientist was not the kind of backup that was going to save the day. Pip needed to act quickly. She drew the weapon from Bob's pocket and recognised it from the cop shows she watched – it was a taser, not a gun. She leapt off him, holding the taser as if it might bite her. Pip was generally not to be trusted with mechanical objects and appliances, let alone a gun. There'd been that unfortunate incident with the electronic stapler when she was in primary school, and things had gone downhill since. She was terrified of handling a weapon. But it had to be done. Bob was a big bloke, and if she didn't act quickly, he would be up. John was still just watching how things played out. Pip knew this type of man – whoever won, that would be the side he was on at the end of the day.

'John!' cried Belinda. 'Get him!'

Belinda still seemed to be under some delusion that John was her knight in plastic armour.

'He's not going to help us, Belinda,' said Pip, and pressed the short black taser against Bob's side. Nothing happened. How the hell did the thing work? Bob had pushed himself up to his knees now. Pip flipped a switch and gave it another try, pressing the device into his side. He shook and went down like a tonne of bricks, knocking her off her feet and twisting her ankle in the process.

'Good work,' Belinda said. 'Now for Sophie.'

Sophie had taken the opportunity of the distraction and was almost out the door.

Belinda stepped in front of her. 'Sophie, the game's up.'

'The game isn't up until I say so!' she snapped. 'Now get out of my way.' She shoved Belinda hard and made for the door.

Just as Sophie stepped across the threshold and made a bid for freedom, Catherine stuck out a leg and Sophie went sprawling. 'That'll teach you,' Catherine mumbled. 'Nasty piece of work. Nasty tea.' With that, she put her head on the floor as if settling in for a nap. Sophie made to get up, but Pip quickly darted over with the taser, gave her a sharp zap, and she fell back down.

Pip surveyed the scene. Three sprawling bodies, two exhausted sweating women, and John still trying to make up his mind about which horse he was backing. It looked like a battle scene from an old oil painting.

'Good lord,' came a honeyed American voice from the doorway. 'What in the hell is going on here?'

CHAPTER THIRTY-FOUR

Into the battle scene came the glowing magnificence that was Madison Price, backlit by the sunlight coming in from the hall, shining and shimmering. Catching sight of Pip, she said, 'Ah, Ms du Bois. I believe you've found Matty. I am so relieved.' She did, it must be admitted, look as relieved as her Botox allowed.

'Ms du...?' said John, his face a picture of confusion.

'All sorted, Mrs Price,' said Pip, trying to sound professional, as if being in a room littered with groaning bodies was all in a day's work. 'Matty is quite well. We are just tying up some loose ends here, nothing to be concerned about.' She hoped she was right. She hadn't seen Matty since the Ming vase came down on her head, and who knew what had happened in the interim.

Madison stepped into the room, followed by her husband, who gushed, 'I'm so relieved, thank you. Really, I can't thank you enough.' He walked towards Pip, arms outstretched as if to embrace her, when he noticed Catherine dozing at his feet. He stopped and surveyed the chaos; the bodies, the side tables overturned on their sides and the scattered scatter cushions. 'Wow, this is um... Should I call the police?'

Both Sophie and Bob were stirring and struggling to their feet at this point. Catherine had opened her eyes and was staring at Madison. 'You look just like, um, what's that actress, you know the one. She was in, what was it? Um... Gwyneth someone, the one with the eggs? No, not her. Not that pretty.'

'Madison Price,' said Belinda and Pip in unison.

'Yes, her. You look like her.' Dawning comprehension broke across Catherine's face. 'Dr Miranda, what's her name. On the telly. You know. The show. Oh my God, you're Matty's mother! Matty Price. Madison… Madison Price. The actress? And you must be the dad!' She turned to Ben, pleased with herself for groping her way to these conclusions.

Pip contemplated her options. The police were definitely needed at this point. Sophie was a kidnapper and a murderer.

'Pip!' Jimmy came barrelling through the door, shaved head gleaming. He stopped, access blocked by the Prices and the prone Catherine. His green eyes found hers and he said softly, 'Thank God you're safe.'

Pip hadn't been so pleased to see someone since that time she'd got herself stuck in the lift in the Empire State Building. She'd have hugged him if the space between them wasn't strewn with bodies and furniture. It really was rather crowded. Bob was up on his knees now, pushing himself to standing.

'Need some help with the big fella?' Jimmy asked, flexing his biceps and gesturing to the guard.

'You won't get no trouble from me, ma'am,' Bob said, showing Pip his palms in a gesture of surrender. Bob seemed to be a man who understood where the power sat in a room at any given time. And that was with whoever had the taser.

Pip was relieved. 'I think I've got things under control,' she said to Jimmy. 'But thank you.'

Bob was not done. Apparently, being tasered had helped him form opinions. 'For the record, I'd just like to say I had no idea that woman was involved in such terrible things.' He pointed at Sophie, who was on the floor propped up next to Catherine, with what could only be described as deep disappointment. 'Kidnapping. Drugging. And that poor girl.'

This sent Ben into a panic. 'What? Kidnapping! Drugs! Poor girls! Where's Matty? I want to see my son. I need to see him now!'

'Matty is fine, I'll send someone to fetch him,' said Pip. It gave her no small pleasure to instruct John, imperiously, 'John, please go and get Matty Price and bring him straight here.' She just hoped Matty really was OK.

'Certainly,' he said. 'Back in a jiffy.' He scurried off obediently. It seemed he was now clear on which way history was going to write this story. Sophie got to her feet to follow him out of the room.

'Oh, no you don't,' said Pip. 'You get back here, *Ms du Bois*.'

'How strange,' said Ben Price. 'She's also Ms du Bois? Are you two related?'

Pip couldn't bear the complications that would arise from an explanation of her multiple identities. Besides, she had her hands full with this cast of thousands. One of whom was once again making a bid for escape.

'Sophie, stop!'

The older woman was moving off at surprising speed. Pip took a step towards her and felt the pain shoot up from her twisted ankle.

'Jimmy, get her!'

The man reached Sophie in one fluid bound, grabbed her and turned her so that her back faced him, her upper arms held firmly but quite gently in his tattooed hands. 'At your service, ma'am,' he said to Pip, presenting his catch. And then to Sophie: 'Am I going to need ties, or are you going to behave?' He glanced at Pip. 'I can break her arm if you want,' he said, somehow making it sound like a very gallant suggestion.

Sophie gave him a withering look. 'No ties,' she said. 'And no breaking my arms. Who are you anyway? And what do you think I am, some sort of criminal? Take your hands off me right now. This is all a ridiculous misunderstanding, you know.'

'You can tell that to the police,' said Pip. 'Bob, call them, please. It's time to put an end to this.'

Bob took out his mobile phone with a self-important flourish and began to dial.

'Oh, don't be ridiculous,' said Sophie shrilly. 'There's absolutely no need for that. Let me go. Sit down and we will sort this whole thing out.'

'You're not giving the orders here, she is,' Jimmy said to her severely, gesturing to Pip. She felt her heart swell with pride. She was giving the orders. Damn straight she was. 'Now if it's all right with her, I will let go of you, but you're going to stand right here next to me and not make any trouble, OK?'

Sophie nodded, her lips pursed and her face a picture of fury.

He looked enquiringly at Pip. She nodded her permission. He gave her a little smile and unhanded Sophie, who shook her shoulders angrily.

'On their way,' said Bob officiously.

Madison, who had been surprisingly quiet, suddenly gave out a breathless shriek. 'My boy, my darling boy!' she said, and ran to embrace the man of the moment, the elusive Matty Price.

Pip wondered afterwards which movie she'd seen that Desperate Mother Reunites with Child in Danger scene in. It was oddly familiar, probably from a hundred films, a hundred mothers finding a hundred children who'd been lost in the desert, or captured by pirates, or huddled under a desk to escape a school shooter. It almost felt like something Madison had rehearsed – the gasp, the graceful dash to meet him, the tender way she held Matty at arm's length to scan his face before holding him to her chest, the fluttering eyelashes with just a hint of a tear.

'Hey, Mom,' Matty said, seemingly embarrassed at all the people and all the fuss. 'I'm fine, really. It was mostly just a retreat, Mom. Meditation and stuff.'

'Mummy,' she whispered. 'British. Remember, we said? We speak British now.'

He sighed with the full force of a teenager annoyed and said, 'Yes, Mummy,' quietly, as if hoping no one would hear.

His father was genuinely effusive, gathering the boy into a bear hug and lifting him off his feet. He was holding back tears and muttering, 'Thank God, thank God you're back.' He pushed the boy to arm's length. 'Let me look at you. Are you OK? Really? Matty, I was so worried. I missed you so much.'

Madison looked mildly miffed at being upstaged by her husband. She might have been the actor, but he was most definitely the more dramatic.

'Dad, I'm fine,' said Matty. And then, even more quietly, 'I missed you too.'

'What's going on here then?' came a voice from the door. A stocky, balding policeman entered the room, followed by a lanky young one with a giant Adam's apple. This was feeling more and more like a movie. 'Who's in charge?'

Everyone looked at Pip. 'She is,' said Catherine helpfully. 'Felicity is in charge.'

'Felicity who? Surname, please,' asked the second policeman, ready with notebook and pencil.

'Well, you see, the thing is—' Pip started, but she was cut short by the first policeman's astonished cry.

'What's Dr Miranda Ray doing here?'

CHAPTER THIRTY-FIVE

Tim came in with a tray and placed it carefully on the coffee table where Pip rested her bandaged leg.

'Earl Grey tea and cinnamon toast,' he said with a smile, looking as if he considered making breakfast the crowning achievement of his life. 'The breakfast of champions.'

'You are so good to me, thank you,' Pip said, looking up into his warm brown eyes. 'I don't know that I could have hobbled around the kitchen just yet.'

'You're dangerous enough in the kitchen on two feet,' he said, sitting down next to her. An affectionate laugh took the sting off the true statement. 'Speaking of absent feet, here's Most. I think he missed you.' The cat jumped up onto the sofa and butted his head against Pip's thigh, purring and dribbling in delight.

Pip wondered if she'd ever been quite as happy as she was now, with Tim on one side and Most on the other, the smell of cinnamon toast in the air, knowing the satisfaction of a job well done. Bonus happy-making fact – she'd just given Tim the month's rent, plus another three months upfront. And she still had a good chunk of change in her bank account. And being out of action for a week, she'd even have some time to catch up on all her favourite Insta celebs and the celebrity news.

Doug Bradford from Boston Investigations had been predictably furious when he discovered that she wasn't in fact an investigator – but then neither was Sophie du Bois, who had also been posing as an expert. And in her case, her mission was to ensure that the missing teens were never found.

Apparently Doug figured that it was worth paying Pip for the job, plus a bit extra for keeping quiet about the fact that one of London's top investigations firms had been duped into hiring a know-nothing imposter who had managed to solve both cases, where the professionals had failed. Not to mention that someone they'd reported as safe had actually died. Plus, there'd been talk of taking her on with a real job at BI. In the meantime, the payment, plus a *very* nice chunk of thank you/keep-quiet-and-don't-go-to-the-papers money from the Prices meant she didn't have to worry about the rent for a while.

Pip took a bite of the toast – delicious – and washed it down with the fragrant tea. It was a fairly blissful combination reminiscent of childhood. Not Pip's childhood perhaps – Mummy wasn't much of a cinnamon toast sort – but someone else's. Someone in a book, or a mummy blogger maybe.

'How are you feeling? How's the foot?' Tim asked.

'Actually, I'm feeling fine. Foot's not sore unless I put weight on it, and I'm pleased that Matty is home safely with his parents. Just sad for Livi's mum and dad though.'

'So Sophie actually killed her?'

'Sophie's sticking to the story that it was an accidental overdose, but I doubt that. The police are looking for Livi's body and hopefully the autopsy will answer some questions. Those poor parents, thinking they'd driven her away when she was actually lying dead in a river. I can't bear thinking about it.'

'What was the drug?'

'We're not sure – the samples from Catherine have gone to the lab. It seems it's some kind of sedative or disinhibitor to make them more docile and susceptible to all those messages Belinda was putting out there, about plastics and waste and so on. It was hectic stuff though; Catherine took ages to get it out of her system and feel herself again.'

'That is so horrible, I'm sorry.' He paused, looking for some way to make Pip feel better. Then, inspired, he jumped to his feet. 'Let me get you some more toast,' he said, and off he trotted to the kitchen.

Her phone buzzed on the table. She reached for it. Jimmy.

'You were amazing yesterday. Absolutely kick-ass amazing.'

She smiled.

'Rocking that taser, girl.'

Indeed, she had somewhat rocked the taser.

'Can I come over? I have something for you.'

The doorbell rang.

'Don't get up! I'll get it!' said Tim from the kitchen. He was the kindest man. In addition to being easy on the eye. 'Coming!' he shouted to the visitor.

He really was most attentive.

It was Flis. She flung herself at Pip.

'Oh my goodness, I'm so pleased to see you. Are you all right? I was so worried. How's your ankle? Is it a torn litigation?'

'Ligament, yes. I tore it in the scuffle. Twisted it when Bob went down. The doctors might have to stitch it up. I just have to rest it now, and we'll see how it heals.'

'Scuffle! Those terrible people. You could have been killed!'

'It was OK, Flis, I had it under control.' This was Pip's story, and she wasn't wavering from it. 'And when the Prices and Jimmy arrived, it was all over. The baddies knew there was no getting away with it.'

Speaking of Jimmy, Pip's phone was still buzzing with incoming messages.

'But who were those people and what exactly were they doing?' asked Flis. 'Why did they have those young people in that place? What was the point of it all? What was the modular opera?'

Pip set about explaining the modus operandi – or modular opera – of it all, and how the young people were all social media influencers with big followings. Belinda got Tara involved right from the start, knowing she was really popular. That helped her reach the others. The Green Youth For Truth movement was a complete set-up. It was designed to draw in young influencers and their followers who cared about environmental issues, and feed them misinformation about waste and plastic, and how plastic was ultimately a good thing.

'It was pretty successful, actually. Belinda knew what she was doing. She would get people all fired up about deforestation, and subtly link that to paper bags. They ran a lot of pieces on recycling and plastic waste management, as if that would save the day – which it won't.'

'I've been reading up on it,' said Tim. 'Quite interesting, really. The way it works is that they muddy the waters. Like straws, for instance. Plastic straws are far from the biggest environmental problem, but it's become a huge thing. People feel they are doing something valuable – they get to feel virtuous.'

'Yes,' said Pip. 'It's at very little cost or inconvenience to the consumer, and it's a minuscule part of the industry. So they'd rather people focused on straws than on something bigger, something that is worth more money to them.'

'And then they use data analysis and AI and bots to maximise their reach and spread the message,' added Tim.

'But if that strategy was working, why did they get involved in all this other stuff? The drugs? Kidnapping people?'

'It seems it all just spun out of control. Sophie was worried about the future of the family business and started putting the pressure on Belinda and John. Belinda was getting desperate about controlling the message. It was her idea to use the retreat to isolate and win over social media influencers. Sophie started looking at ways to make them more susceptible to suggestion and soon she was messing around with the drugs. And then that led to the situation with Livi.'

'What a crazy situation,' said Flis. 'They must be quite unhinged.'

'I think Sophie really is pretty psycho. It seems Belinda and John didn't know quite how psycho. They didn't know about the drugs at first. It all got out of hand.'

'Corporations,' said Flis. 'They are just so greedy. And dishonest.' Her eyes narrowed as she prepared for a diatribe.

Flis's lecture was narrowly averted by the doorbell, heralding the arrival of Jimmy with a giant bunch of roses and a large gift bag.

'Oh,' he said, when Tim opened the door. 'I'm a friend of Pip. I did try to phone.'

'You must be Jimmy,' Tim said with a tight smile. 'Do come in. I'm Tim.' And then, as if as an afterthought, he added, 'I live here. With Pip.'

The roses were gorgeous – a deep red, and lots of them. Proper Valentine's Day vibes. Pip had never been the recipient of so much floral adoration. She blushed and stammered a little. 'That's so kind of you, Jimmy. You shouldn't… I mean… they're beautiful… thank you.'

'Let me put those in water,' said Flis, heading to the kitchen where Tim was opening cupboards loudly, having offered to make more tea.

'I hope I'm not interrupting. I tried to phone. Is that your—?'

'My sister, Flis.'

'I meant the bloke. He said he lives here.'

'Oh, no. That's Tim, he's not… He's my housemate. Landlord. Friend.'

'OK then.' Jimmy smiled. 'Open your present.'

Pip reached into the bag and pulled out a pair of boxing gloves. 'Oh, Jimmy – this is perfect. I'm so keen to start boxing.'

'That's not even the whole present. It comes with personal lessons from the best boxing instructor in London. Perhaps the whole of England.'

'That would be you.'

'That would be me.'

They laughed, flirtily. He really was rather exciting, this Jimmy.

The arrival of Flis and Tim, with roses and tea respectively, pulled them out of their moment and got them back onto the subject of the events of the last week.

'So, Jimmy, you were there when it all happened, right?' asked Flis, who was still trying to get a handle on the confusing events of the previous day. 'How did you know to come?'

'I'd been to the place with Pip before. We went out there on a recce but we couldn't get in. The guard with the gun was a bit of a deterrent,' he said. 'She sent me a message that she'd gone back there, and when I couldn't reach her that night or the next morning I got worried.'

'Belinda had taken my phone by then,' Pip explained.

'So I thought I'd pop over and see what was going on. In case she needed some backup. When I got there, who should I see pacing outside the gate but that hot blonde from the hospital show. Dr Miranda Ray in the actual flesh. Nearly had a coronary myself.'

'Aka Madison Price,' said Pip. 'Before my phone was confiscated, I let the investigations company know I'd found Matty and they let the Prices know. I dropped them a pin with the location. I was going to bring him home with me, but the Prices apparently decided to drive down. They arrived at the same time as Jimmy. Bob the guard was not at his post – he was busy chasing me around the sofa at that point – so Jimmy, true to his name, jimmied the lock. And they all arrived just in time for the dramatic finale.'

'It's not a joke, Pip.' Flis shivered. 'You could have been killed.'

'I wasn't in that much danger,' said Pip. 'It was a little hair-raising, but it ended well.'

'Because you handled it well,' said Jimmy.

'And that awful Sophie woman has been arrested. Thank goodness for that,' said Flis. 'All's well that ends in a bell.'

'What about the others?' asked Tim, who was standing by with reinforcements of toast.

'John and Belinda? They've been taken into custody too. I think they were somewhere between useful idiots and criminally complicit, but who knows. That's for the police to investigate and the courts to decide, I guess.'

'You did great, Pip,' said Tim.

'Really great,' Jimmy agreed.

Pip demurred, 'I couldn't have done it without the rest of you. Tim, your brilliant computer skills helping track the place down. Jimmy, coming to help me find it and then bringing the cavalry. Flis, you gave me a cover story – and even your name for a while.'

'You're going to have to pay for that,' Flis said to her sister. 'I want the first exclusive on that story. The influencer racket, the misinformation, the whole thing. It'll send our ratings through the roof!'

'I'll get right onto that when I've finished my toast,' said Pip. 'I'll have some time this week, while I rest up my foot.'

'Then what?' asked Flis. 'Now you've solved the mystery, what are you going to do next?'

'Fingers crossed I'm going to be working at Boston Investigations. Not as a proper detective just yet, I have to learn the procedures. I'm looking into a course, and Doug said I must come in and talk to him when I'm back on my feet. Said I've got "good instincts for the job", and then gave me a lecture about all the illegal and stupid things I'd done. But he wants me on board. Maybe only because that way it will look like I worked for him all along, but still. It's an opportunity. If everything goes right, I could be a legit sleuth. I think that's what I want to do with my life. It suits me and I could be good at it.'

Most jumped up and sat down next to Flis, butting her hand with his head, asking for a scratch. Flis fluffed his tummy.

'Hey, I thought Most was a boy cat,' said Flis.

'He is.'

'No, she is not. Look at her, Pip, she's pregnant. That's a belly full of kittens.'

Good lord, it was true. Pip had vaguely noticed that Most had been getting rather porky, but suspected Tim of being free with the snacks in her absence. Now she saw that Most's tummy was hard and round. She ran her hand over the cat, and felt the lumps and bumps of the kittens beneath her hands. 'Oh my word! Tim, we're having kittens!'

'I'm not sure I'm ready to be a dad,' Tim said. 'But I'll do my best…'

'Pretty unobservant for a detective,' Jimmy said, nudging her.

They all laughed. Her darling sister. The attentive and beautiful Tim. The exciting, tattooed Jimmy. Her people.

Pip's phone rang. 'The Ride of the Valkyries'. Mummy. She picked up. 'Mummy, I'm sorry I never called back, but this time, I promise, I've got a very good excuse.'

A LETTER FROM KATIE

Dear Reader,

Katie Gayle is, in fact, two of us – Kate and Gail – and we want to say a huge thank you for choosing to read *The Kensington Kidnap*, the first Epiphany Bloom cosy mystery. If you enjoyed the book, and want to keep up to date with all Katie Gayle's latest releases, just sign up at the following link. Your email address will never be shared and you can unsubscribe at any time.

www.bookouture.com/katie-gayle

We hope you loved Pip's adventures, and if you did we would be very grateful if you could write a review and post it on Amazon and Goodreads, so that other people can discover Pip too.

You can find us in a few places and we'd love to hear from you – Katie Gayle is on Twitter as @KatieGayleBooks and on Facebook as @KatieGayleWriter. You can also follow Kate on Twitter at @katesidley and Gail at @gailschimmel.

Thanks,
Katie Gayle

KatieGayleWriter

@KatieGayleBooks

Printed in Great Britain
by Amazon